Death on Carrion Lane

A reunion for murder in Haines Tavern

Sheila agrees to soothe Clara's nervousness by accompanying her friend to the 20-year class reunion for North Bend County High. Nostalgia, good memories, old friendships—this should be fun, right? Ah, but grudges, old rivalries, and long-buried secrets also arise. And before the festivities wrap up, there's one old classmate dead, another being questioned, and enough suspicion to cover several more.

Secret Sleuth series
Death on the Diversion
Death on Torrid Avenue
Death on Beguiling Way
Death on Covert Circle
Death on Shady Bridge
Death on Carrion Lane
Death on ZigZag Trail
Death on Puzzle Place

More mystery from Patricia McLinn

Caught Dead in Wyoming series
Sign Off
Left Hanging
Shoot First
Last Ditch
Look Live
Back Story
Cold Open
Hot Roll
Reaction Shot
Body Brace
Cross Talk
Air Ready
Holiday Bullets
Cue Up

The Innocence Trilogy

Proof of Innocence
Price of Innocence
Premise of Innocence

DEATH ON CARRION LANE

Secret Sleuth, Book 6

Patricia McLinn

THURSDAY

CHAPTER ONE

"YOU'RE READING *The Wizard of Oz?"* my friend Clara asked with no judgment but plenty of curiosity. "Haven't you read it before?"

Crunching leaves would have foretold her arrival … if our dogs' joyous together-again yips and whooshing-past soundwaves hadn't already. My collie Gracie and Clara's Great Pyrenees mix Lulu acted as if this meeting in my back yard came after years of separation, instead of less than twenty-four hours since yesterday's gambol at the dog park.

"I am." I kept reading to finish a passage. "It's well worth re-reading. It's a wise and wonderful book."

"That sounds like the description of the wizard."

"Uh-huh." My pleasure at Dorothy and the crew escaping the fighting trees led by the Tin Man—or the Woodsman, as the book said—was somewhat dimmed by the distracting sound of the wheels in Clara's head spinning.

"You know," she said. "If you look at it one way, *The Wizard of Oz* is all about reunions."

She had a point.

The book starts by stating its protagonist *lived in the midst of the great Kansas prairies with Uncle Henry, a farmer, and Aunt Em, the farmer's wife.* Dorothy spends most of the book learning what she needs to know to get home to her aunt and uncle. And in the movie, home to their hired hands, too, even though they'd accompanied her in the guise of the Scarecrow, Tin Man, and Cowardly Lion.

Without looking up from the book I'd had since childhood, I said,

"I am not going with you to your high school reunion."

I'd expressed the sentiment several times over the past two days.

"It would be a great way to meet more people. You need to widen your circle of acquaintances and there will be lots of people at the reunion who still live in the area."

Not a selling point to me. Widening my circle of acquaintances in North Bend County, Kentucky, or anywhere else, raised dangers Clara didn't know about and I didn't want to think about at the moment. I limited my response to "No."

"Besides," Clara said as if I hadn't turned her down now and all previous times, "it's not only my class. There'll be reunions from before and after my class. You could meet people from different age groups."

"I do that at the dog park."

"You *would* if you talked to more people at the dog park. Gracie has a far better social life there than you do." She slid from earnest to as close to sly as she gets. "Even if you don't want to get to know people, it could be great research. Think of all the murders at reunions."

"In fiction. Most reunions are strictly murder-free."

"Are you sure? Because there are a lot of books with murders at a reunion, plus all those murder games and plays."

Since becoming a virtual author's assistant earlier this year, Clara had developed a deep interest in many aspects of the publishing world. A world I'd been in the middle of until a year ago. Which was a fact about me she didn't know.

She thought I was a former high school English teacher who'd quit and moved here after an inheritance.

"Pretty sure. You could look it up."

"I will," she said. "But it's still good research for you about characters and motives—"

"I'm not writing mysteries. I'm writing romance. I told you." I dropped my voice. Yes, we were in my backyard, but I couldn't be too careful.

Because my writing endeavors constituted another secret, with

Clara the only one who knew about it.

And if you're thinking, *Great. Just what Sheila Mackey needs, another secret,* you're right.

This writing secret I wasn't sharing with anyone beyond Clara. Not my parents, siblings, or great-aunt—definitely not my great-aunt. Also definitely not Teague O'Donnell. First, I wanted to know if I *could* write.

The toughest trick was keeping the fact that I was writing from Great-Aunt Kit, who had always supported herself writing novels.

Why keep it from her?

Not because she wouldn't support me. Because she *would*.

Authors talk a lot about the editor voice in their head nagging at them, which gets in the way as they're trying to create. Add Kit's voice and my head would burst. She would generously share every bit of knowledge she'd picked up in decades writing for traditional publishers and more recently as an independent author.

It would be like someone dribbling a basketball for the first time getting pointers from Michael Jordan.

I needed to get my feet under me and start walking before I could benefit from her advice on skipping and dancing.

Because right now all I was doing was *trying* to write.

When I wasn't sitting in the yard re-reading childhood books.

As for Teague O'Donnell … that was complicated.

Clara said, "I'm glad to hear you're writing romance because there are no murders in *The Wizard of Oz,* so—"

"Except the witches, East and West."

"—I might have thought you were procrastinating." Clara didn't appear to see my wince as she continued. "Those weren't murders, they were accidents. Dorothy didn't steer the house to land on East and she picked up the water bucket that ended West because it was the closest tool at hand to save the Scarecrow."

"That's the movie. In the book, Dorothy throws the water because West has taken one of the magic shoes."

"Anyway—" She relentlessly returned to her topic. "—reunions are even better research for romances. All those pent-up emotions from high school coming out. Crushes revealed. Broken hearts finally mended. Maybe people get back together—true love at last—or realize the high school sweetheart never really was *the one* and they're happy with the spouse who agonized over what would happen at the reunion—"

"Sounds like a murder plot. But the genre doesn't matter, because I'm not going."

"Oh, c'mon. It's not only about doing me a favor because my husband deserted me—"

"Didn't you say Ned's client was hit by a late-season hurricane and needs help getting equipment back on line?"

"A *little* hurricane. Didn't wipe out the whole place, just took off some of the roof, letting rain in on the equipment. Not like the building was lifted up and transported to Oz, leaving only the storm cellar in place."

"That was a tornado."

She steamed past my factual correction. "They could have waited a week. Or Ned could have come home for the weekend."

"You told him not to. That it would be easier on him to stay there and get the work done."

"So, I changed my mind." She sidestepped the speeding freight train of my dog chasing her dog with joyous abandon.

"But you *didn't* change your mind, or you'd have told Ned to come back."

She gusted out a sigh. "Do you have to be so logical?"

"Sorry. Don't know what I was thinking."

"It's okay. You can't help it sometimes. I almost did tell him to come back. They're sleeping in a tent and using the facilities of a damaged motel, poor baby. Only it's really hard to get out of there and then to get back in… But, Sheila, I want to go to this reunion—"

"Great. Go. You know all these people. It's not like you'll be going into a room full of strangers."

"Worse. A room full of people who knew me when I had all the potential in the world and—"

"So did they."

"—a younger, thinner me."

"I empathize, but I'm not going with you."

FRIDAY

CHAPTER TWO

"WHEN DO YOU and Clara leave for her reunion?"

Teague O'Donnell asked the question with an assumption of completely spurious innocence.

He was teasing. Along with not so subtly saying *I told you so* about my giving in after he'd predicted I would when we went to a movie Wednesday night.

"The reunion's not until tomorrow night."

He nodded solemnly. "I know. She's enlisted me to bring LuLu out here tomorrow after I'm done because LuLu will have been inside all day while she primps."

Out here was the Torrid Avenue Dog Park, where we were standing and watching our dogs—my Gracie, his Murphy, and Clara's LuLu—frolic.

After I'm done referred to Teague's plans for the weekend.

He was using his carpentry skills to lead a project adapting a home for a student at the school where he subbed who'd been in a car accident. With considerable therapy, the hope was the boy would walk again. For now, though, ramps, wider doors, and other adjustments would make daily life much easier.

Staff, students, and administration were pitching in to make the necessary changes this weekend before the boy was released from rehab.

"That's Clara primping, not LuLu," Teague added.

"Thanks for the clarification."

This was an accidental meeting. I hadn't known he'd be here with his dog and Clara's, though I might have guessed if I'd given it thought.

Clara had called this morning, asking if I was going to the dog park.

I'd been occupied with … uh, a project on my computer and answered absently that I didn't plan to go today, that Gracie could take a day off from the dog park.

Clara had said okay and reconfirmed what time we were meeting tonight for a reunion eve dinner.

Then I'd gone back to the … project.

I could have predicted Clara would call Teague to see if he'd take LuLu to the park … again, if I'd been thinking about it.

But the project monopolized my thinking. I was only here, with the project temporarily set aside, because Gracie insisted.

You don't think a collie can insist? You haven't met many.

She stood on the other side of my desk with only her ears showing over the edge. She sighed. She moved to another spot where she could stare at me. More sighs. Back to the ears in my line of sight. Extremely expressive ears.

That sounds endearing, doesn't it? Let me tell you, you have never been accused of dog neglect until you've had a pair of furry, cutely tipped ears pointed at you for long, unmoving moments while you tried to concentrate on … a project.

"Clara must be pre-primping now, huh?" Teague asked.

She was, in fact, having her hair and nails done, but I wasn't betraying womanhood by revealing that. "You should be grateful you're included for dinner tonight, and at the Haines Tavern no less. By rights, she and I should be the only ones going, since it's a thank-you for accompanying her to tomorrow night's reunion. You're only in on it because she felt sorry you might be alone on a Friday night. And—" I turned to him with a searching gaze. "—why are you making fun of reunions anyway? You don't go to yours? Have something against the people you went to high school with?"

"Other than the ones in jail, no. Went to the five-year reunion."

His hint of defensiveness increased my satisfaction at turning him away from Clara's insecurities while it also piqued my interest. We'd been dating casually for several weeks. Not casually in the sense that we didn't make plans, but casually in the sense that this relationship deepened at a pace making snails look like Olympic sprinters.

There were reasons on my side.

Secrets to keep, remember?

The first couple weeks I was relieved he didn't push me. Lately, I'd begun to wonder about *his* reasons for taking it so slow.

"No reunions since? Why not? Living down high school trauma?"

"Undercover."

I already knew he'd been a cop in Illinois before moving here last year about the same time I did, after buying a house and adopting a rescue collie. I supposed he'd left police work when he'd been blinded in one eye in an *incident* he had not clarified or described. He hadn't given much by way of detail in other aspects of his former life, either. And I was severely hampered in finding out more because if I asked him questions—including, but not limited to about the pace of our relationship—he'd likely ask me questions.

Not only was an ex-cop sure to be better at it than I was, but I didn't want anybody asking me anything. I was living in the town of Haines Tavern, Kentucky, to blend into the background and not have anyone recognize me as my former persona: The author of beloved and bestselling novels whose releases were events before being turned into blockbuster movies, starting with *Abandon All.*

Except I didn't write that book or those that followed. My great-aunt Kit did.

It's complicated.

"Undercover? That's your excuse for not going to your reunions?"

He chuckled. "Truth. Long hair, scruffy beard and all. Didn't want to take any chances of connecting my undercover life to my real life."

Gracie and Murphy zoomed in close to us and stopped abruptly, staring at each other. The intensity demanded our attention. Gracie took one step closer. Murphy held his ground. Another step closer. Murphy's ears fluttered.

Gracie pounced, hopped backward, then ran past him, circled the table for an extra lap, before looping around for the pleasure of zeroing in and pouncing again. His tail wagging, Murphy scooted under the table.

Teague leaned over to look at his dog.

"I know, buddy. Females are tough." And then, as if I wouldn't have heard, he straightened and continued what he'd been saying to me. "Not to mention my undercover persona would not have been a hit with my former classmates."

"Oh, I don't know. Some people—females in particular—like a little rough."

He turned to me, eyebrows up. "You?"

"I was thinking of my dog." Who now trotted away from us, hip to hip with the lab mix. "I like…" I swallowed against hammering in my chest reminding me how much I liked him as he was. "Uh, clean cut."

"Good." His voice dropped on the single word, adding a new drumbeat in my chest.

He'd shaved off the beard he'd sported for a few months, with interesting timing.

He hadn't done it immediately after Clara told him I didn't like beards. Not after he first asked me out, either. Not even after Clara repeated something else I'd told her—the theory that women, in particular, won't vote for men with beards or other facial hair because the men appear to be hiding something.

The beard disappeared after our third date.

As if he'd wanted to be sure this had a chance of going someplace before he gave up the facial hair.

But then why no, uh, developments?

Now, he cleared his throat. "Just don't go finding anybody clean cut or otherwise tomorrow night. What time did you say you were leaving?"

The quick follow-up question eased the seriousness, but left me wondering about the almost-not-quite intimation toward exclusivity.

"Clara's coming to my place at six-forty-five."

"Thought you were driving."

"I am, but she said she'd come to my house and we'd leave from there." I was the designated driver so she could relax and drink as much as she needed to relax.

"Doesn't trust you to get started on your own, huh?"

I zapped him with a look. He grinned.

"I won't renege. I agreed I'd go, I'm going." I turned and picked up Gracie's leash from the nearby picnic table. "Speaking of which, I should go get ready for tonight's dinner."

CHAPTER THREE

CLARA WAS WAITING at a table when I arrived at the Haines Tavern—
Historic Haines Tavern, according to locals, who usually called it that or
simply The Tavern, distinguishing it from the town named after it.

I learned of Clara's previous arrival from the hostess who stood
behind a small lectern at the bottom of the stairs to the second floor of
the 1830s building. A hallway to the right of the stairs led to the back,
with a doorway farther to the right to the bar.

What always caught my eye from this spot was the line where the
ceiling and wall met above the stairs' mid-point landing. Well, *line* in
the loosest sense.

I'd had my share of issues with elements of my seventy-plus-year-
old house not being perfectly square. But the comparison to this
toddler's sketch of a line—slanted and irregular—always cheered me
up.

The smiling hostess led me through the front room to the slightly
smaller back area of what must originally have been a double parlor.
More dining was available in rooms upstairs or on side and back
porches, but this was our favorite. Unless we slipped into the bar
across the entry hall for a quick meal or drink.

"You look great, Clara. You'll knock 'em dead tomorrow."

She turned rosy under her newly trimmed and styled hair.

"Thanks. Teague will be here soon. He messaged me. The hair and
nails are probably overkill, but I had the appointments, so…" She
shrugged with would-be casualness, then said in a low voice, "I'm so
glad you're going with me tomorrow."

"Have you kept in touch with a lot of people from high school?"

"Can't help staying in touch. A lot of them still live here, too."

"Then why go to the reunion?"

"Some of them haven't," she said simply. "I'd like to know what they've done."

"Wondering about the road not traveled?"

"You mean what I might have done if I'd left North Bend County? Not at all. Missing out on the life Ned and I have? No way." Her lips lifted in a small, private smile.

"How about your close friends from high school?"

"Didn't have anyone I'd call really close. There was one girl who used to come with me sometimes to play cards and board games with Gran, her friends, and my cousins. She died a few months after graduation. My classmate, I mean. Not Gran." I'd figured that, since Clara's gran was in Belize with a newish *boyfriend*. "I mean I was sad— of course I was—although she'd stopped coming over a year before she died. I was already at college when she died, so it didn't have the emotional impact it would have if I'd still been here, had been hanging around with her, went to the funeral and all."

"When you came back after college, did you rekindle high school friendships?"

"No. I worked at the library a couple years. One before, one after Ned and I got married. Then his mom's MS turned worse and she needed help." She tipped her head. "I guess you could say I became part of Irissa's circle. She'd been a real social person and to keep her spirits up, her friends came to her house and played cards and bingo, or did crafts, or watched movies, or did a potluck dinner, and I was included. When she got worse and needed help available around the clock, we moved her in with us, and all her friends came along, too. I became accepted as part of the group."

I thought about her telling me when we first met about Ned getting her LuLu and insisting she take a break after his mother's death.

Was he conscious not only of the toll caring for his mother took on Clara, but also her mourning the connection? Or was it instinct? Either way, it was further proof he was a good and caring man.

"Those ladies became my friends. The people from high school, I mostly wave hello to in the grocery store. What about you?"

"Oh, like you said, waving at the grocery store."

Only in my case, I worked hard to make sure there was no opportunity for more during the few times I'd visited my hometown after Aunt Kit hired me to be a secret surrogate for certain books. I went there to see my family and stuck close to home. Far more often, they came to visit Kit and me in New York, where they—and the arrangement Kit and I had—could fly under the radar of general indifference to the ins and outs of neighbors' lives. Unlike in my hometown.

Teague arrived then, coming in behind a couple who took the table across from me and behind Clara. Other than that, they didn't register, because my attention was on Teague and trying not to let my reaction to his easy gait, tousled hair, and sharply attractive face show too much.

He grinned at me.

Oh, hell. Let it show.

✧　✧　✧　✧

THE FOOD, AS usual at The Tavern, was excellent. Our conversation was easy, wide-ranging, and interesting. Dogs were not the sole topic, but they garnered a good share of our attention.

During the meal, Clara waved and said hello to several people.

But now the room had mostly cleared out, leaving only us and the couple in my line of sight, who'd been served about the same time we were.

The man tucked into a steak with every sign of enjoyment, wielding the restaurant's signature steak knife with intertwined H and T marked into its oddly comfortable—as I knew from experience— triangular handle. While the woman picked at her salmon salad between tossing him searching looks he appeared not to catch.

My curiosity—or nosiness, depending on your angle—lost out to interest in our table's conversation.

Until Clara's sweater slid off the back of her chair.

She twisted to pick it up, then stilled as she straightened.

"Oh." She tentatively raised the hand not holding the sweater, but fully smiled as the people from the other table looked over. "Glenn? Glenn Selka? Is that you? I'm—"

"Clara. Clara Prentice." The man had sandy colored hair, expertly cut, and pleasant but ordinary features.

"Yes. Clara Prentice Woodrow now. It's so nice to see you. You must be here for the reunion? Would you…" She glanced at me, then Teague. We each gave a tiny nod. "…like to join us? Dessert? Or coffee?"

Glenn Selka checked with the woman with a look. We couldn't see her face from here, but it must have been a yes, because they picked up their coffee cups and joined us.

He introduced the woman as his wife, Kirstin. She had dark curly hair, decided eyebrows, and large hazel eyes whose varied colors conveyed shades of emotion. She was pleasant, though her focused attention on her husband made it feel as if the rest of us were peripheral.

Clara introduced Teague and me, with less embellishment than usual. For which I was grateful.

"I'm so glad you came back for the reunion, Glenn."

He flicked a look toward his wife, then said, "Wasn't sure I would, but…" That trailed off into something he wasn't going to express. "How have you been, Clara?"

"I'm good. Really good." She filled him in on marrying Ned, the two of them happily settling here, but his inability to be here this weekend.

After that the conversation dipped into a *what the heck do we say next* silence.

Our young server came and went, casting an eye over the new seating arrangements—noting, but not judging. He looked around at the rest of the otherwise emptied room. A frown flitted across his face, but it didn't seem to be the result of anything in the room, because he turned and went out the door at the back to the central hall.

Teague broke the silence, directing a question at Glenn. "Are you looking forward to seeing your former classmates tomorrow night?"

"It's good to see Clara and there are a few others I hope will be there." He sipped his coffee. "But not a lot of them."

"Then why come?"

Glenn flicked a look toward Teague—if he thought that was a less than casual delivery, he was right, but well short of interrogation. Though those not familiar with Teague's background might not easily recognize the difference.

Glenn addressed his answer to Clara. "Maybe I wanted them— some of them—to see me, more than I wanted to see them. But it is good to see people like you."

He delivered the statements easily, yet his wife had a tuck of worry between her eyebrows.

"What have you been doing since high school, Glenn?"

My question drew a reaction ... from Teague. The slightest tightening of the corners of his eyes. He liked the question.

"College. PhD. Post-doc. One startup. Sold it. Second startup. Sold it. Third one was the big one." He shifted his gaze to his wife. "Married this amazing woman, who's a brilliant therapist, between the post-doc and the first startup. Best move ever. Two boys and a girl and—"

"Who has him wrapped around her little finger." For the first time, I had the impression Kirstin relaxed.

"—a rescue dog," he finished.

I knew I liked him.

"Those are great achievements," Teague said.

"Especially the rescue dog."

Everyone chuckled a little, even though Clara wasn't entirely kidding.

The gaze between husband and wife shifted slightly. I couldn't read his. Hers once more held worry in its depths, yet a go-ahead on the surface.

He interlocked his fingers and set them as if guarding his coffee cup. He leaned forward slightly, looking only at Clara.

I reassessed my impression of his features being ordinary. Especially his eyes. They burned with intelligence and determination.

"There's something I'd like to ask you. I hope you don't mind." But his tone and manner said he was proceeding anyway. "What happened to Heidi Holmes?"

CHAPTER FOUR

THE QUESTION CLEARLY had more import to Glenn, his wife, and Clara than a casual enquiry about a past classmate.

I hadn't heard the name before.

"I never got the whole story," Glenn added. "I was already at college and with my family moving away from here that summer, I never came back until now. And there wasn't much online."

Clara pulled in a long, slow breath.

Movement beyond our table caught my attention and I looked up as a man, apparently a customer, stumbled into Glenn and Kirstin's now deserted table. He must have come from the hall by way of the door in the room's back corner.

Like the walls, the floors of Historic Haines Tavern weren't close to level, though thankfully not as bad as the stair landing. But I had a feeling this stumble stemmed less from what was outside the man, who was dressed in jeans and an untucked beige shirt, than from what he'd recently put inside.

The man didn't fall over or make enough noise for the rest of our table to notice, but his weaving unfurled a flag that read *drunk*.

Our young server must have been paying close attention from somewhere out of my sight. He zoomed in from the doorway.

He put a shoulder under one of the man's arms and levered him upright immediately, as if he'd been doing it forever, his hair falling over his forehead. In the same motion he turned the man, who clutched a napkin from the table, toward the back exit and hustled him out of view. No fuss, no noise.

Clara's next words pinned my attention back to our table.

"Oh, Glenn," she said on an exhale that matched her inhale for length and depth. "I probably don't know much more than you. I'd started college by then, too. And we hadn't been in touch most of senior year." Clara's look took in the three of us who hadn't graduated from North Bend County High School. "One of our classmates—one of our friends—died a few months after graduation from a fall."

It had to be the girl she'd mentioned before, didn't it? The one who'd played cards and board games with Clara, her gran, and their assorted relatives.

"She really fell?" Kirstin Selka asked.

Why would she question it?

Clara nodded solemnly. "The papers had the official report and it said she slid down an embankment behind the parking lot of the apartments where she was living. At the bottom of the embankment, there was a 20-foot drop-off to a paved path."

"But why would she…?"

"It was raining that night. A lot. A thunderstorm with winds and lightning. They said she might have dropped something or it blew away from her, and she went after it without thinking. The ground was so slippery and she went down and couldn't catch herself. They said it was an accident."

Glenn's head came up.

His wife watched him, but he looked straight across the table at Clara.

"An accident? She didn't…? It wasn't deliberate?"

"Oh, no. You thought she committed—? No." She reached across the table and touched the back of his hand.

"You said *They said*. Like you might not believe it."

"I didn't mean that at all, Glenn. I have no reason to doubt the reports. The authorities said there was no note and no indication she *meant* to. That was in one of the newspaper articles my gran sent me."

"Do you still have the articles?"

She withdrew slightly at his urgency, probably not even aware of her reaction. "I can't imagine I do. All these years later? No, I'm sure I don't."

"What do you think, Clara? You knew Heidi. Do you think she could have committed suicide?"

"I have no reason to doubt the official reports," she repeated. "But could have? I don't know, Glenn. Truly, I don't know. She drifted away months and months before the end of school. But on graduation day, she did tell me she was really happy."

"She did?"

"Absolutely. I hardly said more to her than congratulations, good luck, and good-bye."

He sat back. "Me, either. And that was more than I said to most. Not very talkative then."

She smiled. "I know. I recognized you right away, but I wouldn't have remembered your voice. Probably because I rarely heard it."

He chuckled slightly and his wife relaxed as conversation turned more general.

SATURDAY

CHAPTER FIVE

MY PHONE RANG shortly after five o'clock the next afternoon.

That made me jump. Not because of the sound, but because of the realization that it was after five o'clock.

Or maybe it was the caller ID announcing Kit on the other end from her new home in the Outer Banks of North Carolina that made me jump. Not guilt. Not exactly.

To my hello, Great-Aunt Kit asked, "What are you doing?"

Not writing.

Non-writers might not realize it, but not writing can be quite an active state, in which you are doing a whole lot of other things while not writing. Or maybe non-writers do realize it, because their entire lives are not writing. Although they don't feel guilty about it.

"Not much. How are you, Kit? Did you—?"

"I heard music when you answered."

"Sorry. Just some music. I've turned it off."

"I wasn't complaining about the volume. The Righteous Brothers. *You've Lost that Lovin' Feeling.*"

"How do you know—?"

"Distinctive voices. I remember those songs. I should. Heard them often enough. They were my older siblings' era." Kit was younger than my grandmother and her other siblings by a decade and more. "Why were *you* listening to them?"

"Just something I came across on the Internet."

"Ah."

I did not ask *Ah, what?* I stayed quiet.

Didn't stop Kit. "How'd you come across the Righteous Brothers?"

"Oh, um…"

"Can't imagine there's much video of their TV appearances or concerts." After an impatient pause, she added, "Had you found those?"

"Not exactly."

"What exactly, then?"

Sticking to as few words as possible hadn't stemmed her questions, so I went the other direction.

"I stumbled across videos of young people hearing the Righteous Brothers for the first time. France, New Zealand, South Africa, UK, and of course from the U.S. Some are funny, like the guy who said nobody ever told him Ken from Barbie dolls could sing. And a young woman who said she thought a lot of babies were made listening to the Righteous Brothers. But it was also interesting to see them get excited and emotional about the music. One girl said if a guy sang like that to her, they could work it out, no matter what the problem was. And I learned *You've Lost That Lovin' Feeling* was reported to be the most-requested song of the Twentieth Century."

"You were looking that up?"

"Not exactly. Sort of fell into it." I rushed past that. "And, of course, people mentioned *Unchained Melody* as another of their hits, which brought up the movie *Ghost*, when it became a hit again—first a hit in the mid Sixties, then in the early Nineties. Amazing. People listening to the guy with the higher voice doing *Unchained Melody*— Bobby Hatfield—asked did the guy with the deep voice—that was Bill Medley—do anything solo? And that led into people bringing up *I Had the Time of My Life* from *Dirty Dancing*, which Medley sang with Jennifer Warnes, who—"

"Where did you fall from, Sheila?"

"Hmm?"

"You didn't enter the rabbit hole looking for the Righteous Brothers, *Ghost,* and *Dirty Dancing.* You were already down the rabbit hole before you found that particular corridor. What else was in that rabbit hole?"

"Oh, some other reactions."

"To?" The woman should have been an interrogator.

I took my medicine fast. "The Tomb of the Unknown Solider, post 9-11, patriotic songs, Jim Croce, Steve Goodman, Simon and Garfunkel, musical analysis, Don McLean."

"Good grief."

"And baby stoats."

"Baby stoats." She made that sound like I was doing drugs. "How long? And don't say *How long what?*—how long were you down the rabbit hole?"

"Uh, I don't know exactly."

"When did this start?"

"Yesterday morning."

Apparently, she had no trouble hearing my low voice, because she snorted. "At least you stopped to go out to dinner last night, but it is—"

"And the dog park before that." I'd thought I'd broken the spell of this rabbit hole last night, but when I got home from dinner, I opened my laptop in bed and didn't turn it off for four hours. Then, it was so handy when I woke up, right on my bedside table... "Plus, I've been to the dog park yesterday and today. It's not—"

"—*not* a good sign—"

"—like I've been doing it non-stop."

"—you're back at it today." The accuracy of that arrow stung. "Are you dressed?"

"Yes." I packed more indignation into the word than it deserved, since I was dressed again in yesterday's clothes—not what I'd worn to dinner, but my dog park attire of shirt and leggings. And I hadn't taken a shower. Yet.

"You're avoiding something."

Two somethings. Trying to write and telling her that I was trying to write.

I'd tell her someday. Preferably at a point when I wasn't still referring to it as *trying to write*, thus inviting her version of the Yoda *There is no try* speech.

"No, I'm not," I lied. "I—"

"Why weren't you out with your ex-policeman last night?"

"He's not my—"

"Your mother says you've been dating, though she can't tell if you're serious or not."

"It's too early to know if—"

"So you haven't broken up with him."

"Why would you think—?"

"Because it's what you did time after time when we were living together in Manhattan. As for whether this is serious or not, you won't find out by *not* spending time with him. You're avoiding something." My denial hadn't made a dent in her assurance. "Is it him?"

"No. In fact, he was there last night. Clara invited him to dinner, too."

"Huh. Then why are you going to Clara's high school reunion tonight instead of out with your guy?"

"Ned—Clara's husband—is out of town and she asked me to go with her. Anyway, it'll be interesting. On top of which, Teague is spending the weekend making a house wheelchair-accessible." The days, anyway. Not the evenings. Or nights. But we weren't on a level where nights mattered. "I should get going now to get ready."

She snorted, but did not dispute my agenda with words. "We'll talk more later."

Oh, goody.

The trouble with Aunt Kit, I decided as I showered, was that in some ways she knew me better than anybody else in the world. My parents, my siblings, of course, knew me. But they had not been there day to day for most of the past decade and a half as I'd become the person I was now.

Sort of.

Because for all those years I hadn't been myself. I'd been a construct created by Kit and embodied by me.

That character—which I played—presented herself as the author of *Abandon All*, described as this century's *To Kill a Mockingbird*. Something I'm comfortable saying because Kit wrote the book. She did the creating, I did the public role.

In the past year, since Kit retired the persona I'd portrayed, I'd changed. A lot. And not in name only, though I had shed the recognizable name and taken different parts of family names to form Sheila Mackey.

Sheila—*I*—could look back on quite a year.

Like a teenage boy's growth spurt, though, there was no telling when or how the change would stop.

CHAPTER SIX

"YOU SAID YOU'D be ready ten minutes ago," Clara complained mildly as I completed preparations for leaving Gracie alone. Closing some doors, opening others, ensuring she had fresh water, filling a kong with kibble and a couple treats that would take her two minutes to empty, but signaled, yes, I was leaving. "I don't want to be late."

"You don't want to be early," I said.

"What?"

"Nothing. Go get in the car. I'll be right there."

She barely sighed a couple minutes later when I slid in behind the driver's wheel and backed out of the garage.

But she truly didn't want to be early to an event like this where *awkward* swirled around for the first fifteen, twenty minutes. If you were lucky.

A little late was far better, a tactic learned in my days as Kit's public-facing alter ego.

But Clara wasn't the kind to protect herself. So, she wanted to be early.

When I signaled to turn onto the short-cut to the back of the high school, she said, "Don't turn. Keep going straight."

I obeyed, eyeing the crenelated brick building that, fortunately, hadn't taken the castle theme to extremes and so passed up arrow slits for good-sized windows.

"Why didn't we turn at—?"

I broke off, because I'd caught sight of a street sign for the road the building fronted on.

"Carrion Lane?" My voice climbed. "They named the street the high school's on *Carrion* Lane?" Either I hadn't approached this way before or I'd somehow missed the sign.

"No. It was already called Carrion Lane when they built the high school. In fact, I think the land was donated. A long, long time ago. I don't know details."

"Donated or not, putting a school on Carrion Lane ... What's the mascot? A buzzard? A vulture?"

"I know teams use birds, but never heard of a buzzard or vulture as a mascot."

"They're the only appropriate choice for a school on Carrion Lane."

"Tigers is much nicer. Besides, we're not going to the high school tonight. Now, at the next light, turn north."

The reunion was at a mid- to upper-scale chain hotel—nice but not remarkable—not far from the airport, tucked into the northeast corner of North Bend County.

"All the reunions are held here," Clara said. "We get a deal because they cater to business travelers, so they aren't very busy on weekends."

Signs out front welcomed alumni from three different classes. if my quick math was right, a five-year reunion and a thirty-five-year reunion bracketed Clara's twenty-year reunion.

Inside, another sign welcomed North Bend County High School alums and directed all to the left. We followed a glassed-in hallway along the front of the building for what seemed like a block. At last, the hallway turned right, then, from a compact central area, branched three ways.

Clara tugged me into the central branch. As we walked down the short hall, I lagged back slightly to let Clara be greeted by classmates.

No one greeted her.

A clot of people surrounded a table set across the hallway leading to a room labeled "Central North Bend Ballroom." Clara couldn't get past them. Beyond the table and near the ballroom entry, I spotted a sprinkling of people well and truly caught in first-few-minutes awkwardness.

The hallway cloggers were not. They were ebullient, ecstatic even. Female voices went high in delight, male voices laughed loudly.

They paid no attention to Clara.

"Excuse me," she said.

Nobody moved.

"Excuse me," Clara said more strongly. *Atta girl.*

Two women and a man on the outside of the clot stepped back, smiling, and giving her a path. Trouble was, that still left the table—which held nametags, packets of information, and other registration materials—blocking her. Stupid place to put the table.

"Clara…" I caught up, then stepped ahead, catching the edge of the table with my thigh and pushing.

"Uh-oh. Sheila, the table…" Clara reached for the edge to hold it in place.

I shoved harder. "You're right. It'll be much better against the wall. Let people get through and avoid this gridlock."

As the table pivoted, the other end nudged a few people. They made noises, but as long as they didn't use their words to protest, I figured no harm, no foul. The three people who'd opened ranks to let Clara past stepped forward and helped pivot the table, so Clara wasn't the only alum associated with my furniture moving. In case anyone got cranky. The new arrangement shifted enough people that we could see the table's contents.

"Here's your name tag, Sheila." Clara handed it over her shoulder.

A short woman in a dress that vee'd near her waist intercepted it. The movement allowed a wide-open view of her not-quite-so perkies to anyone taller than she was, which was pretty much everyone.

As she backed away with her prize, I realized her height-challenged status was despite wearing four- to five-inch heels.

I used my longer reach to pluck my nametag back. At the same time, I read her nametag: Debi (Eads) Norris. And saw from her attached high school graduation photo that she'd been a pretty girl.

"It's much easier for the attendees to see all the nametags and reach them with the table this way," said one of the women who'd helped move it. A short, sleek hairstyle emphasized her great cheekbones.

Debi glared at her from under eyebrows sharp-edged and thick enough to have been carved into a pumpkin. "Is not."

The woman with the cheekbones gave the tiniest shrug, not engaging with the short woman's pugnacity. The woman with the cheekbones headed for the ballroom, along with the other two table-moving helpers.

"You can't just take a nametag," Debi snapped at me, while giving the back of the alum with the cheekbones a dirty look.

"She's already taken it," said a guy standing off her right shoulder, which gave an unobstructed view of what she had on display. Unlike me, he took full advantage. "What you two girls need to do is mud wrestle for it."

He was not among the rare people who can get away with using *girls*. He wore an untucked blue shirt, his thinning hair in a Caesar cut, stubble nobody would consider fashionable, and a smarmy smile. He triggered my *eww* response.

The woman named Debi said, "Shut up, Marcus."

"Don't worry, Debi," Clara said. "I checked off Sheila's name, see? Sheila Mackey. Now I need my nametag."

Debi took the printed list from Clara and held it in front of her own face. "What's the name of the North Bend High School alum?"

That was a power play. Clara had acknowledged remembering Debi. Now the woman was declaring Clara wasn't important enough to be remembered. If all Clara's classmates were like this, I regretted not bringing sharpened knives along.

"Name?" the Debi woman insisted.

Clara looked quizzical, but said, "Clara Prentice. Now Woodrow."

"How nice for you, but there's nothing on the list, the official, master list. If you're not on here, you're not signed up."

The guy named Marcus tried for another survey down the front of her dress, foiled this time by the paper.

"What about her?" Debi's gaze flicked to me with avid curiosity, thinking thoughts not hard to read. And ignoring that not only did I have my nametag, but Clara had marked me off on the vaunted master list.

Clearly unaware of the other woman's speculation, Clara said, "My husband was unable to attend. Sheila's new to North Bend County and I thought it would be nice for her to make more friends. Where better than reunion weekend?"

"I'll be her new friend," the guy said, bumping his hip against Clara's. Definitely *eww*.

She murmured an *excuse me* as if she'd been at fault and restored normal spacing.

He closed the gap. "In fact, I'll be both your friends. The three of us can—"

"I'm not seeing a nametag for anyone named Cara." Debi's voice topped the guy's. Oblivious to his patter? Or trying to stop it?

"It's Clara," my friend said, "with an 'l' after the 'c'."

"Don't see that, either."

Except Debi wasn't looking at her list. She'd lowered it, reclaiming the guy's attention and his renewed allegiance, judging by his next words.

"Maybe you've got the wrong reunion, Cara. Sure you went to North Bend High?" He smirked, pleased at his supposed cleverness in inferring he didn't remember Clara.

In that moment, he struck me as familiar. In fact, as an all-too familiar type I particularly disliked.

Chuckles rippled through about half of the group still milling near the table. But several non-chucklers broke off and headed toward the room.

"I am sure," Clara said. "Otherwise how would I know you're Marcus Etchells and your nickname was MarcAss? Although I suppose your reputation could have extended beyond North Bend County High School."

She looked so innocent.

In many ways she was. But not entirely.

Some of the remaining chucklers guffawed. The *eww* guy I now knew was named Marcus—or MarcAss—Etchells didn't look happy.

"Oh, there it is, Clara." I accompanied my jovial declaration and pointing finger with a sidewise slide along the table for a hip check into Debi. To regain her balance on those heels, she staggered back and unbalanced Marcus.

He swore at her, even as they clung to each other to keep from falling.

In the meantime, I secured the nametag.

"Thank you, Sheila." Clara picked up an envelope from a stack on the table's corner, took her nametag from me, smiled, pivoted on her heel, and marched toward the interior room.

I caught up with her with a low-voiced, "Well done."

"Silly games." She drew out a list of names from the packet. "After you moved the table, it was clear someone purposefully jammed up the hallway. Heaven only knows why."

So people had to maneuver past, which made others acknowledge them and, some might say, acknowledge their claim to the territory.

"Ado Annie!" a voice from inside the ballroom called with affection and excitement.

Clara called back, "Aunt Eller!"

After enthusiastically hugging a dark-haired woman, she hurriedly explained they'd been in the high school's production of *Oklahoma* together. I knew she'd been in high school plays, but her musical talent was news.

I left them happily catching up. As far as I was concerned, the evening was already a success.

CHAPTER SEVEN

I **MEANDERED IN** a circuit around the room a few times, stopping now and then for brief chats with people who were temporarily solo. Those were my good deeds for the day, easing awkward standing-alone moments before another alum came up and the memories were off and running. Then I eased away.

Maybe they weren't such great good deeds, because they weren't difficult assignments. People were friendly and pleasant, if momentarily bemused by the presence of a non-alum. From what I could tell, few spouses were here, though I spotted Kirstin with Glenn Selka and waved at our tablemates from last night.

During my meandering, I'd picked out a table at the far end of the room, near a double-doored exit to another hallway, which allowed in a nice breeze to fight off any temptation to doze. Better yet, the table provided a good view of the assemblage, including of the entryway.

Perfect place to while away the evening in people-watching.

Before I settled, though, I decided to visit the nearest cash bar.

It was interesting being at a function like this without anybody wanting anything from me—me in my persona as author of *Abandon All*. At those events, I never went to the bar myself, because someone always jumped in with the offer to get me a drink, whether an official host or someone who thought plying me with liquor might earn them an interview (reporter) or The Secret of Publishing (aspiring writer.)

Here, not only was I on my own, but I wasn't an object of attention.

I could down a dozen drinks and it wouldn't even warrant a mention in a gossip column.

If I weren't Clara's designated driver.

And if Haines Tavern, Kentucky, had a gossip column.

"What can I get you?" the young bartender asked. He had blond hair that flopped over his forehead, reminding me of last night's server.

"A club soda with a twist of lime, please."

Feeling quite the adventurer in this unfamiliar territory of bar chat, I boldly asked the bartender, "Keeping busy?"

"Not really. For most of the people, these reunions are more talk than drink. Except for a couple frequent customers."

"Hearing anything interesting?"

"Nah. What happens at a reunion stays at a reunion."

We both grinned.

"Do you work a lot of these?" I asked.

"All the ones that're held here. They're most of my hours for the hotel. People remembering high school is helping me pay for college."

I tipped him more than he'd charged for the drink.

He brightened. "Thanks. Want more lime?"

I chuckled. "No, thanks. I'm good."

"Hey. You got yours. Let somebody else in for—" I turned to find Marcus, the guy who'd made the crack about Clara being at the wrong reunion, hanging over my shoulder. I had the misfortune to be close enough now to inhale his stale-alcohol essence. "Oh. You."

I stepped aside to let him up next to the bar. That took the strain off my nose and—big bonus—kept him from trying to look down my top.

Unfortunately, I failed to secure my glass and Marcus blocked my access to it. I stuck around to retrieve my drink.

"Another double bourbon. No, two," he ordered.

"Marcus," Debi shouted from twenty or thirty feet away. "Get me one, too. I paid for your last round."

"Make it four doubles," Marcus said to the bartender.

Apparently, he knew Debi's drink order. But how on earth was he going to carry four glasses?

Almost before the question formed in my mind, he answered it by chugging the first glass.

The bartender quickly named the price of the drinks, possibly afraid the proof of his serving would disappear.

Marcus pulled out loose bills crammed in his front pocket. It took him another moment to choose two that came closest to his bill and drop them on the bar.

With him distracted, I reached for my glass.

That's where I made my mistake.

I didn't anticipate his quick turn to me.

"You know you're not half bad, babe. Hey, if you want a good time—"

"I'll be sure to find it elsewhere."

Before I could step away, he bracketed me, with a hand on the bar to either side of me.

"Excuse me."

I made as if to step forward. He didn't budge and I didn't follow through because I didn't want front-to-front contact. Or any contact.

"We could have a lot of fun. My car's out in the parking lot."

"Now, there's a head-turning invitation."

"I bet that mouth could talk dirty real good."

We'd gone from head-turning to stomach-turning.

He was going to make me push him to get free. I had no issue with pushing the jerk, but I'd rather not cause a scene that might mar Clara's reunion and call attention to me.

"Your change, sir."

The bartender's words immediately redirected Marcus' attention, whether from the mention of money or a reminder of the awaiting alcohol.

I moved enough to have an escape route, though I was not going to scuttle away.

He took the money, pocketing all of it with zero tip, picked up the three glasses with practiced but not entirely steady hands, and left.

I added another bill to the kid's tip jar.

"No need, but thanks," he said.

"I appreciate the diversion."

We grinned at each other again.

With my club soda, I headed for the table I'd scoped out earlier, noticing on the way that Marcus delivered one glass to Debi and kept two for himself. By my count that was three double bourbons and presumably at least one earlier to justify his order of *Another double bourbon.* Eight bourbons and there were hours more to go.

I DIDN'T MAKE it back to the table right away.

Shorter interruptions came because a couple people Clara had introduced me to stopped me to introduce more people.

The longer interruption in my journey happened when I spotted the dessert table.

Clara had told me the invitation stated "heavy hors d'oeuvres" would be served. That meant eat beforehand or prepare to go hungry. Between Kit calling and Clara arriving, I'd made and eaten a sandwich, leaving dessert unaccounted for.

I approached the dessert table and immediately spotted my target.

A woman in a black and white print shirt dress stood between me and the mini-tarts that surely were chocolate under the decoration of meringue. She wasn't even looking at the table, but turned partly away from it, her gaze landing on cluster after cluster of attendees.

"Excuse me."

She didn't move, she didn't acknowledge my presence.

I stepped into her line of sight, smiled, and added a vague gesture toward the table. "Excuse me."

She looked back, not moving.

From this angle I could see her nametag included a high school graduation photo, so she was an alum. But I couldn't read the name.

In the interests of not damaging Clara's relationship with a former classmate, I kept smiling as I edged closer, hoping my encroachment on her personal space would prompt her to move to one side. "Hi. You're a North Bend County grad?"

She did not move. Other than being able to read the name tag— Josepha Viedux—the only thing I'd achieved was making myself uncomfortable by being so close and wondering how her last name was pronounced.

"Why else would I be here?"

Interesting delivery.

Just flat enough to avoid snarky, so most people might not pick up on the snarkiness. Yet also with a *soupçon* of sharp amusement.

I took a closer look at her.

She was medium height, weight, hair color. No distinguishing marks. The dress didn't help. Its black and white blurred together toward gray.

I could have lunged past her, grabbed a tart or two, and been on my way.

"This is great, isn't it? Such a nice event," I said, probing a bit. "The organizers must have worked hard to put it all together. Get in touch with everybody. Make all the arrangements."

She returned to her survey of the room and its chattering groups of people for a long beat. "They get what they want out of it."

"A fun time for their classmates?"

Her look intimated an eye-roll without making the effort. "Running things. Just like high school."

"Which they seem to have done well, since this is coming off without a hitch." Except for the table blocking the entry, but we'd taken care of that. "Besides, if they're willing to do the work…"

"Oh, yes. Let them do the work. Let them follow their little plans for all these people who are obsessed with who they once were because they haven't had a new thought since high school, if they had one then. The beauties, the brains, the jocks, even ones who still consider themselves immune to it all. None of them are. Not immune at all."

The ends of her mouth lifted. Perhaps her version of a smile.

"Not that I object to their having no thoughts. It makes everything so much easier."

I took it back. This woman did have a distinguishing mark.

Not visible. Internal.

I reached past her. Grabbed two tarts before her presence curdled them. Didn't even say excuse me.

CHAPTER EIGHT

AFTER CONSUMING MY chocolate mini-tarts—not bad at all—and moved by a sense that my reaction hadn't been sufficient counterpoint in the karmic ecosystem to the harshness from the woman in the print dress, I endeavored bridge-building after spotting Debi standing alone.

As I approached and said hi, she didn't look around and replied only with a grunt.

I persisted. "Looks like everything's going well. A reward for all your hard work."

A corner of her upper lip lifted. Not quite a snarl. "It better go well or I'll have that idiot hotel coordinator's job."

I cast around for another topic. "You and Marcus were high school sweethearts?"

"Sweethearts?" She scoffed harshly. "Learned that lesson right after prom. He'd screw any skank who threw herself at him."

With a smile she might have noted was not genuine if she'd bothered to look at me, I tried a more neutral topic. "How's the turnout?"

"Fine."

"From the list you gave attendees, it's less than a third of the class."

I'd switched from bridge-building to *The Bridge on the River Kwai* moment of blowing up my own creation and wondering why I'd built it in the first place.

"We knew some wouldn't come. Hiding at home because they didn't like high school."

"Because they were bullied?"

"Because they weren't popular. Can't stand coming back and see-ing the popular kids."

I suppose it was understandable at least some folks who'd been popular in high school aimed to retain their status. But she'd snapped my last shred of understanding.

"According to his own account, Glenn Selka wasn't popular in high school, but he came back. And he's doing great for himself."

She sniffed. "So he says. How do you know when he lives way out wherever?"

"Phoenix. In Arizona. It is fairly well known. And his company is on the Internet."

"All sorts of scams on the Internet. People making up things all the time. Why hasn't he been part of the Facebook group these past years? Then we'd know what he's really been doing."

Worried about Internet scams, yet she'd rely on Facebook posts for accuracy?

"It's … weird. Like he never did anything here, at home and had to go way out there to accomplish anything."

"He was valedictorian here."

"Like that means anything."

"Staying here didn't guarantee other people accomplishing any-thing."

I thought my comment was plenty pointed.

She didn't see the point. "Them? They weren't ever going to do anything. That was clear in high school."

Was I tempted to ask what she'd done?

Oh, yes. But I restrained myself.

Did I feel more empathy with the woman in the black and white print dress?

Couldn't push myself that far.

I trudged on, trying a different path. "It's been fun to talk to the people Clara has introduced me to. Hearing their stories from high school and all the wonderful things they've done since."

"Who?"

"Clara Woodrow. Was Clara Prentice."

"Oh, yeah. Her. I suppose nobody actually *hated* Clara Prentice, not like some of the others." She didn't even recognize she'd betrayed remembering Clara. "When they noticed her. She just kind of *was*. Boring."

Tipping my head slightly, which gave the impression I was less threatening, I said, "Exactly the nuanced and deep kind of personality that people who aren't at all perceptive will pass over, because only the blatant gets through to them. Ah, excuse me, I see someone calling me."

Some*thing*, rather than some*one*, to be precise. Another chocolate mini-tart.

If Debi were brighter, she might have gotten huffy before I excused myself, but I figured this sting wouldn't land until well after the reunion was over and she sobered up. And even then she wouldn't be entirely sure she'd been insulted … if she thought about the exchange at all.

This called for another mini-tart. Even if I did fall into a sugar stupor.

Clara popped up at my side as I took two.

"Hi there. You should try these. And fast, before I eat them all."

"Is this horribly boring for you?"

"Not so bad."

"I saw you talking to Debi."

"Ill-judged attempt to be friendly with a barracuda."

"She and Marcus, some of the others were cool in high school and they're still—They think they're still cool." Somewhere deep in her heart, she wondered if they actually were. She hadn't totally escaped the pull of the teen orbit.

"They do. But so what? Do you want to be them?"

"No." Genuine horror suffused her face.

"Their supposed coolness is part of a package. Take the whole thing or leave it. Besides, being cool might be important in high school to some kids, but out in the real world, other things matter."

"See? This is why I wanted you to come with me. To remind me what's important when I get a little crazy and—"

A short woman rushed up and clutched Clara's arm, followed more sedately and with no arm-clutching by the much taller woman with the great cheekbones.

"*Clara!* That *was* you I saw on TV talking about some horrible murder." She might as well have said *thrilling* instead of *horrible*. Her nametag said Mary Jo Anderson Hubble, though the final name was emphatically X'ed out. "I was here in the spring, visiting my brother. I never thought you'd be on TV before me, but there you were. But with a different name."

"I'm Clara Woodrow now. My husband—"

"Yeah, yeah, we've all had one of those—or more," she added with an out-of-tune trill of laughter. "But you were on TV. It must have been the high point of your lifetime, looking into the camera and knowing people were watching you for once. Not like when everyone watched us cheering, because, let's face it, people watch TV while they're doing all sorts of other things, so they're only half watching. And then it's forgotten. Not like when the stands are filled with people all watching us cheer."

Or possibly looking past them to the sporting event.

"They said she solved that murder," said the taller woman.

"Not me alone. It was—"

Before I could interrupt Clara's attempt to draw me into the conversation and shovel credit on me, Mary Jo did a thorough job of it with a flutter of her hand, followed by, "The reporter you talked to— someone should tell her that her eyeliner needs to turn up at the corners, not down. She looks so *grim*."

Because everybody wants to see a reporter with perky eyeliner reporting about a murder.

"They said it was brilliant detecting. Not even the police had figured it out," the woman with the cheekbones said.

I peered at her nametag, catching Ancella as her first name. Something long and complicated after it.

"The police?" Mary Jo shuddered artistically. "Anyway, the important question is if you're going to be on TV again."

"I, uh, I don't know."

"You have to pin them down. Don't let them give you vague answers. And tell them about me. I can do local reports on North Bend County. I know all the news here."

"Don't you live in Michigan now?"

She ignored Clara's question.

"Anytime they want. Now that you have connections, I'll give you a call. Oh, there's Julian. I must say hello. You know his brother almost won an election for something."

"School board," Ancella said.

Mary Jo economically waved that off and used the same gesture for farewell to Clara, never having acknowledged me, and hurried off toward a man I'd bet had hair in high school or Mary Jo wouldn't have been interested in him—near miss election to the school board in the family or not. Because this guy would make even the most ardent bald-lover rethink her position.

"Polly was looking for you earlier. She has photos to show you. I can take you to where she was sitting. Both of you." Ancella included me with a smile.

"Not me, thanks. I'm staying here by the desserts. You two go ahead."

"If you're sure…"

"Sure. Go. Talk. Have fun," I ordered Clara.

It might have been wrong of me, but I was starting to enjoy myself. For reasons beyond Clara's pleasure.

Kit had taught me by example about collecting bits and pieces of behavior, traits, gestures, expressions, and phrases for application to characters. Not only was this a flea market of such collectibles, but I cared about only one person here, so I wasn't hindered by knowing the real people.

I heard chatter about whose job was more important than someone else's, about children being either the best or worst ever, about marriages made and broken.

But two themes recurred the most.

One was how much the airport had changed since the flyer-ins last used it. The North Bend County stayers responded either that the airport was a savior with runways (a minority position espoused by county employees) or a pain in the ass bad neighbor (everybody else.)

The second was dead classmates, starting with Heidi Holmes, a few months after graduation.

They followed her name with a list of military deaths, accidents, and a couple from cancer.

Hard to tell from their expressions if the attendees taking in the sad roll were mourning or internally celebrating they weren't among the fallen, or both.

CHAPTER NINE

I **HADN'T LEFT** the dessert table—or as I thought of it now, the tart table—when I watched Josepha ease up to a position across a nearby hors d'oeuvre table from Glenn. I shifted along the dessert table to get closer, even though this end had no chocolate mini-tarts.

"Surprised to see you here, Glenn Selka."

"Surprised to see you, too, Josepha Viedux." That answered one question—he pronounced it *VY-ducks.*

"But I live locally and you came all the way from Arizona."

A flicker of reaction crossed his face. At her knowing where he lived? Surprise? Annoyance? Pleasure?

Probably not pleasure. I didn't get high school honeys vibe from them—especially not with his interest last night at dinner in Heidi Holmes.

"Not such a big deal with those modern flying machines they've got nowadays."

She ignored that. "Stayed away because of Heidi's death?"

"No," he said calmly.

"Probably wise to stay away, considering how things changed." An undercurrent of frustration edged her words. He was balking her of some point she wanted to make. "You never came back before."

"It's nice you noticed."

His hint of humor was not appreciated.

"If not Heidi and the end of the great romance—though she seemed to move on, didn't she?—must have been because of what Debi, Mary Jo, and Marcus did."

"What did they do?" This time, he failed to mask the strain as much as he likely hoped.

"Tried to get you removed as valedictorian. Didn't you know? Or did you? They said *they* were the class leaders and you were a nobody. The three of them told Principal Ingram you shouldn't give the speech because you weren't part of class leadership and the valedictorian should be a leader, not a hermit."

After a brief, tense pause, Glenn chuckled with what struck me as genuine amusement. His previous strain was gone. "If only I'd known. I would have been ecstatic to be spared giving a speech at graduation. Although to pick someone from their social group, they'd have to slide right through good grades and dig down deep into mediocre grades. Guess they didn't know valedictorian was based on grades."

"We should talk more about this tomorrow at—"

"Sorry, I'll be spending all my time with my wife."

My peripheral vision caught him moving away from her.

More of my vision could see her expression.

She was not amused.

Momentarily.

Then sharp interest replaced dissatisfaction.

I swung around in my chair to follow the direction of her gaze.

Marcus and another man crossed paths in an open space. The second man was neatly dressed in pressed jeans and a polo shirt, un-logo-ed and tucked in. He had a sharp nose, brown hair, and pale skin.

Marcus clapped the man on the back. As the clappee turned to see who'd delivered the blow, Marcus yanked him into a bear hug. The other man's arms hung at his side.

"Wesley Oshmann, you son of a gun. Great to see you. Been too long. Way, way too long." The standard reunion greeting. It was a testament to Marcus' personality that the words seemed imbued with an unpleasant context.

"Marcus." The man named Wesley made it an entirely neutral greeting.

"Can you believe all those people croaked? Heidi Holmes to start and on down to that guy last month. Who was he? Swear I never heard of him. Lucky we're still walking around, right?"

Proving the *eww* response was gender neutral, Wesley tried to duck away from the arm still around his shoulders. Proving Marcus' social tone-deafness also was gender neutral, he tightened his hold.

"This guy was the best wingman ever," he declared to a third man walking past, who showed no interest. Marcus addressed the room at large. "Never tried to edge into my spotlight. Never worried about him trying to snag the babes I wanted. Left my lane wide open so I had my pick. Was always there when I needed him. Kind of thing ties us together for life. Right, Wesley Oshmann the Assman?"

Marcus Etchells truly thought he was charming, I realized.

"It was a long time ago," Wesley said.

"*You.*"

I looked around at the peremptory word no one would mistake for a greeting.

Debi Norris. Looking at me.

In my vicinity, anyway, because her focus was well short of pin-point.

I'm no aura reader, but I could almost see a miasma of alcoholic fumes around her.

"Fix my zipper." She turned her back to me and gestured over her shoulder.

The zipper on her dress was down to her waist. That loosened the material in front so she had to hold it to her chest to keep the whole thing from sliding down to hobble her ankles.

Gee, I wondered how that happened.

I wondered less when the bald guy Mary Jo had fluttered off to see came in from the back hall with a sheepish expression and tucking in his shirt.

I stood behind Debi and grasped the zipper firmly. Pulling the material away from her back gave a view all the way down. Either she'd started the night commando or she'd lost her underwear along the way.

I edged around a bit and she followed by necessity, giving both of us a direct view of Marcus and Wesley Oshmann. They hadn't moved, though I might have missed some dialogue.

"Hey. That hurts," Debi griped.

"Hold still." I wasn't about to apologize to her.

Marcus' unchanged grin said he remained delighted to see his old classmate. "Still applies, still applies, my wingman. Tied for life. Nothing changes with Assman. Assman, Assman. Sounds like you liked butts." He laughed uproariously.

I didn't get why that was funny to him.

"Excuse me. I want to say hello to a friend from elementary school." Wesley walked away.

I started pulling up Debi's zipper. "Who was that with Marcus?"

"Wesley Oshmann." Her reply held no particular interest.

"They're friends? Were friends?"

"He *worships* Marcus. Follows him around like a little puppy. Always has. As if giving him rides was enough to make *Wesley* one of us."

Had she not seen what I did?

With the zipper up, she stepped away and shimmied her shoulders to settle herself into the dress, also resetting her decolletage at maximum exposure.

I looked down at her face, surveying the room with a studied air of unconcern that didn't curtain the avid urgency of a bird chasing a worm. I felt sorry for her in that moment.

"Oh." With that worm-sighting syllable, she darted away.

No more inclined to thank me than she would a hanger holding the dress in her closet. And everyone knows, hangers can't feel sympathy.

I looked back to the tall man who'd escaped Marcus. He'd joined a group that included Glenn Selka and his wife, talking with apparent pleasure.

A friend from elementary school? Or a spur of the moment excuse to separate from Marcus?

Wesley slipped the bonds of the Marcus cult sometime in the past twenty years.

The blinders had lifted.

Surveying the room's pockets of conversation, I bet a lot of blinders had lifted as they saw each other as people, rather than potential threats to their status or—more widely—potential sinkholes in the bumpy road to self-assurance.

But what about the greater challenge of removing their blinders about themselves?

If I'd had a magic wand at that moment, I'd have let every one of them see themselves as others saw them as they were now—for good or bad.

I'd bet most would be astonished to realize they were viewed as full-fledged, functioning adults with about the same number of insecurities as everybody else, rather than the hormone-rattled kids of high school. On the flip side, a few would be astonished to realize they weren't viewed as teenaged gods and goddesses.

I knew which camp I'd put Marcus in. Especially as I watched him horn into the group with Wesley and Glenn.

CHAPTER TEN

DEBI NORRIS HELD the microphone like it was the answer to all her prayers.

She called for everyone's attention and got cranky when they didn't respond immediately.

"Shut *up!*" she shouted into the mic.

That did it as people stared at her.

"Good. Stay quiet while we're doing the awards."

Debi herself snagged *Most Involved*, which might be accurate, and *Looks the Same*, which was not.

Came the Farthest displayed the award committee's lack of geographic knowledge when it went to a guy who'd been among the hallway-blockers at check-in. He'd come from Georgia ... compared to Glenn's trip from Arizona.

I'd hoped *Most Hair Lost* would go to Marcus, despite there being a few bald heads. After all, other awards weren't constrained by reality.

Instead, it went to Ancella, the woman with the cheekbones, who'd had a mane of hair according to her high school photo and now had the sleek, short cut. I applauded for her.

My attention flagged as it became apparent each member of that group had an award coming—no matter how much of a stretch. One moment caught my attention. Debi put her arm around equally short Mary Jo Anderson while handing her some award I'd missed, Mary Jo ducked and jerked away. She also exited the area around the microphone, while most of the others lingered.

Finally, Marcus and Debi preened on stage as a poor-quality video recaptured their glory as homecoming king and queen, followed by prom king and queen.

They were still at it when a member of the audience shouted, "Oh, look, it's Mr. Z," effectively ending the awards presentation.

I turned to see a man who could give George Clooney a run for his money on gray-haired appeal.

Debi and Mary Jo, trailed by Ancella, rushed toward him. The first two grabbed his arms with clear self-satisfaction.

Except Debi saw Mary Jo had an equal hold and glared across at her, then proved her instinct to assert higher status by throwing her arms around the man's neck with full frontal contact.

"Mr. Z." Her squeal pierced the surrounding noise.

Ancella pulled up short and smiled at him. He returned it over Debi's head while he disentangled himself with practiced ease, pivoting out of their holds with the balance and élan of a professional dancer.

It brought him face to face with Josepha Viedux.

"Mr. Z. Are you here alone?"

"Officially, I'm not here. I'm next door at my own reunion. Just came in to say hello to you all."

"My, and you said hello to the girls first? That's a change."

He didn't color, but the flesh over his cheekbones tightened. "Ah, but some things don't change. Like you, Josepha Viedux."

Before she responded, more alums circled round, saying hello to Mr. Z and he was telling them to call him Lovell. From the chatter, I gathered he'd taught history or whatever they called it these days that involved historical events, coached something to do with running, and his full last name was Zelig.

He was surrounded by smiles and I found myself smiling at the group. In their interactions, the teens they'd been resurfaced in a kind of renewed freshness.

It struck me as rather sweet.

Josepha watched the press around Mr. Zelig with intense interest. She wasn't smiling.

Then my peripheral vision caught one figure cutting across the room to intercept another headed toward the cluster around the teacher.

The interceptor was Marcus, with a teeth-baring grin that made me think of an ominous jack-o'-lantern. The other was Wesley.

Curious, I wandered their direction to pick up Round Two.

"Hold on there," Marcus demanded. "Hear you got a nice setup. Live in a nice place. Good job. Cute kids. Loving wife. More than you ever thought you'd have, huh? Was really looking forward to you bringing the wife."

His use of *the wife* rubbed me the wrong way, a response inculcated in me by Kit. She maintains switching *your* wife to *the* wife turns a person into a category.

"Been wanting to meet her forever. Since you didn't invite me to the wedding."

That could have sounded teasing. It sounded harsh. Probably as a result of those double bourbons.

"Told you, it was a very small wedding."

"Yeah, yeah. Well, who needs women anyway. You and me'll party hard. Staying a couple days? We can really go. Tonight's not so hot, with these jokers at the bars watering the drinks. But I've got the good stuff out in my car."

"No thanks."

"C'mon, don't be a wuss."

"Sorry. Going to say hi to Mr. Zelig. Know you don't like him, so see you later."

This short Round Two ended with a string of muttered curses from Marcus, but no other drama.

SEATED AT MY favorite table, with mini-tart sugar jangling through my bloodstream, my attention perked up when a female voice came from behind my left shoulder.

"…like a bad dream. Except you don't wake up the next morning. A bad memory lasts forever. Like a nightmare that keeps coming back. Or a bill you have to pay every month. And you will. Every single month. Forever."

The words might sound sad, or even ominous, but the tone struck me as—I grappled for the right description—*triumphant.*

"Not here." That harsh whisper wasn't identifiable as male or female.

I turned. Too late. The shadow of a figure disappeared around the corner into the hallway, followed by a glimpse of a black and white print dress.

CHAPTER ELEVEN

I HESITATED, BUT not long. I followed, perfectly willing to sacrifice one of nine lives to satisfy my curiosity.

Oh, wait. That's cats.

Well, just have to take the chance.

Too late to turn back without having my movements look less than casual—if anyone happened to be watching me the way I'd been watching them.

Alas, *too late* also applied to learning more about that exchange.

Neither the shadow figure nor Josepha's print dress was in sight. I took several quick steps in the direction they'd gone, but then heard a door close ahead.

Yet I still heard the burble of voices from around a curve in the hall. Another minute took me around the curve, to where I could see one of a double set of doors open to another room like the one I'd left. Was the closed door the one I'd heard?

This must be one of the other two reunions. Standing partly behind the open door, I peered inside.

The five-year reunion, I decided, based on the attendees looking like babies and on me hating their music. Isn't that always the way?

Contemplating how the passage of time rolls into cycles with one generation looking askance at the next, I started to turn away, a move that morphed into a jump a foot off the ground when a voice came from behind me. I completed the turn in an arm-flailing whirl.

"What's wrong, Sheila?"

"*Clara.* Good heavens. Don't sneak up on people. Especially when they can't hear anything over that noise."

"I saw you leaving. Are you okay?"

"Absolutely fine. No reason for you to check on me. Now, go on back and be with your friends."

"*You're* my friend."

"I know, but you see me all the time. This is a rare chance to see these folks."

"My best friend. Probably the best friend I've ever had, except for Ned, of course."

I took her arm and turned her back toward the twenty-year reunion room. "Same back at you. Except about Ned, of course."

"I can't thank you enough for coming with me tonight. I probably shouldn't admit it, but I might have turned tail and run from the registration table if it hadn't been for you."

"No, you wouldn't have. Especially not if there'd been a dog to rescue or a wrong to right on the other side. You just needed a nudge to remember you're worth fighting for, too."

She hugged me. Over her shoulder, I spotted the outline of a door in the outside wall that mostly blended into the surface. Was that where Josepha and whoever she'd been talking to took their discussion of bad memories, nightmares, and bills to pay?

"I'm having a great time," she told me, as if that would be news to me. "Everybody's so friendly and *interesting*. But I wish you'd stick around with me and let me introduce you to everyone."

"Clara, this is for you guys and all your memories. I'm doing great. It's prime people-watching, as you predicted. And I've chatted with very nice people. Besides, as I said, I'm around all the time. Those people are a limited commodity. Spend time with them. Store up the memories so you can tell me all about them later."

As we walked past the door set into the outside wall, I picked up snatches of words. From outside? Beyond us down the hall? Behind us?

"…truth… hiding. I go, you go. … Want to lose…?"

Another voice. Maybe. No words though.

Then "Told you. It's all set."

I saw no handle in the door. I slid my hand over the surface. Nothing. I looked behind us. Nothing there. Nothing in front of us, either.

"Sheila? What's the matter?"

"Did you hear that?"

"Hear what?"

"People talking. At least one person talking."

She shook her head, but willing to believe me asked, "Who? What did they say?"

I exhaled. "I don't know who. Not even male or female." Or real or imaginary. "It was probably nothing. You know how sometimes your mind makes words out of sounds that are just sounds? That must be what it was."

We'd neared the door to her reunion room.

Before we could enter the room, though, two figures burst into view from around the hallway curve leading to the third reunion ballroom.

"—told you and told you, I didn't. Stop yapping about it." Uncharacteristically, Debi's voice, while recognizable, came so low it barely reached audible.

"I don't believe you. I never believed you. You have no morals." That was Mary Jo. Mascara-blackened semicircles under her eyes. Tears trickled down. She, too, kept her voice low.

"What difference does it make? You divorced the guy. Why are you still harping on this? Water under the bridge." Perhaps recognizing that didn't reinforce her denial, Debi added, "Because I never slept with your husband—your ex."

"He's out of my life now, but you're still in it. You were supposed to be my best friend. From *kindergarten.* That's what difference it makes."

"For God's sake, stop going on about it. I told you and told you—"

"That you didn't sleep with him and I don't believe you. You did. Admit it. Friends since kindergarten and the minute I turned my back—"

"Well, that's your problem."

Before I finished forming the thought that it was pretty darned cold of Debi to say it was Mary Jo's fault for turning her back for a moment on her husband and best friend, she had more to say. "If you don't believe me, if you don't want me in your life, then leave me alone."

Debi pushed Mary Jo, jostling her arm, sloshing the drink she held over her hand. Mary Jo stepped back from the liquid and bent slightly at the waist, trying to keep it off her clothes. It almost looked as if she'd bowed to Debi, who made full use of that to start to swan past her like royalty.

Then she spotted Clara and me, frozen in place.

"You are the meanest—" Mary Jo's eyes filled with more tears.

"Shut up." Debi gripped the other woman's arm and jerked her past us.

Mary Jo appeared too miserable to recognize our presence, much less acknowledge it. Debi spared us a general glare and kept going.

They disappeared into the reunion room.

Clara and I remained where we were.

"Wow. Those two fighting. And over…" Clara barely moved her head to look at me. "You don't really think Debi would…? Her best friend?"

Considering she'd already been out of her dress at least once tonight, I really thought she would. I didn't say that. "Guess best friends forever didn't work out for them, huh?"

I cupped her elbow to start her toward the door to the middle ballroom.

Instead of following my steering, she continued on down the hallway. To keep contact with her, I did the same.

"Let's go see what's going on with the other reunion," she said.

"But…"

"I don't want to go in right behind them in case people figure out they're fighting and think we know something. C'mon."

Following her to that third door, I was thinking we did know something. Not a lot of something, but something.

Also, I was thinking this group's music was a huge improvement over the newbie alums'. As we got closer, I realized a major factor might be they had the volume much lower. Almost as if they wanted to talk to each other.

Standing at the open doorway, we could also see the lighting was better, and many small groups talked, laughed, mingled.

I barely had time to speculate that the additional years under their loosening belts had brought these North Bend County alums far greater ease than a swath of Clara's classmates had attained, when two voices called out simultaneously, "Clara."

"Carole, Linda, how are you?"

Hugs ensued, followed by introductions. Clara explained they were among her late mother-in-law's close friends.

"Did you come to see us all?" Carole asked. "How smart of you. This is the place to do it."

"That would have been smart, but I can't claim it. My twentieth is next door."

"Twentieth? No. You're just a baby," objected Carole.

"You must be knocking their socks off, because you look fantastic. Absolutely glowing," added Linda.

Clara blushed slightly as she smiled. "It's been too long since I've seen you all. I feel so bad for not keeping in better touch."

"Nonsense. You needed a rest after Ned's mom passed. Nobody could have done more for her than you did. I know Ned was concerned about you and how you gave and gave."

"He's been terrific. He insisted I not work at all for a while, and now I'm setting up my own business online and he fully supports it. We all have to plan a lunch together soon. In fact, I would love to start coming back to your lunches—If you'll have me. I don't want to horn in on your group or—"

"Darling, you are a breath of fresh air every time you come around us old fogies, and we would love to have you come now and then. But we should not be your core social group. You need people your own age."

"Too," Carole said.

Linda and Clara turned to her with faint, puzzled frowns.

"Too," she repeated. "She needs people of her own age, too. In addition to us." Carole looked at me and patted my arm in a friendly way. "We were so happy to hear you and Sheila—this is Sheila Mackey we've heard so much about, isn't it?—have become friends. Double dates, even."

Both she and Linda grinned at us. "Donna, of course," Carole finally said by way of explanation.

And all was clear. Donna and her placid senior retriever named Hattie were the acknowledged doyennes of the dog park. Apparently, they ruled a wider realm than I had been aware of.

"You two go on back to your fellow youngsters, and we'll call you about the next lunch so you both can come."

"That would be great. Wouldn't that be great, Sheila?"

"I look forward to it."

They seemed like a lot of fun, even though they might be too sharp for my comfort in this ongoing charade. But how much could one lunch hurt?

CHAPTER TWELVE

WE RETURNED BY the back hallway. As we rounded its bend, we heard voices.

Clara and I exchanged a *Déjà vu?* glance.

Not lowered voices this time. Though we quickly saw one belonged to a repeat performer—Debi. Marcus provided the other.

They were close together and he appeared to be trying to undo my good deed, trying to manipulate her dress zipper, one-handed and over her shoulder.

Sure glad my zipper duty hadn't included those obstacles.

"…fine for you to say, but why's he avoiding me?" Marcus complained.

"You're crazy. He'll want to hang out at the after party. He always wanted to be around us because of who we are and he's a nobody." She tried to look over her own shoulder. "Are you ever going to—"

Clara clomped loudly, disrupting the tryst. I might have let it run a little longer to see their reactions when we made ourselves known.

Marcus leered at us over Debi's shoulder. "Like watching?"

Clara kept going, which brought her into Debi's field of vision.

"You two again? What are you doing back here? That's weird."

The fact that seeing us meant she was back here, too, clearly eluded her.

Rather than faulting her former classmate's logic, Clara answered her question. "We visited the thirty-fifth reunion."

"You have something for old people?" Without a breath, she added, "And, speaking of weird, why'd you bring your *girlfriend* to the reunion?"

"As I said earlier, my husband, Ned, couldn't come at the last minute and I had the ticket, so I thought she could meet more people from the county, since—"

"Couldn't come at the last minute, huh? Heard that one before. Like he was ever going to come."

"He was. Urgent business kept him out of town for the weekend."

"Ha. Ha." Marcus said. "More like urgent blonde business."

He cackled at his witticism. Debi continued watching Clara like a snake at a mouse hole.

I watched Clara fight—and win—the urge to respond.

Debi might have seen it, too. So she let loose another arrow. "Even with the husband AWOL, I don't get why you brought *her*. Unless there's something kinky going on."

Clara coolly stared her down. "Haven't you ever had a friend, Debi? No," she said with deliberation, "I guess you haven't."

Grinning, I took her arm and continued on our way. "Way to go, gunslinger. You shot her down but good."

"Wish I could have shut up Marcus, too. Implying Ned… well, you heard."

"Shutting him up is not worthy of your efforts. He's three-quarters of the way to shutting himself up by falling into a coma."

I SENT CLARA off to have more fun with those among her former classmates who'd turned out to be pleasant adults, watching her enjoyment from my seat at the well-situated table.

Unfortunately, unconsciousness did not claim Marcus, though his drunkenness progressed.

By the time the bulk of the group was exiting, he was well past *eww*.

He put a bit of a damper on what struck me as a touching reluctance to disperse, with clumps of alums lingering to chat on the sidewalk outside the hotel's doors. He lumbered around with no apparent aim, disrupting the congenial knots.

"Watch out," he shouted after he'd smashed into one of the alums

Clara had introduced me to. Fae Ballard was an IT security specialist, who'd learned a lot about self-presentation since her high school graduation photo.

She ricocheted into the teacher, Mr. Zelig, who steadied her with a hand under her elbow. Mr. Zelig had joined this group after his own reunion broke up a few minutes earlier.

Marcus sneered at them. "If you weren't so fat, you wouldn't need a fairy's help. Fat Fae and the fairy."

"Shut up, Marcus," came from several directions.

"Boo hoo hoo for Fat Fae and the fairy. All of you. Buggets— *Buckets* of tears. Crybabies."

Fae turned and walked away on the sidewalk along the front of the building. With her head down, she removed her purse strap from her shoulder and held the purse in front of her, out of the sight of the rest of us. Looking for something to wipe tears?

"Fae," Mr. Zelig called, frowning at her departing back.

"Yeah, yeah, everybody go crying after Fat Fae," Marcus mocked.

"*Should* someone go after her?" I kept my question to an undertone only Clara would hear.

She shook her head. "Give it a minute, because—"

Clara was drowned out by Marcus.

"Aw, poor baby. Poor boo hoo baby. Goin' off all by herself." With his accent now slurred and thickened, he then said a word I heard as "Oscillating herself."

Oscillating herself.

It took another beat to add context, then subtract his thickening accent and slurring to recognize it as *isolating herself.*

He didn't wait for anyone to decipher what he said.

"Fancy clothes, big job, stayin' at the fancy-dancy B&B, and for what? Nothin'. Because all that can't hide what she is, always has been. She was fat in high school, now she's even fatter. How's it even possible?" He laughed, the sound broken off by a cough. Those around him withdrew. "But I don't get it. How does anybody get that fat?"

That was egregious even by the standards I'd come to associate with Marcus Etchells during our brief acquaintance.

He didn't seem *that* drunk.

Something tickled at my memory.

"How does anybody get this stupid?" someone muttered, drawing sounds of agreement.

Turning to try to spot the speaker, I saw Josepha Viedux—definitely not the speaker—watching over someone's shoulder, her eyes alight with interest.

"Yeah," Marcus said with no apparent inkling the comment was directed at him. "Fat *and* stupid."

His denseness earned a few disgusted sounds.

He appeared to take them as encouragement and laughed even louder, this time ending by spitting on the sidewalk.

Those in the immediate vicinity widened the gap around him. Other attendees started to move away. Dividing to the sides, as if avoiding a rock in a stream, to head for the parking lot.

Debi screamed at him. "Don't be gross."

Nice that she protested spitting, but not his nastiness to a fellow alum.

No one seemed surprised by any of this. Including Fae Ballard, who at that moment returned to the outer ring of the group.

She showed no sign of tears. No blotchy cheeks, no red eyes, no marred makeup. I indulged a moment of envy, since I am a champion ugly crier.

"Gross? I can do better than that." He grabbed the waist of his pants, as if about to open and drop them.

Debi squeaked a protest.

Wesley stepped up and tried to take his arm.

"Don't touch me." Marcus jerked away, unsettling his own precarious balance and stumbling toward Debi.

For a second it looked like he'd take her out—albeit accidentally.

Instead, she braced her legs and shoved him hard in the chest, sending him backward three steps.

"Marcus, call a ride." Wesley said with more patience than anyone else seemed to feel. "It's past time you left."

"Leave? Yeah, yeah. Us. The gang. Leave these losers behind for somethin' better. But I don't need a ride. I'm driving. I'll get you in the party, Oshmann the Assman, just like the old times, whatever the rest of them say," he said in one of those abrupt reversals of mood those worse the wear for drink can do. "C'mon, we'll go now. Just gotta know where's the after party, huh?"

"You know where it is, you idiot. Senior Hill," Debi snapped.

"You should come, too." Josepha's voice came unexpectedly loudly. "You'll be very interested. You really, really should come. You won't want to miss this."

Surprised she would be part of the group going to an after party, I shifted and realized she'd addressed Mr. Zelig.

Marcus, sticking to his own thread, scoffed, "Forget lame Senior Hill. I mean someplace hot. Now. Right now."

Nobody responded to him.

"Fine, you bunch of losers, I'll go find my own after party. You were wusses in high school. You're still wusses."

He took a step, then three more choppy ones, as if on a downhill slope.

Clara nudged me and whispered, "Look."

She tipped her head toward the entrance from the highway, where a sheriff's department vehicle was arriving.

The bulk of the main building cut it off from view almost immediately.

"You can't drive." Wesley stepped into the gap around Marcus.

"Great driver. Ga-reat. Nobody can say different."

"You *won't* drive."

With perfect timing to reinforce Wesley's statement, the sheriff's department vehicle came around the corner of the wing and slid to a gentle stop.

"The hell I won't." Marcus pushed at Wesley's shoulder.

Wesley retreated a step.

Marcus swore at him, advanced, and pushed his shoulder again, harder.

With an eye on the official car, Wesley retreated another step, apparently hoping to avoid a confrontation. He was hampered by other attendees behind him. He moved to his left.

"What? Tryin' to run away?" Marcus pursued with shuffling steps and bobbing head. "You're the biggest wuss of all. Don't know why I ever let you hang around with me in the first place."

"Because he's the only one who'd put up with your bull," Mr. Zelig said under his breath.

With surprising speed, Marcus reached across the gap and punched Wesley's shoulder.

At that moment, a deputy I didn't recognize emerged from the vehicle at a deliberate pace, settling his utility belt as he assessed the situation.

His task probably became easier as the remaining reunion attendees receded, leaving Marcus as a center stage soloist with his percussive swearing.

He lunged toward Wesley again with his right hand fisted.

"Marcus. That's enough," the deputy said with impressive authority.

"What the—?" Marcus tried to look over his shoulder, which threatened his balance. He broke off with another string of curses.

"Back away, Marcus. Everybody else, step back."

Marcus turned to face the deputy, who maintained a distance. "Nobody needs you here. Nothing's going on."

"Must be something going on. You've got all these people here. What is it, Marcus?" the deputy said easily.

"Reunion. High school." Though it came out as *shool*. "All friends. No trouble." As much as Marcus tried to be casual, his tone yo-yoed from truculent to whiny, while he swayed as if on a rocking boat. "No reason for you to be here."

"That's the thing, Marcus. We were called, then add in that I saw you punch that gentleman."

"That doesn't mean anything. He won't complain."

"Why don't you come on over by the car and we'll talk about it, while your friends go on with what they were doing."

"We were gonna go—"

"Not now. You can see them later." The deputy nodded to the rest of us in clear dismissal.

"You don't understand. Really, he won't complain. He's my friend." Marcus' face contorted like an old TV losing its signal. He waved toward Wesley. "Tell him. Tell him you won't ever complain."

The deputy said, "C'mon, Marcus. Doesn't matter. I saw you do it, so—"

"He won't complain. He does everything I say, because he knows what's good for him."

Marcus did not appear to recognize he'd undercut anything Wesley might say on his behalf.

Or maybe he did recognize it belatedly, because he abruptly lunged toward the deputy. "You don't understand."

The lunge clipped the deputy's arm, but he retained his balance. In fact, he used Marcus's momentum to propel both of them toward the official vehicle, while obtaining a firm grip on his subject.

Without missing a beat, he resumed addressing Marcus in a firm but soothing tone, too low to pick up words.

"I'm sorry, Wesley." Clara touched his arm.

He grimaced from a gray face. "I'm okay."

As he moved away, I saw Josepha watching with a cold, glittering interest.

The rest of us broke up into transport units—how we'd arrived and how we would be leaving. I thought I heard exchanges about seeing each other again, but I focused on the interaction between Marcus and the deputy.

From my car, I watched in the rearview mirror and saw the deputy guide Marcus into the back seat of the vehicle. Something about both men's movements made me think of an often-performed dance.

CHAPTER THIRTEEN

PAYING ATTENTION TO the rearview mirror along with making sure I didn't hit anything ahead of us as vehicles funneled toward the exit kept me occupied.

"Where did you go back there?" Clara asked.

"Huh?" With us stopped, waiting for traffic to clear, I blinked my focus back to her. "Go?"

"Mentally. Your attention. You were dialed in, watching Marcus making a scene like a hawk—"

"You make me sound like Josepha Viedux."

"—and then you sort of glazed over and—" She flipped one hand. "—disappeared."

"I don't know. It felt like something tugged at me, but whatever it was didn't gel."

"It'll come back eventually," said my optimistic friend.

In the rearview mirror, I saw the deputy sitting in the driver's seat, though the official vehicle didn't move. Absently, I said, "Maybe it's not meant to. Maybe there wasn't anything there in the first place."

Clara tsk'd at me. I didn't listen to her optimism scold. My mind slipped away to unknown territory as I continued watching the mirror with occasional checks of the lack of movement ahead.

"…why you insisted on staying on the fringes," she finished, having shifted at some point to scolding me about not being sociable.

"The thing about sitting on the fringes is you hear all sorts of interesting conversations."

"Like what?"

"We both heard one woman accuse another of sleeping with her husband when the first woman—the wife—was out of town."

Clara groaned.

"That wasn't all I heard," I said quickly. "There was a conversation about memories."

"Oh, that's nice. People remembering the good memories."

Some bad memories last forever. Like a nightmare… bill you have to pay every month.

I wasn't repeating that and souring Clara's mood.

She continued, "I had such a good time. And what surprised me was it wasn't only the people I remember as friends who were great to see. It was wonderful to hear what lots of people have done and see how they've turned out. Plus, there were people who were happy to see me." Her eyes widened at the last word.

"From what I heard, you were a favorite, Clara."

"Oh, no. I wouldn't say that at all. But it was fascinating how much more comfortable I was. Especially with the boys. Well, men now."

"Some of them."

She might have missed my mutter.

"I used to be so nervous to talk to them. Terrified. But it was fun talking to them tonight. They're great. I mean regular guys, but great. Know what I mean?"

"Yeah. Amazing how a few years can change perspectives on the opposite sex."

She grinned. "And being married to Ned."

"I can't judge how being married to Ned might change attitudes toward other guys."

She giggled. "No, but you know how dating Teague has changed your attitude to other guys."

Not interested in them.

Whoa, where had *that* come from?

We were dating, sure, but not long. Surely too soon to rule out other possibilities.

"Getting back to your reunion…" I said, drawing a knowing chuckle from Clara.

"After Fae went off by herself, what was on your mind when you said to wait?"

"Oh. I wanted to see what she did, because she wasn't going to walk away and do nothing. She wouldn't have in high school and the accomplished professional she is now certainly wouldn't. I'm sure she called the sheriff's department."

The vehicles ahead moved. I gave the rearview mirror one more look—no movement there—then tuned back in to Clara.

"… so I can drive tomorrow. I can pick you up if you want. Or—"

"Pick me up for what?"

"Oh, didn't I tell you?" Clara often was innocent. This time her innocence was entirely spurious. "The reunion continues tomorrow with a picnic lunch at the high school, then a tour by the assistant principal."

I heard her voice saying on the way here, *We're not going to the high school tonight.* Had she emphasized *tonight?* Enough that it should have warned me? Along with Debi's exchange with drunken Marcus about some *after party* tomorrow.

"Clara—"

"No, really, it's part of the official reunion. You said you'd go with me to the reunion and you always live up to your word…"

✧ ✧ ✧ ✧

"HOW WAS IT?"

Teague didn't call me every night, but when he did, he showed an uncanny knack for picking the time when I was in bed but not yet asleep. Mostly reading. Occasionally watching TV. At the moment watching videos of people reacting to hearing the Righteous Brothers for the first time.

Don't judge. I had moved on from *You've Lost that Lovin' Feeling* to *Unchained Melody*, which only features one Righteous Brother, so that's only half bad, right?

With that phrase on the tip of my tongue, I responded. "Not half bad."

Gracie, who'd raised her head at the phone ringing dropped it back down, wriggled her side more firmly into her bolstered bed, and gusted a sigh.

"Not an enthusiastic endorsement."

"I felt a bit like I was in the land of Oz."

"Yellow brick roads? Talking scarecrows? Melting witches?"

"The witches definitely didn't melt."

"Uh-huh. Bet you singed them if they picked on Clara."

"She handled it beautifully herself."

"Good for her. What made it Oz-like?"

"Maybe I should have specified that I felt like Dorothy in Oz. As the outsider, many things seemed strange and worth marveling at to me that everyone else accepted as routine."

"Ah. Remember, Dorothy's observations made her the one who exposed the Wizard as a humbug."

"Actually, that was Toto. Knocking over a screen curtain."

He chuckled, low and smoky. He really shouldn't be allowed to do that on the phone. "The dog to the rescue. Should have known."

"Yup. And Dorothy didn't even realize the magic shoes were her ticket home, which were silver in the book, by the way, not ruby. She needed someone else to point it out."

"Uh-huh. So is that what you were doing when I called? Contemplating *The Wizard of Oz?* Re-reading it? Re-watching it?"

I ignored the Righteous Brothers frozen on my laptop screen and said, "More like working on acceptance that what I thought was the end of the story is only Part One, with Part Two tomorrow."

I told him about the picnic and tour of the high school awaiting me.

"What were you doing when I called?"

I fibbed. "I was looking up buzzards and vultures. Did you know buzzards eat mostly live prey? I always thought they were like vultures and ate carrion."

"Carrion?"

"Yeah, the dead flesh of animals."

"I know what carrion is. I'm a little at sea about why you're delving into the topic after spending the evening at Clara's high school reunion. The Oz connection I got—sort of—but carrion?"

"The high school is on Carrion Lane."

"Really?"

"See. That was my reaction, too. Clara acted like it was normal."

"When you grow up with certain names you stop thinking about what the word means and accept it as the thing, the place, the whatever you know. Like how you don't drive on a driveway but you do on a parkway."

"That's not the same as naming a street after decaying animal flesh and then putting the high school there."

"You're kind of wound up about this, aren't you?"

"No. But it was part of the Oz-ness. It was like being in a parallel universe where no one else thought the odd things were odd."

"That was a big topic of conversation at the reunion?"

"I wouldn't say big," I confessed.

"Anybody other than you talk about it?"

"Not exactly. They were caught up in memories."

"Which made you think of dead animal flesh, buzzards, and vultures?"

"There *was* tension. Especially surrounding this one woman, Josepha."

"Return of the Mean Girls?"

"I don't think so. From what I can tell she wasn't part of the in crowd."

"*In crowd?* Are you from the 1960s? You must be older than you look."

"Ha. Ha. She was ... separate. It was like..." I mentally replayed watching Josepha slide around and through the chattering groups.

"Like?" Teague asked quietly, making me realize he'd waited quite a while.

"Like watching a shark cut through schools of fish. Not attacking, but everyone involved knowing it could whenever it wanted to." I shook my head hard enough to shudder my shoulders, even though he couldn't see it. "Dramatic. Sorry."

"No apology. You made it vivid."

"Oh, heck, I'm probably dramatizing to keep things interesting."

"Could be. Not your usual style, though."

"Thanks."

More smoky laughter.

He really, really shouldn't be allowed to do that.

Nor, after telling me about the progress made today on the accessibility project, to drop his voice that way when he said good night.

I told myself I'd shaken off my reaction to Josepha Viedux, but to tell the truth, I dreamt—in Picasso-esque surrealism—about coming face to face with a shark with two feet in black pumps, melting after the high school fell on her.

SUNDAY

CHAPTER FOURTEEN

"**OH, WAIT UNTIL** you hear what I have to say," said Polly, the dark-haired woman who'd played Aunt Eller in *Oklahoma!*

Followed closely by Fae Ballard, Polly had arrived with a covered dish whose foil covering dazzled in the just-past-noon sunlight.

The light came through leaves turning red, orange, yellow, and brown. It dappled the ground of this knob of a hill with a view to the back of the high school in one direction and the football field in another. A half-dozen picnic tables and trash barrels occupied the flattish area identified as Senior Hill by a sign.

The sun was better at dazzling than heating today, with everyone wearing jackets or sweaters against a brisk chill. Polly added her dish to the cloth-covered table designated for the buffet offerings, along with the necessities of plates, napkins, and utensils at one end.

Clara drove today, so we'd arrived in time to make her dish among the first wave on the table.

When we arrived, Debi had been ordering around the woman with the cheekbones and the great haircut—Ancella—about arranging items on the table.

We'd pitched in and helped Ancella. Now, we stood among the other fifteen or so early arrivers—Oh. Unless they weren't the early ones, but the only ones.

"Smart idea," Fae said to Glenn Selka with a nod toward the bakery box he held. She lifted a paper plate wrapped in plastic to reveal squares of what appeared to be breakfast casserole. "I begged this off our hostess at the B&B."

Glenn, with Kirstin beside him, apparently awaited instructions from Debi before adding their contribution to the spread. Wesley Oshmann stood a bit to one side with his hands dug into his jeans' pockets, presumably having already dropped off his dish. The rest coagulated into two clumps. One not far from Debi, the other noticeably far from Debi. Clara and I maintained a neutral stance in between.

"What do you have to say, Polly?" someone from the far-from-Debi group asked.

"I was talking to my younger brother this morning—I'm staying with him while I'm here for the weekend. He's always had this habit of tracking arrests in the county. Started as a kid, taking police reports from the free newspaper that used to come 'round and putting them into a spreadsheet he had on his very first computer. He's kept it up to this day, using the county website reporting arrests now. You should see the pie charts and graphs he has. The county should hire him to analyze—"

"Polly," Clara said with mock sternness. "Just tell us what you said you were going to tell us."

Hands now free of the dish, she gestured with one. "Last night was not the first time Marcus was arrested for being drunk. Not the second or third or fourth time, either." She looked around for dramatic effect. "Eight times."

Debi scoffed audibly, then flounced away to the far end of the buffet table, where she rearranged still-covered dishes. She couldn't know their contents, which meant she couldn't be grouping like together or making any other reasoned change.

Was this information about Marcus news to her? Or was she reacting to the news being spread?

Talking over a few murmurs, Wesley Oshmann said, "Sad."

He looked around, as if challenging anyone to disagree.

Glenn said quietly, "It is. It's also not surprising."

Wesley frowned. But neither he nor anyone else contradicted Glenn.

"Speak of the devil," Polly muttered—loudly enough that everyone turned toward where a dilapidated taxi discharged a passenger in the parking lot at the foot of the hill.

Marcus Etchells.

✧　✧　✧　✧

BEFORE HE WAS halfway up to us, everyone must have recognized he wore the same clothes he'd worn the night before and without benefit of washing. Worse, far worse, as he passed among us, we all knew his skin matched the clothes.

Both exuded old booze and sweat.

The other alums parted to give him a wide berth as he shambled toward the buffet table or Debi or both. But he wasn't swaying the way he had last night.

"You took a taxi right here? Really?" Debi asked.

"Had to. Impounded my car. Can't get it until Monday."

She scoffed. "You think that's your biggest problem? Not yet," she snapped without looking at him. "We're not ready to serve."

One hand extended toward the nearest dish, he stopped, his shins not quite touching the back of the table's bench covered by the cloth that reached the ground.

"Come back here and fix this tablecloth. It's totally uneven." Debi turned her back on her homecoming and prom consort to fuss loudly at Ancella, who'd joined the not-near cluster right before Marcus' arrival. "You should have evened it out before putting food on it."

"Food was already on it when I started," Ancella said. "Besides, I tried to adjust the tablecloth and it wouldn't budge."

"Well, not from this side, you idiot. You pull it from the short side. I'll do it. You move the dishes while I do."

Ancella sighed, but returned to the table. "Stop tugging, Debi. Give me a minute."

"I can't wait all day." Debi had folds of material in her hands.

This was not going to be pretty. It promised to shape up as a slow-mo disastrous attempt to pull off a tablecloth while leaving the dishes intact.

Turning away, I intercepted Clara on her way to volunteer to help.

I intended to save her from herself. And from Debi, who was certain to ensure the good deed did not go unpunished.

A piercing, high-pitched siren went off in my ear.

The sound seemed to come from everywhere at first.

"What on earth—?"

It took an ear-shattering second to realize the noise emanated from behind me.

I spun around to see Ancella, apparently riveted in place by the same sound. Couldn't blame her. She was even closer to the source.

Debi stood in a stiffened version of yoga's mountain pose on the far side of the buffet picnic table. Her eyes closed. Her fingers spread. Her mouth open ... and out of it coming that glass-shattering noise.

Several of us rushed toward Debi.

I was in the lead, but pulled up when I reached the far corner of the table, where the tablecloth was flipped back.

Voices jumbled together.

"Debi?"

"What is it?"

"What's wrong?"

"Stop that."

She kept shrieking.

I gripped Clara's arm and said in a harsh whisper, "Under the table. A body."

Thanks to the corner of the shortened tablecloth on this side being doubled back, we saw Josepha Viedux under the table, rolled onto her side, with the handle of a knife sticking out of her.

CHAPTER FIFTEEN

"DON'T TOUCH ANYTHING. And stay back," I ordered the others.

"Why?"

"What's going on?"

"What is it?"

"She could need help," a female voice said.

She was past that kind of help. But I didn't say that. For one thing, the voice couldn't see Josepha and clearly meant Debi, who still shrieked.

I took Debi, still at full volume, by the shoulders from behind and advanced her toward the others, issuing another order. "Call 911. Get them here as soon as possible."

Let them think the call was for Debi. For now.

"Who is it?" Clara asked from behind me. I realized I obstructed her view. But with more people streaming in closer, I didn't want to risk giving up my spot blocking them and their view.

"Josepha Viedux. Stabbed." I kept it low enough that only Clara heard.

"Dead?"

Automatically, I checked back with the sight under the table. In addition to the knife handle protruding from her chest, she was an odd color, and very, very still. "Uh-huh."

Though there wasn't a great deal of blood. Because the killer had left the knife in place?

I stared at that knife handle.

Was it...?

Could it possibly be…?

I leaned in closer, trying to be sure.

Then a couple others peered past me and saw under the table. More shrieks went up. Pale shadows of Debi's, but still adding to the din.

Fae Ballard said, "For God's sake, get another tablecloth and cover her up."

I vetoed that. "We don't touch anything. And nobody leaves. But somebody should go down and stop anybody arriving for the picnic from coming up here." Two vehicles had pulled into the lot since the first note of shrieking.

Glenn and Wesley volunteered, going halfway down the slope and standing with arms akimbo and feet planted slightly wider than natural, in apparent unconscious mirroring.

Some of the others grumbled, but no one broke ranks and fled, instead, splintering into sub-groups and whispering to each other.

Ancella took Debi by the shoulders and shook her. At first it only rumbled the shrieking, like your voice when you talk into a box fan. But a bit more and the shrieking shredded, then nearly stilled into noisy gulps.

She led Debi to the bench of a nearby picnic table and sat her down there. Someone else gave Debi water.

This sequence I watched while I lowered my voice to ask Clara, "What was Josepha like in high school? Was she close friends with anyone? Part of a particular group?"

I was thinking ahead to the likelihood that we'd be kept otherwise occupied and I wouldn't have the chance to ask for hours and hours.

Her shock-hazed eyes cleared a bit at the questions.

"N…no. Not a part of any group. But she … she always seemed to know things. About people in all the groups. Are you sure she's…"

"Yes."

From the body's position and the angle of the knife, my best guess was she'd been left under the table with her body anchoring one end of the tablecloth, while the rest of it was brought up and over the table. From the back of the table, she might have been visible, but that was toward the steep slope down to the football field. Everyone would have approached via the gentler incline from the parking lot, seeing only the tablecloth.

I suspected Ancella's effort to even out the cloth from the front side partially rolled the body, with the protruding knife handle resisting the full roll, prompting Ancella to give up.

Only Debi's insistence on overhang equality forced the issue.

Which raised very interesting questions.

I caught Ancella's eye.

She glanced at Debi, who now stared straight ahead in absolute silence, then came toward Clara and me.

"Is she okay?" Clara asked before I could get in my question.

"Your guess is as good as mine," Ancella said. "She's not responding, but at least she's quiet."

"Ancella, you said you tried to move the tablecloth before, right? What happened?"

Maybe that hadn't been the best lead question because the other woman blanched, her cheekbones now a knife's edge under muslin skin.

"It gave a little, then it wouldn't come any more. I thought it was stuck on… a nail or something." Anything but a dead body's dead weight. "I didn't want to risk tearing it, so I stopped tugging."

"Is it Debi's cloth?"

"I have no idea. It was on the table when I got here."

"With the front side down to the ground?"

"Uh-huh."

"Did you go around to the other side?"

She shook her head. "I don't like heights and it's not the most secure footing beyond the table."

"Who got here first?"

"No idea. When I got here, Debi was already here."

"Who else?

She squinted, remembering. "Mary Jo, Wesley, Fae—"

"But she arrived after we did," Clara interrupted.

"Yes. She forgot her dish and left almost immediately to go get it from the B&B. She came back just after Glenn and his wife arrived." She glanced toward the Selkas, then away. "They stayed right by the table."

"Anybody else?" I asked.

"No."

"Did you notice the blue van in the parking lot when you arrived?"

Clara cut me a sharp look.

Ancella shook her head.

"You didn't see Josepha here?"

"No." She glanced toward the shielding tablecloth. "Do you think—?"

"We don't think anything," I said firmly. Then I redirected attention to the parking lot. "Here comes the sheriff's department."

ARRIVING DEPUTIES GRUMBLED about trampling around the site, but it took on an official tenor when Deputy Hensen came on the scene.

"Get those people out of here and into a contained area down in the parking lot, with supervision. With this mess, we're going to have to take shoe impressions of half their graduating class."

A young deputy gestured to Clara and me to move ahead of him.

Deputy Hensen said, "Not them. Not yet."

Did he sound like he was looking forward to the moment when *yet* was over and he could dispatch us, too? Maybe a little.

"Don't know if it will make you feel any better," I said, "but it already was trampled before she was found—people bringing dishes, arranging the table. At least a dozen."

"Oh, I'd say more." Clara gestured toward the tabletop. "Look at all the covered dishes, plus a couple boxes. Probably closer to twenty."

It was a testament to Deputy Hensen's strength of character that he did not groan.

"Take these two over there." He tipped his head toward where the path from the parking lot reached this level of the hilltop. In other words, as far from the table in question as possible without descending the hill. "Stick with them. I'll talk to them shortly."

Clara watched the activity around us, assessing. "You all are much better at this than you were," she said kindly to the deputy.

He blinked.

"I mean better than the first time I saw you all at a murder site."

He looked at her without responding. I wasn't sure he could.

"At the dog park. Oh, maybe you weren't with the department then," she said kindly. "We—Sheila and I—found that body, too."

The deputy flicked a look toward me. I didn't meet it. I squeezed my eyes closed.

Clara continued chattily. "Actually, our dogs found the body, but we called 911. This time we didn't call 911, but Sheila told other people to. I suppose you could argue Debi found this body, but all she did was scream, while Sheila recognized what happened and got things started. You wouldn't be here if it weren't for her."

He didn't appear particularly thankful.

Having directed other deputies to various tasks and with scientific types taking over around the table, Deputy Hensen came to us.

"Should've known you two were involved, since you—"

"We were not *involved* precisely," Clara objected.

I backed her up. "Completely innocent bystanders."

"—were around the ruckus at the reunion last night."

"So the deputy who took Marcus Etchells in last night told you about it."

"We don't know him. How'd he know us?" Clara asked.

"You two are famous in the department. Never miss one of your TV appearances," he said dryly to her. "Now, tell me what happened."

"It's my reunion," Clara started. "North Bend County High School, of course. We were at the hotel last night with two other classes having our official reunions. Today is—was supposed to be a potluck picnic then a tour of the high school by the assistant princi-pal—Oh. We need to let him know—"

"We'll take care of that. Get to finding a dead body under your picnic table. Starting with who she is."

Clara gave him the name.

I added, "There's a blue van in the parking lot with what looks like a temporary sign for her business. It's got to be hers."

DEPUTY HENSEN TOOK us back over what led to finding her body. Twice. Then, back to last night's event. He slid in good questions about interactions and relationships.

He showed strong interest in the order of arrivals today. He even stopped us long enough to instruct the young deputy to round up Debi, Ancella, Mary Jo, Wesley, Marcus, Fae, Glenn, and Kirstin.

When we'd gone through it again, he called to a different young deputy.

"Take Ms. Mackey and Mrs. Woodrow to the department and have someone wait with them until we get their statements. I want more from you two, which will have to wait until I've covered more ground."

I pointedly looked down at the clump of people in the parking lot then to the outnumbered law enforcement vehicles. "Wouldn't it be more efficient for Clara and me to drive over in her car so we don't waste spots in one of the department vehicles?"

He followed my gaze, then turned to the deputy. "Go with these two in their car to the department. Bring another official car back. And since we're being *efficient*, take that one, too."

He jerked his head toward Fae Ballard, who was pale but looked irked, having been questioned by Deputy Eckles, a very literal-minded young man, who often brought out that reaction in me, too.

CHAPTER SIXTEEN

ALONE AT LAST after hours of waiting to give our statements and no longer hindered by a chaperone, Clara and I climbed into her van in the sheriff's department parking lot. Fae, we were told, had already departed.

"I need dog park therapy." Clara pushed her hair back with both hands. "We'll stop at my house for LuLu, then swing by yours and pick up Gracie."

"Good call. And change our clothes."

Unspoken was that we could talk en route and likely at the dog park.

I started by asking, "Anything?"

"You mean from their questions? Not really. They seemed to be vacuuming up every detail. Today, yesterday, twenty years ago. Just kept asking *What else?* until I was wrung dry. Deputy Hensen came in for a while, but didn't stay."

"Me, too. I had the impression he was a floater, checking in with the ongoing interviews."

"You know what I was thinking about while we were waiting? You probably figured this out the second it happened, but it took me that time of sitting there quietly to think through the timeline. If Marcus was arrested as we all left the reunion last night and he showed up at Senior Hill in his same clothes and unwashed and without even his car, doesn't that mean he came straight there from being released from jail? Which means…"

"He has one heck of an alibi."

She sighed deeply and shifted conversational gears. "Did you keep anything back from the sheriff's department?"

I waited for her to complete a turn to the left, then shifted a quick gaze to her. "Nothing factual."

She gripped the steering wheel tighter. "You've got something."

"I wouldn't say that. More like a question. Did you recognize the knife?"

"I didn't see the knife. You were in the way—not that you meant to be, I'm sure. But you were." At a stop sign, she swung around to face me. "Wait a minute, *did* you recognize the knife?"

"Maybe not *the* knife, but where it came from, yeah. It had the same handle as the steak knives at Haines Tavern."

She deflated. "That doesn't help much. Everybody goes there."

"Including everybody who was in town for a weekend to go to their high school reunion?"

"You mean—? You can't mean—Glenn?"

"One possibility. He did have steak Friday night."

"I don't believe it."

"You haven't seen the guy in twenty years, Clara. You don't know him at all."

"I don't believe it."

To avoid direct conflict about Glenn Selka, I broadened the issue.

"I have to agree with the sheriff's department that looking at people at the reunion—which their questions made clear is where they're starting—makes sense, even though that's an awful lot of people."

"The reunion? Why?" Her indignation wasn't all for the deputies, sparing a good dose for me. Yet it lacked something. As if she were trying to persuade herself more than me.

"For starters, because she was killed at a reunion event."

"Not *during* the event."

I resisted rolling my eyes. "If she'd been stabbed during a reunion event, we'd probably have a pretty good idea of who did it. But she was killed between events and at the location of the next event."

"It could be a fluke. Somebody who was mad at her found her there. If she gathered information like she did in high school, she could have all sorts of enemies. Lots, lots more than the people who were at the reunion. It doesn't have to be associated with the reunion."

She emphasized that point by engaging the parking brake with far more enthusiasm than required.

Still, she was cordial when she invited me into her house. "You want to come in?"

"No, thanks. I'll wait here for you and LuLu."

Before she returned, with LuLu leaping joyfully around her, I'd decided forcing the issue that this killing likely connected to the reunion wasn't worthwhile at the moment.

There were more important questions.

I'd also sorted through questions Deputy Hensen asked me, especially those I hadn't had an answer to.

Clara handed me a paper bag as soon as she got behind the driver's wheel. "Made sandwiches, since we didn't get lunch. I hope the deputies ate all that food left there."

"Probably not. It's part of the crime scene."

"Well, they'll have to get us back our dishes."

I didn't mention doubting that was high on their priority list.

As Clara backed out of her driveway and LuLu tried to lick my face—or possibly to get my sandwich—I focused on the most basic question.

The victim.

"Tell me more about Josepha Viedux."

"I've been thinking about that, too. I didn't know her well at all— our paths didn't cross much even in school—but from what I knew… Well, I hate to say it, but she wasn't a very nice person. Nothing overt, not outwardly mean to people, but maybe that would have been easier to deal with because you could sort of see it coming."

"What did she do?"

"Like I told you before, she knew things. Dug up secrets about people." She crinkled the corners of her eyes. "I think she liked the power of knowing, if that makes sense."

"It does. And it fits." It fit each snippet of conversation I'd overheard last night, her separateness, and others' reactions to Josepha

Viedux.

Then another aspect hit me.

…dug up secrets about people.

…the power of knowing…

"Fits what? And why does your face look like that?" Clara asked.

"Fits what I saw and heard last night. As for my face, hearing you say that creeped me out. Because that's what *we* do, Clara."

"No, it's not," she said indignantly.

"We find out things about people, secrets they've been keeping."

"Well, yeah, but only because we think they committed murder."

"You know who would say that makes it worse?"

"And more dangerous," she contributed. "Ned and Teague. But we're cautious. And it's not worse, because we're working for the good of North Bend County. For the good of the wider community, for the world, even. Besides, we eventually tell law enforcement what we find to help bring a murderer to justice."

"But in the interim we hold onto a lot of secrets. And some of those secrets are ones we keep holding onto because the person involved isn't the murderer we're looking for. But that still might not make them comfortable with us holding their secrets."

She considered that. "Most of them don't know we know their secrets, though, right? And a lot of the others are just glad they weren't accused of murder. We don't use the secrets we find out to have power over people. Well, unless it's to get them to confess or something."

I could imagine Teague's and Ned's comments on *that* distinction.

As evidenced by her next words, Clara's thoughts went back to an early issue. "Josepha doing the sort of things she did—which were totally different from what we do—would make lots of people unhappy with her. Far, far beyond people here for the reunion."

"I don't disagree she likely accumulated enemies. But if she has been snooping or information-gathering—and it sounds like she has—consider that nobody killed her until your class came back for the reunion."

She stared down at her hands a moment, swallowed hard, then said one, succinct—and for her very rare—swear word, before looking up.

"Does that mean people from out of town are more likely because they didn't have an opportunity to kill her until this weekend?"

Attagirl, Clara. Not only had she accepted reality, but she'd made a great point.

"It's a good place to start."

CHAPTER SEVENTEEN

Saturday and Sunday are amateur time at the dog park.

The owners bring out dogs who have been cooped up all work-week, taking out their boredom and frustration on carpets, shoes, or door jambs. The owners hope their dogs will expend enough energy to make the coming week calm while the animals try to run, leap, and play out their excess energy from the previous week.

This causes heightened alert on the part of the DPRs (dog park regulars) for several reasons. First, as I said, the amateurs' dogs have enough pent-up energy to fuel the Ohio River Valley's streetlights for a year. Second, the dog park amateurs' dogs have a better than even chance of being poorly trained. Third, the amateurs' dogs don't know the mores and unspoken rules of the dog park. Fourth, the human amateurs don't know the mores and unspoken rules of the dog park. Fifth, the human amateurs have a demonstrably poor likelihood of being able to read.

Or else they would follow the rules posted by the gate, starting with pick up your dog's poop.

When the weekend corresponds with unseasonably good weather, it seems to trigger some latent *Need to Go to The Dog Park* message in the brains of every dog owner in the region.

It was that kind of Sunday. The lot was jammed—though no sign of Teague's truck. If his project finished early, Murphy would have persuaded him to come out, for sure.

The big dog enclosure was particularly popular today, resulting in a dog crush around the entry, which also happened to be near the drinking fountain.

At home, I made sure Gracie and her visiting four-legged pals had clean, fresh water on each level of the house, as well as in the backyard during outdoor fun times.

Here at the dog park, the water came from a drinking fountain in each of the four enclosures.

The DPRs rinsed out and filled bowls that did not bear too close a scrutiny. I figured drinking from those bowls was better than swallowing the mud, which was Gracie's favorite go-to snack.

The drinking fountain had two levels—theoretically one for humans and one for dogs. But the one for dogs either trickled or arched beyond the catch bowl, with nothing in between. Few humans were brave enough to use the other one for themselves. Especially after watching more water-centric or less patient dogs plant their front paws on the edges and drink from the spout.

The fountain rested atop a concrete slab that appeared to be slowly rising above the surrounding ground. What was actually happening was the ground was being transported away, bit by bit.

Overshooting spray, dripping mouths, and—especially—enthusiastic paddling in bowls, produced and retained a mud wallow worthy of a connoisseur pig. Each dog's coat picked up some measure of mud, and transported it away, like slow but persistent earth-movers.

While operating the water fountain for the dogs, Clara and I talked only about dogs.

We weren't going to mention murder in this crush, even if half of the crushers were canine.

Gracie poked LuLu's side with her nose—a long, pointed nose perfect for poking—and LuLu took off like a scalded cat, if a scalded cat looked back over her shoulder at what scalded her and said with her eyes, *Chase me, Chase me.*

Gracie obliged.

We sauntered in their general direction. Both picnic tables were already clogged with humans—easy to tell the amateurs, they sat on the benches, which male dogs routinely christened.

When our dogs disappeared into a low area by the far fence called

Las Vegas—because nobody responsible knew what really happened there—Clara and I exchanged a look and followed with more purpose.

We had Las Vegas to ourselves. We could stand partly down the slope and keep an eye on our dogs below as well as most of the main area if they decided to explore there.

And we could talk about murder without being overheard.

I told her what I'd heard last night—including the *bad memories* snippet. No sense trying to shield her from possible unpleasantness concerning her fellow alums when the victim was one of them, as were the likely suspects.

"She was stirring up trouble," she summarized.

"Poking the bears and finding pleasure in it," I agreed. "And those are only the ones I overheard. Who knows how many other people she poked."

Clara breathed out slowly. "That doesn't help us much, then, does it? I mean, we can concentrate on the people we know about from what you overheard, but there could be others."

"It's a place to start. Along with why she was killed where she was killed."

"Could she have been killed somewhere else and taken there to make a point?"

I considered that, then slowly shook my head. "It would have been hard to transport her without disturbing the knife. And if they killed her somewhere else, took the knife out, moved her to under the picnic table, then put the knife back in, I'd think there'd have been no blood, because it would have come out when they took the knife out."

"I'm sure you're right. I mean, to kill her somewhere else and carry her up that hill? That would be really hard. And why? It doesn't make sense. It's not like it was a great place to hide the body so it wouldn't be found for a long time." She nodded decisively. "I'd say it was someone who came in the same way we did and met her there."

"What about coming up from the football field side of the hill?"

"Too steep," she said immediately. "It's not so bad at the bottom, but at the top, there are no handholds and kids got stuck or, worse, fell from there. I know of several attempts and they all ended in failure, a couple kids going to the hospital. There's no way to fence it off, but there are bright lights focused on it, dusk to dawn, to discourage stupidity."

"Are there lights showing the picnic area at the top?"

"No."

"Okay, so we're thinking it was someone who went up that hill from the parking lot, most likely with Josepha or to meet her by the tables—the odds of a chance meeting up there are astronomical unless it was just before other people started arriving for the picnic."

"In other words, Debi." She raised a hand to stop my waffling on that point. "If it was an accidental meeting before the picnic, it had to be Debi, because she was the first one there. Anybody else would have had at least one witness."

"Do we know for sure Debi was first?"

She considered. "Not absolutely. We can check. But I bet she was because of the being in charge thing. Harder to boss people around when you get there after them and they're already working."

Tacitly agreeing, I said, "Plus, since we don't know the time of death, there's the possibility of someone who met Josepha there or went up there with her during the night."

"But would Josepha have met someone up there during the night?"

"Would she? You knew her—"

"I didn't really."

"Better than I did. But you asked a good question. Let's think of the kind of person she seems to have been. What kind of meeting place would she want?"

"Someplace where she was in control. Definitely not an isolated spot at night."

"In other words, unless we find out the time of death contradicts it, we theorize she was killed there and it happened sometime after sunrise and before Debi arrived, if she's not the murderer, or before whoever was second arrived, if Debi is the murderer. Agreed?"

"Agreed. Because Mary Jo is a follower from way back, but I don't see even her letting a murder happen in front of her and staying silent."

"There's one more factor," I said. "The tablecloth. If Debi's there first and she's the murderer, it makes sense that she used a tablecloth she brought to hide the body. But for her to *not* be the murderer, there needs to be an explanation for that tablecloth to be there and to be used to cover the body. Where did it come from?"

"Oh, that's good, Sheila. I never even thought of that. What I want to know about is what you heard in the hallway last night about it being *all set?*"

"Could have meant anything, could have been anybody and that's if I actually I heard those wo—"

"Clara! Sheila!"

We had been spotted.

CHAPTER EIGHTEEN

AMY KACKLEY, WHO lived across the street and a few houses down from me, made a beeline for us.

"Hi, Amy. Don't often see you out here with Sadie," Clara said of Amy's mature English setter.

"She was so antsy and not knowing if we'll have many more days like this before spring, I wanted to get her out."

Sadie, placidly sniffing several yards away, turned her head and gave Amy a *don't blame this on me* look.

"Makes sense." Clara meant it. To her it always made sense to bring any dog to the dog park.

So, she might have been surprised, but I was not, when Amy said, "I heard you two were out at the high school when they found that poor woman dead today."

"Uh-huh."

"But they've already questioned you and let you go, so you must not be suspects."

"Us? Suspects?" Clara repeated in astonishment. "Oh, no."

"Well, I hear they are still questioning several people. Marcus Etchells, Debi Norris, although she was treated by medics first. And then the one that takes my breath away. Glenn Selka." She placed a hand to her throat. "*Glenn Selka.* I can't believe that. I just talked to him yesterday when he came into the library. He seemed absolutely fine and I was delighted to see him after all these years."

"You know him?"

"Of course." Amy and Clara gave me the non-verbal equivalent of *duh.* "His older brother was on baseball teams with my son. We sat in a lot of bleachers with the Selkas."

"And Glenn?"

"He didn't play baseball. They'd bring him to the games some-times, but he preferred staying home on the computer. They worried about that, so unlike his brother—" She hurried into the next words. "—but they were proud of Glenn, too."

"They must be especially proud of him now."

Amy looked blank at Clara's comment.

"Because he's so successful," Clara expanded.

"Is he? I know he's married with a few kids—"

"And a rescue dog."

With a sideways glance, Amy ignored my interpolation. "—from his mom. We've stayed in touch since they moved. I know the older boy's in Paducah and he's had rough breaks with jobs, but he's driving people around now. Still living with his grandma, but doing lots better."

Yet the Selkas hadn't brought up Glenn's success?

Family dynamics? Or something else?

"Did Glenn go the library to say hello to you?" Clara asked.

"No. He was at the library and asked my help finding back editions of the newspaper."

"Which editions? What stories?"

Clara's urgency unsettled Amy. "I shouldn't talk about patrons' research. It's a matter of privacy."

I saw the explanation that we were on a mission to solve the mur-der welling up in Clara. I cut in before it overflowed. Amy wouldn't like the idea of exposing Glenn to suspicion, and she might use library policy as her excuse for not sharing ... not unreasonably.

"How about we tell you which editions and you let us know if we're right?" Not waiting for acceptance of my suggestion, I said, "Ones from twenty years ago that had to do with the death of a recent graduate of the high school."

Amy's expression confirmed my speculation immediately, her words came slower. "How did you know?"

"Lucky guess. We shouldn't have any problem having another librarian finding them for us today, should we?"

"Library isn't open Sundays."

"The main library is," Clara said.

If anyone else had said it that would have been a dig, since the main library had been moved to the bigger town of Stringer. Haines Tavern residents called the branch in our town the Old Main Branch, clinging to that much of its previous prominence in the county.

"I suppose you could go there." Amy made it sound like a trek up and down the Amazon, rather than a twenty-minute drive each way. "But they close at five. Tell you what, come to the library—the Old Main Branch—tomorrow morning and I'll have those editions ready for you."

AFTER THANKING HER and getting out of Amy's earshot, I asked Clara, "Do you know more about why Glenn is so interested in what happened to that girl—Heidi?"

"Heidi Holmes. They dated. Most of senior year. That's why she stopped coming to Gran's. Too busy dating. I guess you could call it dating."

"You guess?"

"They hooked up to start. She told me all about it—even though I didn't want to hear. About how she'd discovered sex was the way to get and hold a guy. After a while they started going out." She tipped her head. "Glenn was so shy then, maybe that was the only way it would work. Couldn't see him asking anybody on a date unless he already knew they'd say yes. You know what I mean?"

"Uh-huh." My mind, however, wasn't absorbed by Glenn's mating habits from two decades ago. "But why now? Why his interest in her death now? It's not like he was curious about meeting up with her again at the reunion and suddenly found out she'd died back then. He said he knew around the time it happened, which is when most people would want to know more. So why wait until now to be curious?"

"I see what you mean. Especially since he seems happily married."

"With the caveat that nobody ever really knows what goes on inside a marriage—sometimes including the two people involved—I agree. Plus, Kirstin seemed to encourage him to find out more. You saw the little exchange Friday night before he asked about Heidi?"

She nodded. "Checking in with Kirstin and Kirstin saying go ahead."

"Although…" I started, but didn't finish.

"*Although* what?" Clara answered her own question, relieving me of the need. "Oh. You mean because she was worried at the same time. But I don't think she was jealous. It was worry for him and what he might find out, but knowing he needed to find it out."

I grinned at her. "You look so sweet—you *are* so sweet—even I forget sometimes how sharp you are."

She grinned back. "That's why I married Ned. He's the only person who never forgets."

"That might be the most romantic thing I ever heard."

Her phone rang. Before answering it, she clicked her tongue and said, "If that's true, Teague better get on the ball."

Then she chuckled and answered.

"Hello." Listening to the response to her greeting, her eyebrows rose and she looked over at me. "We'll be there then."

She ended the call.

"That was Kirstin Selka, Glenn's wife. She wants to talk to us."

CHAPTER NINETEEN

WITH AN HOUR left before the time we'd meet Kirstin Selka at the Amber House Bed and Breakfast, we picked up burgers after leaving the dog park, along with extra French fries. I was the designated fry tosser to the poor, starving dogs in the back on the way to my house.

Eating at the small wall-mounted table in my kitchen, I said, "We agree Josepha spread seeds of discord throughout the reunion and the most likely scenario is one of those seeds sprouted into a motive for murder, right?"

She tipped her head. "Yes. It seems to me she was more subtle in high school."

"Had more time. At the reunion, she had to cut to the chase. Just one night to get her pointed barbs in before she lost all those targets who are usually out of reach. That's going to be a problem for us, too. If something she said to someone Saturday night is a motive, we're going to need to try to track down all those people and get them to tell us what nasty things Josepha Viedux said to them or intimated about them."

She groaned. "Some already left after last night."

"We have plenty of people still here to get through before worrying about the ones who weren't at the picnic today. And—" I waggled my last chunk of burger at her. "—we won't go at them direct, asking what she said about them. We'll ask what she said or asked or intimated about other people."

"Oblique. I love it. Mind if I use your powder room to clean up before we go meet Kirstin?"

❖   ❖   ❖   ❖

As soon as Clara went into the powder room, I searched online for information on Glenn Selka.

What I found confirmed what he'd said about his success. But there could be a story behind these headlines.

I quickly messaged my great-aunt and asked Kit to use her connections for a deeper look at the business side of Glenn Selka.

Turning back to making my own searches, I didn't find any of his family on the main social media sites, which indicated a rare amount of reticence.

Or something to hide?

❖   ❖   ❖   ❖

I'd liked Glenn and Kirstin Selka from what I'd seen of them Friday night at the Haines Tavern and last night at the reunion. Now I had something to thank them for.

They were staying at the Amber House Bed and Breakfast in a building that boasted being among the town's oldest homes and having golden windows at either side of the front door that gave it its name. A crop of large red brick houses surrounded it in the area east of the town's central square, which had once been the most fashionable area, fell on hard times, and now was gradually reimagining ways to use the historic buildings with impressive footprints.

Its website showed an appropriate, gorgeous, and comfortable interior renovation. Rumor had it the food was on par.

I'd been wanting to see inside and thanks to the Selkas I did.

Different circumstances would have been nice, however.

Clara surged ahead of me, zeroing in on a woman coming toward us from the back of the house. She was assured and graceful, making her plain features and extra weight unimportant.

"Hello, Ottalie. We're here to see one of your guests, Kirstin Selka."

"Yes, she's waiting for you in the small dining room. You'll have privacy there. Right this way."

Darn their efficiency, I barely had time to look around and confirm my impression from the website was accurate or, possibly, even underselling it. In person, the textures invited sitting, the artwork demanded closer attention, the light from the windows pooled warm gloss on the wooden floors.

This is what I aspired to with my non-historic house. It had a long way to go.

I followed Clara and the woman named Ottalie Bishop she introduced me to.

The small dining room held a wide, shallow sideboard, a square table with four chairs around it and two more at the ready on either side of the sideboard. Over the fireplace hung a large landscape that looked as if it might represent a scene in North Bend County. Another wall held a large window onto a side garden, which was softly lit.

I coveted this room. I would gladly take every bit of its furnishings, its proportions, and its view and plunk them down in my house.

"Thank you for coming."

Kirstin's voice, calm but strained, shook me out of my decorating envy abstraction.

"You said Glenn's still at the sheriff's department? But why?" Clara asked as soon as we sat.

"They let us talk for a moment and he said they wanted to ask him more questions. I don't understand why. We never saw that woman who died, Josepha, except last night and only for a moment then. That's what I told them when they asked me." Her brows dropped. "They seemed particularly interested in our dinner Friday night at the tavern."

"What about it?"

"The police—"

"Sheriff's department."

"Sheriff's department. They asked why we chose to eat there, when we arrived, when we left, what we ate, who—"

"What you ate?" Clara repeated.

For a second, I was afraid Kirstin would recognize the dismay in Clara's voice. She'd put it together that the sheriff's department had already connected the murder weapon to the tavern and likely already knew Glenn Selka had used one on his steak Friday night.

But Kirstin didn't appear to take in the emotion behind the words. "I know. Strange. They also asked who we talked to. I did tell them about you." It wasn't an apology. "Their reaction is why I called you."

"Someone at the *sheriff's department* told you to call us?"

"No. I should have said their reaction first made me *ask* about you. They froze and looked pained. When they said I could leave and I returned here, I asked Ottalie Bishop, the woman who runs this B&B, about that. She knew you—" She looked at Clara. "—had been interviewed a couple times about investigations. She called someone named ... Donna?"

We nodded in unison at the reference to the grande dame of the dog park.

"I spoke with her as well. She said to call you."

Chances were good that wasn't all she said. But what the rest of it might have been—in praise or caution or otherwise—there was no guessing.

Before Kirstin could think about our reactions too much and get cold feet, I redirected to what I wanted to know about.

"You said you talked to Glenn. What did he say?"

"It was short and there was a deputy there. He asked about me, the kids, and changing our reservations—I told him that was all okay. He said they asked him for his fingerprints and DNA. He said he told them of course, because he has nothing to hide. But..."

"They'll ask for lots of people's fingerprints and DNA," Clara said. "As for making you sit there waiting forever before they even ask you questions, that's the usual procedure."

Kirstin looked at her a little oddly. Likely wondering how innocent-looking Clara could know the *usual* timeline of being interviewed by the North Bend County Sheriff's Department. Explaining would take us down a rabbit hole, even though it truly was a matter of in-thewrong-spot innocence for both of us.

"They've been questioning him for hours. When they first told me to go. I didn't. The rest of you all left. I watched you go, one after the other while they kept him. Then the woman who found the body left. And the man they took away last night. I don't think anyone was left except Glenn. The deputy came out and said I should leave. He didn't quite say I had to, but close. Said I should go rest—*rest*—and they'd let me know. I asked if he meant they'd let me know when I could pick up Glenn and he repeated that they'd let me know."

"And you're worried. That's understandable."

"I wanted to call a lawyer, but Glenn said no, he had nothing to hide."

"Kirstin," I started.

She shook her head. "I know. I called a friend who's finding us possible lawyers here. But…" This pause became a definite silence. We didn't push her. "I don't know…"

Neither of us pursued that, leaving her the time she needed to sort out what she did and didn't know.

"I don't think Glenn would want me to talk to you. He's so used to holding things inside. Even with me. But especially about anything to do with North Bend County. I was so stunned when he said he wanted to come to this reunion." Her mouth compressed. "No way was I letting him come alone. But now we need more help, we need the kind of help I can't give him. As I said, I checked on you. Looked you up." She directed that at Clara. "You've helped solve murders before. We need you to solve this one. To show it wasn't Glenn."

Clara put her hand over Kirstin's.

"We can't guarantee we can solve this," she said. Before I could release my held breath from relief, she added, "But we'll do our best. Tell us everything you know."

"Clara—"

"You're right, Sheila. That's too broad. Why were he and—?"

She was coming in too hot, too fast.

"What made him decide to come to the reunion?" I asked.

"Oh." From the darkening of Kirstin's eyes, I might have come in too hot and too fast, myself.

I eased back. "It didn't sound like he had the best time in high school."

"Do the brains ever have a great time in high school?"

Her tone indicated she knew the answer from personal experience.

I filled in with more words. "You said you were surprised he wanted to come to the reunion. Why?"

CHAPTER TWENTY

"HE DIDN'T SPEAK much of his high school years. When he did, it wasn't entirely happy. I've found in counseling that a lot of how people become who they are as adults—for better or worse—traces to adolescence." Kirstin slid into professional speak, clearly a comfortable mode. "Not solely high school, but it is the core period. It's not that we're stuck in always being who we were in high school, but the processes we develop often endure. Especially if we don't disrupt them.

"It's a core period in other ways, including what's called the reminiscence bump. Given random prompts, adults' recollections will disproportionately come from the teens and early twenties. An aspect of that is people's preferences in music are often set in that period for the rest of their lives. A phenomenon that's kept a lot of aging musicians in business."

Clara and I both echoed her quick smile. But I didn't want to let this go too far down the track of her shop talk.

"What was Glenn's process?"

She was silent so long I started hearing phrases in my head about professional confidentiality, not to mention husband-wife confidentiality.

I threw out another potential starter. "How did he become who he is as an adult?"

"He grew into his intelligence. He was always smart. How he handled it in high school was to be quiet, especially about the things that most interested him, including technology. He did his best to blend into the background. He once told me—" She flicked a look toward Clara, as if prefacing what she was about to say with *Is this true?* "—that when he was announced as valedictorian, students said there must be a mistake because there was no one by that name in their class."

"I never heard that," Clara said. "I—"

"I did," I interrupted. "A variant of it, anyway." I related what I'd heard of the conversation between Glenn and Josepha Viedux. "I wonder if the sheriff's department knows…."

Kirstin made a small sound of protest.

"Their knowing should help him," Clara said. "From Sheila's account, he obviously wasn't the least bothered by Josepha's attempt to get under his skin."

I kept my gaze down. Afraid it would show that I was thinking it might make the sheriff's department wonder if Josepha Viedux had made a second attempt and been more successful.

"Let's back up and get the background," I said.

We started with a more organized rendition of what we'd gathered Friday night, including the names and dates of businesses, their address, Glenn's degrees.

Remembering the dearth of information online, I asked, "How old are your kids?"

"Eight, six, and three."

"Oh, dear, who's taking care of them?" Clara asked.

"My mother and father. They're there at the house with them. So they're okay."

"That must be such a relief to know they're well-cared for."

"It is. Without my parents there…" She didn't need to explain that this would be even more difficult, perhaps dividing her loyalties, certainly wanting to be in two places at once.

"You must be all over social media to share photos of the kids with family," I said.

"No social media. I had accounts before Glenn and I got together, but he's adamant about not using it. Certainly not with the kids. He's very security conscious, especially about our digital lives. It's also important for business reasons to keep his online presence in line with his professional standing."

That made some sense. I still wasn't completely convinced.

"Do you know of any connection to Josepha Viedux?"

Her right eyelid twitched. She'd expected another question. A harder one. "None at all that I know of. He's never even mentioned her name."

I hit her with the harder one.

"Tell us about Glenn and Heidi Holmes."

She'd been ready for that from the start.

"They dated their senior year, but broke up before the end of the year. Never had contact after."

"Who broke up? Why?" I asked.

She jerked her head to the side. "That's Glenn's business."

"If we're going to help—"

"She died twenty years ago. What can it possibly have to do with this?"

Good question.

Except it certainly had been the focus of Glenn's interest Friday night at The Tavern and Saturday when he went to the library.

Clara eased the taut silence. "Tell us about who you and Glenn talked to at the reunion and what you talked about."

It was a great question. I listened carefully to what Kirstin said. But didn't harvest anything more than reunion chit-chat.

From Kirstin's account, Glenn's only encounter with Josepha had been the brief one I overheard. That didn't mean there hadn't been another that neither she nor I witnessed.

After we stood to end this meeting, I said one more thing to the worried woman.

"Kirstin, whatever Glenn said, you need to call those lawyers."

CHAPTER TWENTY-ONE

KIRSTIN LEFT US to go up to her room by a back stairway.

I dragged my feet on the way out, gawking at details that went together so well. Also coveting a round drop-leaf table in the corner.

My slowdown proved to be propitious.

The front door opened and there was Fae Ballard.

Clara didn't miss a beat, while I was imagining the round drop-leaf table by my front door. Was it walnut?

"Fae. Hi. We were hoping to have a word with you."

"With me? Why?"

"We didn't get a lot of time to talk at the reunion," Clara said.

"If I'd been smart, I wouldn't have had time to talk to anybody there. Nothing personal, Clara, but I never should have come. It's not like I had a great time in high school that I wanted to relive. Unlike everyone stuck at seventeen years old."

Clara tipped her head. "Is that truly how you see everybody?"

Fae's expression said she was going to say yes.

Clara didn't give her the chance. "I wonder if, you know, we see what we expect to see in cases like this. We expect them to be the same as high school—how we viewed them in high school—when, if we tried to have a relationship, we'd see they'd turn out to be real people. Don't you think?"

What I thought was Clara was truly a real person and probably always had been.

But she wasn't asking me.

"Relationship?" Fae echoed with a hint of mockery. "No, thank you. Don't want one now and never had one back then, other than being in the same place at the same time."

"About Saturday night—"

Fae cut me off.

"Yes, I'm the one who called the police. Marcus thought—you all thought—I was off crying about the mean guy calling me names. I was calling law enforcement to pick up a drunk. I put up with bullying back then. Can't do anything to change that. But I'm not putting up with it now, especially from a drunken fool like Marcus Etchells."

"Clara figured you were calling the sheriff's department," I said.

"Did she?" She studied Clara. "Maybe she did."

"Feeling this way, why *did* you come to the reunion?" I asked Fae.

"To test my theory. And I was right. That cadre is never leaving high school, mentally or emotionally. There are exceptions," she added grudgingly.

"Including Josepha Viedux?" I asked.

Clara made a sound of protest.

Fae, though, got the glassy-eyed look of someone gazing into memories. "Interesting. She *was* an exception. Not like Clara. More like she never really was in high school. It was like she was apart from the rest of us."

"When did you get into town?"

"Friday afternoon. And, before you ask, as the deputy did repeatedly, I had dinner in my room here at the B&B—had it delivered—so I could do some work before the weekend's frivolity." She didn't stint on the sarcasm.

"Besides, why would I kill Josepha Viedux? She never bothered me. Not back then and not now. I wasn't worth anything to her. Now, if it were Marcus who'd been murdered..." She sighed, possibly with regret about what she was about to say. "No, I wouldn't kill him, either."

"Wish you could?"

"More like a daydream you'd never pursue in real life. No, not even that. I look at him and feel sorry for him. That he felt the need back then to try to diminish other people to feel better about himself. Still does it now, which is sad. Did you know studies have shown something they call the reminiscence bump?"

The same phrase Kirstin had used. Interesting.

"What's that?" Clara asked before I could.

"It's how they describe the fact that adults' memories from adolescence—basically high school and college—are disproportionately recalled compared to any other period of life. That is also the period—especially high school—of the greatest dopamine activity in a human lifespan, which makes the experiences and memories more intense."

She had to have learned this from Kirstin. Idle B&B chatter? Or more?

"Think about that. All those kids learning how to become an adult while they're being told who they are based on standards of fleeting athletic ability and facile prettiness. I fought hard against that back then, learning to see myself for my accomplishments, not the opinions of—*them*." She brushed the air with one hand. "I certainly won't put my self-worth now in their hands. A group of should-be-adults stuck in adolescence."

"I don't think they're stuck," Clara said. "They want to be there. Clinging to it. Because they enjoyed their power from that time."

"Very astute, Clara. You always were a good observer."

Startled, she asked, "Was I?"

"You were," Fae said firmly. "Not part of any of the cliques, yet accepted by most. And watching everybody."

Clara flushed.

"Fae," I asked, "what did you mean about you not being worth anything to Josepha Viedux?"

She didn't answer immediately, then gave a short nod. "What I said about Marcus diminishing other people to feel better about himself? Well, Josepha Viedux did a variant of that." She looked across at Clara. "You know."

"I don't—"

"Yes, you do."

Clara frowned, but not at Fae's contradiction.

Fae continued, "That group gossiped, spread rumors. Josepha

didn't. But… She didn't tell a lot of things, but when she said something, it was true. She gathered intelligence with the aim of evening the odds—no, of putting herself ahead of someone who thought they were superior to her." With matter-of-factness Fae added, "So she never gathered any intelligence on me. I wasn't worth it."

Clara expelled one breath. "Me either."

"What did she do with the intelligence she gathered?" I asked.

The North Bend County High School alums looked at each other, then shrugged in tandem.

Clara added, "Like we said, she didn't share much of it."

"But she did use it." Fae Ballard left no doubt. "I saw her do it with a senior when we were freshmen. The senior was bossing her around and Josepha said something I didn't hear, but that senior did and backed off. Immediately. Another time, I wasn't clear what happened in the moment, but later, running it through my head… By then we were juniors and she might have been smoother."

"What was it?"

"I don't remember. It wasn't important enough to me. But I remember thinking Josepha was someone to steer clear of."

Remembering a moment Saturday night, I asked, "Ever see her do it to Lovell Zelig?"

"Mr. Zelig?" From surprise, Fae's expression quickly transitioned to something more closed off. "You mean because he's gay? But everybody knew that."

"I didn't know. Not back then," Clara said.

"Well, he was your teacher. You weren't supposed to know about their private lives."

"Didn't think they were allowed to have them," I said dryly.

"Pretty much aren't. Still, she couldn't have done her worst to him about being gay. That was too widely known. It wouldn't have given her leverage."

"Could be something else. Something that would give her leverage," I said.

Her expression hardened. "You're thinking abuse?"

Clara's head whipped from Fae to me. "Abuse? You think Mr.

Zelig—?"

I raised my hands. "I don't think anything. I'm asking."

"No," Clara said.

She and Fae looked at each other.

Slowly, Fae turned toward me. "It would be a major, major piece of intelligence for Josepha. But I never heard even a hint of that." She gave her head a quick jerk, as if to shake off a bothersome fly or realign the parts inside. "Anyway, Lovell Zelig wasn't at the potluck picnic."

"He knew about it," Clara said. "In fact, Josepha told him about it Saturday night. I heard her. Said he really, really should come. That he wouldn't want to miss it."

"She would." As if aware she sounded surprisingly sharp, Fae quickly added, "But that doesn't change that he wasn't there."

Not being there, however, didn't change that he could have killed Josepha at any point between the breakup of the previous night's event and when people started arriving at Senior Hill. Killing her there, leaving her body partially under the picnic table, anchoring one side of the tablecloth that obscured the body from view.

"Anything more recent Josepha might have known about people in your class? Any scandals?"

She scoffed. "Run of the mill scandals? That wouldn't suit Josepha." Fae put one hand on the round top of the newel post. "I'm going to my room now. Good night."

CHAPTER TWENTY-TWO

CLARA BARELY WAITED for us to get into her vehicle to protest.

"I can't believe Mr. Zelig would abuse any of the guys—or anybody. I know, I know. That's what everybody says when these things happen. But I can't. I'm sure he didn't."

"It could explain Marcus' animosity toward him."

"Marcus? No way. More likely he'd be—No, I'm not going to say that. It's too… No."

No need. I got her drift. Marcus was more likely cast as a sexual predator than a victim.

After a silence, I said, "That was interesting what Fae said about you being accepted by all the groups."

"I tried to get along with people, but…"

"But what?"

"I never felt comfortable in high school. You know, sure of who I was."

I laughed. "That puts you in the same camp as the vast majority of kids. Maybe all of them with the exceptions of psychopaths and … well, honestly, I don't know who else felt sure of who they were."

Clara wasn't laughing with me.

"What?" I asked her.

"Remember what Fae said about Josepha never really being in high school the way the rest of us were?"

"Uh-huh."

"She was right. She *was* sure of who she was. And then what you just said about psychopaths… But it wasn't like she was *dangerous*.

Or—Oh. I suppose she must have been dangerous to at least one person or she wouldn't have been murdered. But she wasn't *crazy*."

"Psychopaths can be very charming and—"

"She wasn't that, either," Clara mumbled.

"No. But they can fly under the radar. Especially women."

"Your aunt?" She meant was Kit my source for this information, not if she was a psychopath.

"Of course."

"Huh. What else?"

"They're narcissistic, though not necessarily overt about it, while all the time thinking they're better than everybody else. Especially smarter."

"Oh, yes."

"Often manipulative. Maneuvering other people to get what they want. They want to be the center of attention. They know about social interactions and normal human emotions, but they don't feel them or have empathy for them. Mostly they imitate them to manipulate or present a *normal* front, while often feeling they're a weakness."

"Definitely not the center of attention for Josepha. She'd stand back and watch people. It was kind of creepy, like she was memorizing what they were doing. The rest of what you said fits."

We settled into our own thoughts for several blocks.

"Clara, did you keep the list of attendees they passed out last night?"

"Hmm? Oh, yes. I've got it at home. I'll make a couple copies and bring you one."

"Thanks. But what's bothering you?"

"Something Fae said."

My hopes rose. She'd picked up something I'd missed. *Great.*

"Fae said she was bullied by her peers. But that's not true. I mean, if she says she was bullied, I believe her, but by how many people? Three? Four? Even a dozen? That's horrible and should never happen. But she put everyone in our class into the same category. I was her peer and I never bullied or insulted her. Same goes for a lot of other kids. It's handing the power to a small group to define not only yourself—which happens when you're a kid—but to define everyone else in the class. Even now, when we should be grownups."

"You are very wise, Clara."

TEAGUE MESSAGED THAT they finished late, but they *had* finished the project. He was turning in because he'd agreed to substitute teach all week. He'd be in touch.

The easy tone of his message told me he had not heard about a death associated with the reunion picnic.

I replied, wishing him a good night and a good day teaching. Okay, also hoping he shut off his phone for the night before a specific piece of news reached him.

Sure, I didn't want to disturb his rest. I also wanted a little more lead time before he knew Clara and I had been at another murder scene, even if we did miss the honor of finding the body.

WHEN MY PHONE rang at this hour, it was either an emergency or my night owl great-aunt.

I was relieved to see the name Kit pop up on caller ID.

Even though her greeting was, "What exactly are you up to?"

"I'm looking up *reminiscence bump* and other things someone said about adolescence."

"That's not why you asked for the rundown on Glenn Selka's professional standing and reputation. Details," she demanded.

I supplied them, from start to finish.

"I'll let you know when I get something back on Selka. For your suspect named Fae—"

"I don't know that she's a suspect. Or Glenn-."

"Of course they are. Both of them. The wife, too. Along with that shrieker and a few others I can think of."

Before I could ask her to name names, she moved on. "Anyway, Fae gave you accurate information about the reminiscence bump. I've read those studies."

My reaction fell between a sigh and a chuckle. "Of course you have."

"You know my opinion of high schools. They're like four years of *Lord of the Flies* in brick buildings. Pack those kids in, mostly devoid of adult company, and they're bound not only to create their own hierarchy, but to make a thorough mess of it. I believe English teachers include *Lord of the Flies* on their reading lists so often because they know they're living inside its plot."

I stored up that last line to use in my guise as a former high school English teacher.

Kit promised to report back with any more about Glenn and declared I would update her.

Before I turned off the light, I searched online for anything about the reunion on social media and found several postings, most simple announcements of when and where.

One site offered more, with ongoing posts over the past few years.

Josepha promoted a self-named company that offered cleaning services. One endorsement came from Debi Norris.

A couple other companies presumably run by alums, also advertised. None as prominent as Josepha's. A spattering of baby announcements. Four or five messages from posters looking for a specific past classmate. Beyond that it was The Debi Show.

Photos of her house, which ran to swoopy, dark-colored floral drapes, and lots of fuss. Photos of her on vacation, which showed big, white teeth against over-tanned skin at beaches that all looked alike. Photos of her at events, which revealed the startling moment the current rendition of her eyebrows appeared.

A couple of the shots caught a male figure in one corner, mostly exiting the frame. Thinning gray hair on top, with an unremarkable form. None of the moments caught his face.

MONDAY

CHAPTER TWENTY-THREE

YESTERDAY'S SUNSHINE HAD given way to morning clouds.

Thanks to Clara picking me up, we were at the Old Main Branch of the North Bend County Library shortly after it opened.

We found Amy on the second floor. She took us right to the station where we could access digitized editions of local newspapers.

The initial reports we found didn't add a great deal to Clara's memories. The first was five paragraphs with the bare essentials, all attributed to law enforcement sources. The second was longer, with a few quotes from neighbors about how hard it was raining that night and had been for two days, how there should be a big fence or wall where "that girl" went over, how it was a tragedy, but they hadn't known her more than seeing her move in a while back.

My phone vibrated. An incoming message from Teague.

Clara raised *Are you going to check that?* eyebrows. I shook my head and we resumed reading.

The headline on the second article referred to a *Tragic Fall* and that phrase returned in a third and even longer story, which said she died of a broken neck. It had photos of Heidi Holmes from high school and one of her significantly younger.

It also had quotes from people who had known the victim.

The first was from Debi.

I reached it first and apparently made a noise, because Clara said, "What?" After a minute more of reading, she said, "Oh."

I can't get my head around someone I've known most of my life dying so shortly after we left the fabulous experience of high school, while I remain, vibrant, young, and happy.

"She's so broken up about it she can't see past herself," I muttered.

Clara's narrowed gaze focused on the screen, but she wasn't reading. "That part about knowing Heidi most of her life… If I remember correctly about where they each grew up, that could be true. I think they would have gone to the same elementary school."

"Any other connection you know of?"

She shook her head. "Don't remember Heidi even mentioning her name."

We both returned to reading.

Four paragraphs later, we hit a quote from Lovell Zelig.

A vibrant girl, just finding out how terrific she was. This is a tragedy. And she will be missed.

We looked at each other. "Did she know him well?"

"I don't remember. I… I think she liked him, but most everybody did. I didn't know about any special closeness." With self-blame edging in, she said. "Or I don't remember it."

I bumped her shoulder with mine. "It's not your fault, Clara. Did she try to keep your friendship going while you were still in town? Did she contact you after you left? No. You said she pulled away during your senior year. That happens. With kids, with adults."

"I know, but—"

"Let's finish reading this and see if there's anything else."

There wasn't. Nothing more of interest in that article and only one additional bulleted item saying her death had been officially ruled accidental.

Clara, though, didn't look up. She went back to the longest article. With her finger, she traced up the paragraphs to Lovell Zelig's quote.

She sniffled. "I'm not sure she was. Missed, I mean. I had moved on to college. Glenn was gone. She never had much family and I don't even know what happened to the ones who were left. They never cared about her alive, so how could they have missed her? Maybe my gran missed her the most, but even that was part of missing me. That's the real tragedy."

❖ ❖ ❖ ❖

OUTSIDE THE LIBRARY, I checked my phone.

Teague had messaged. Someone at the high school where he was subbing—not North Bend County High—must have blabbed.

He'd sent one word with punctuation:

Again?

❖ ❖ ❖ ❖

"ISN'T THAT KIRSTIN?" I asked as a car passed us going the other direction.

Since we'd been heading to the Amber House B&B for an update with her, that was a pertinent question.

"Yes." Clara made a U-turn with admirable elan.

We caught up with Kirstin in the parking lot of the courthouse.

The worry in her eyes had spawned dark circles beneath them that showed despite impeccable makeup.

She started when she saw us, as if yanked out of difficult thoughts back to a present she did not find any more appealing.

"What are you doing here?" Harshness strained her voice.

"We saw you and wanted to touch base to see how things are going," I said.

"They aren't. Not so far. I'm meeting a lawyer who happens to be here for a court hearing in ten minutes. I had meetings with two other lawyers in Cincinnati and one in Stringer. I can't say any impressed me. I hope this one… But I have to choose someone and get them on the job to make the sheriff's department release Glenn."

"Is he officially in custody?"

"I don't even know. Surely he would tell them he was done and leave there if he wasn't."

Neither of us posed a guess about that.

Instead, we told her we'd been talking to people about what happened and starting to dig.

She nodded, though I wasn't sure she'd fully taken in our words.

"How did you decide to go to Haines Tavern for dinner Friday night?" I asked as casually as I could. I was not ready to let anyone else know about the knife coming from there.

"I overheard the owner of the B&B tell someone else they could get dinner delivered from there and she said it was the best food in town."

"Who?" Clara asked.

Kirstin blinked. "The historic tavern—Haines Tavern. Or do you mean who said it? That was Ottalie Bishop, the owner. Actually, I don't know if she's the owner, but she's running it and—"

"No, I meant who was she telling about the tavern?"

"Oh. Sorry. I haven't slept much. Um, it was one of the alums. We had a couple chats over breakfast. I should remember her name, but… She was the one Marcus went after when we were all outside leaving the hotel Saturday night. And she walked away to call the police."

Fae Ballard.

Kirstin might be short on sleep and might not have remembered the name, but she noticed things, picking up on what Fae had done.

"I'm sorry. I have to go to the ladies' room before I see this lawyer." She started away, then turned back. "As much as I appreciate your looking into this and trying to help us, all my energy right now is needed to get Glenn released. Maybe later you can fill me in?"

She didn't wait for an answer.

We watched her go inside in silence.

"What next?" Clara asked. "Fae?"

"Let's try to get more information before we go back to Fae."

CLARA KNOCKED ON Debi Norris' front door. We waited. With no response, I rang the doorbell.

The door yanked open.

"What?"

We both micro-recoiled. Less at her shout than at her appearance.

She was generally pale, but now irregular red blotches stood out starkly and those eyebrows looked like black paper cutouts pasted onto a white background.

"What do you want?"

I blurted out, "Were you the first one at the picnic site yesterday?"

"Of course. I was in charge."

"Did anyone come up the steep side while you were there?"

"Like what? An orangutan? Or dropped from a helicopter? Idiot."

"Or go down the steep side?" Though why someone would while Debi was there… But I wasn't letting her truculence stop me from asking.

"Idiot," she repeated.

"The tablecloth on the buffet table—" That hid the body. "—you must have brought that with you yesterday—"

"Shows how stupid you and those deputies are and why *I'm* in charge of everything. I think ahead. I brought all that out in a box Saturday so I didn't have to worry about it Sunday."

Debi started to swing the door closed.

"Wait." Clara braced the door open with her spread hand. "What did Josepha know about—"

The red blotches darkened.

"—other people?"

Then faded.

"What the hell business is it of yours?"

"If you don't know if she knew things about Mary Jo, Wesley, Glenn, whoever, then you don't know. Though it's rather surprising you're in the dark…"

"I'm not in the dark. I just don't care about shit she had on other people."

Other people. Implying Josepha also had information on Debi?

"Did you employ Josepha's cleaning company?"

"Not long."

"When?"

"Last spring."

"Why did you stop using her company?"

"She did a shit job."

"Did you notice her van in the parking lot by Senior Hill?"

"She didn't have a van. Just a cheap little compact." She tried again to push the door closed.

Clara pushed back harder. "Tell us, where are people staying?"

"I was far too busy to memorize where everybody was. Some at that jumped up B&B, I suppose. Some at the hotel. Some at those cut-rate places off the Interstate in Stringer or with family. I couldn't care less."

She slammed the door in our faces.

CHAPTER TWENTY-FOUR

"HAD SHE BEEN ... *crying*? Over *Josepha*?" Clara asked in a shocked whisper.

"If so, it definitely qualifies as an ugly cry, but I'd guess she was crying for other reasons."

"I suppose we answered the tablecloth question anyway. If we believe her, the cloth was there in a box of supplies and the murderer had access to it to hide the body."

"Who leaves a box of supplies at a public place the day before?"

Clara turned a confused face to me. "Why not?"

"It'll get taken."

"Who'd take somebody else's picnic supplies?"

Sometimes I forgot I was in North Bend County. "But—while I bow to your superior knowledge of local customs—why didn't Debi wonder why it was already on the table?"

"Hungover."

An all too plausible explanation. "Okay, who else do we want to talk to?"

"Mary Jo to help pin down the order of arrivals. I wonder if Ancella could add anything. Wesley, since he was an early one there, too. I suppose we should talk to Marcus, too. Even though he has an alibi?"

"Yeah. But we can put it off until we talk to the others. Who knows, maybe we'll get something that breaks his alibi."

"Being in jail? That's awfully hard to break. We should be so lucky." Her nose wrinkled, perhaps in memory of Marcus' odiferous presence at the picnic. "Let's try the hotel first and see who's staying there."

✧   ✧   ✧   ✧

THE HOTEL WHERE the reunion had been held was a bust.

We tried name after name for people on the reunion list who were from out of town. To several of them the clerk said, "Checked out," including Mary Jo Anderson. According to the alumni list Clara had, she lived in Traverse City, Michigan. We would have to call her in Michigan if we wanted to talk to her.

The lone exception was Ancella. But she did not answer her room phone when the clerk rang it.

Next, we headed to Stringer, the biggest and most influential town in the county. Haines Tavern had held onto the county seat and its history, but Stringer had the growth from its location alongside the Interstate connecting Cincinnati and Louisville.

Two chain motels had nothing. The third, though, had a Wesley Oshmann registered. And he answered his room phone.

"Uh, sure," he told Clara, speaking loudly enough for me to over-hear. "I'll be right down, meet you in the lobby and we can get coffee there. Just give me a minute."

When she hung up, I said to Clara, "Did he sound nervous to you? Like he was afraid you wanted to go to his room?"

"Maybe it's a mess. Besides some people get that way talking about murder."

When he joined us in the lobby he smiled at Clara, but I also no-ticed his hands jerked. As if aware of me watching, he put them in his pockets.

"Let's go to the restaurant next door for our coffee," I suggested. I'd seen the setup in the lobby and wasn't impressed, though I had another reason for the suggestion.

"Okay," Clara said, confused but willing.

I didn't mind confusing her because Wesley's eyes flicked toward the direction he'd come from.

Encouraging them to precede me and confident Clara would keep him occupied, I followed slowly, twisting my neck in a good imitation of the *Exorcist* scene and was rewarded by spotting a figure crossing the parking lot toward a vehicle.

Settled around a table with coffee and a plate of cracker pizza appetizers in the center, Clara eased into the conversation.

"I noticed on the list of attendees that you were added on, Wesley."

"Didn't decide to come until the last minute."

"We didn't have much of a chance to talk Saturday night. How are you doing these days?"

"Good. Nobody would've expected it in high school, but I've done real well. Have a great family, two boys and two girls, a wonderful wife, and a job I'm good at." He kept his smile small, while pride showed in his eyes.

She beamed at him. "Of course we expected it. I'm so glad it's turned out well for you. Sounds like you have a wonderful life."

"Pretty much, yeah. Maybe you expected it, Clara, because you looked for the best in and for everybody. But not most of them. Or me, for that matter. Considered myself pretty much a loser back then."

I inserted my first question. "Was that why you came to the reunion? Show folks how you turned out?"

"No—Or, uh, tha—." He stumbled on the syllables. Thrown off stride because he'd forgotten I was here? He stopped and took a deep breath before starting again. "Sounds pretty arrogant put that way. I suppose that would have to be some of it, though. And to catch up. It's what you do, right?"

Seemed to me it wasn't what the majority of their high school class had done.

"Are you aware of Josepha knowing private information involving your past classmates?" I asked.

"Did she? I'd have no idea. Nobody said anything. As for her, didn't do more than say hello Saturday night."

"Of course," Clara soothed. "Have you stayed in touch with friends from our class?"

"Not sure I had any friends. No real friends."

Clara's mouth formed an O. "But you and Marcus…"

"Friends? Never really were. And we all outgrow certain … things from adolescence."

His slight hesitation before *things* had me mentally jumping the gun to supply the phrase *bad habits*.

"You've outgrown Marcus?"

"I have. Finally. Sure would have gotten more out of high school if I'd done it earlier."

"I thought you two… I guess I assumed. Didn't you bail out Marcus on Sunday morning?"

"No." He shook his head to reinforce the word. "Probably his mom did. Unless things have changed radically since high school."

"I don't believe they have changed for him. Not the way they have for you—the way you've changed things for yourself."

"Thanks, Clara."

"Just stating the facts. Did you know Josepha back in school?"

"Not really. Didn't cross paths with her much then and not at all at the reunion. Saw her, of course, but not to talk to. Hard to believe, somebody from North Bend County High getting murdered like that."

"It is—and when we were all planning to have such a nice potluck picnic and then see the updates at the school. We're trying to make sense of it. Weren't you one of the first to arrive at the picnic area, Wesley—?"

"Not the first. Other people were there when I got there."

"Who?"

"Debi Norris, Mary Jo Anderson, Fae Ballard, though Fae didn't stay long. Debi made a pointed remark about her not bringing a dish and Fae said she'd forgotten it at the B&B. Debi prodded her to go back and get it, so she did."

"How about a van in the parking lot? Blue. Did you see that when you got there?"

"Didn't really pay attention, you know?"

"Did you notice anything particular yesterday, Wesley? Someone acting tense? Or something strange? I mean before Josepha was found."

"Nothing."

"Anyone acting odd or—?"

"No. Seemed to me they were acting just like high school. Debi bossing people around. Mary Jo toeing the mark. Fae defying with passive aggression. Nothing was out of the ordinary at all. Not until…"

Clara grimaced. "Until we found Josepha's body."

✧ ✧ ✧ ✧

"LUNCH? FAST FOOD okay?" Clara asked after we'd parted from Wesley and watched him head inside the motel.

At my double yesses, she started the engine and headed out.

"You got awfully quiet back there," she said.

"Guess who I saw walking across this parking lot from the motel rooms to a car when we were going for coffee?"

Her eyes widened. "Debi? Oh. No. Marcus?"

"Why would you say Debi?"

"Because Wesley always had a thing for her. She didn't give him the time of day—unless she wanted something from him."

"Huh. But your second guess was the right one. It seems Wesley Oshmann is not completely estranged from Marcus Etchells."

"Or Marcus was trying to get Wesley back under his thumb."

"Under his thumb? Everybody else talked about them being friends."

"Marcus bossed him around all the time."

"Taking lessons from Debi?"

"I suppose, though she bossed *everybody*." She tapped a finger against her cheek. "You know, last I heard, Marcus works not far from here. After lunch, do you think…?"

"I do."

✧ ✧ ✧ ✧

SOMETIMES, KIT MAINTAINED, cliches were cliches because they were true.

Marcus Etchells worked at a used car lot.

A slightly seedy used car lot along a decidedly unscenic stretch of highway.

He came out of the office as we pulled to a stop, with the same smile as Saturday night, but thankfully not the same clothes.

"Good thing you came by here today, ladies. Just so happens I can do real well for you on a trade-in for that—" His eyes caught up with his mouth, as he recognized us. His smarmy smile faltered, then returned. "Especially for a fellow North Bend High alum. Glad you came to see me. I can help you out."

"We're not here for a car, Marcus," Clara said sternly.

"Cars are our business, so—"

"Were you really in jail Saturday night?" she asked.

He looked over his shoulder, then closed the gap to us. "Deputy making a big deal out of nothing like they always do. Didn't get out until lunchtime. That's why I went straight to Senior Hill. Didn't want to be late and piss off Debi."

"The sheriff's department records will back that up?" I asked.

He shifted to a smirk. "Check in and check out times, on the dot."

"Are you involved with her—Debi?" Clara asked.

"I'm a free agent when it comes to babes."

I noticed he'd shifted from ladies to babes, now that he knew we weren't potential customers.

"What were you doing at Wesley Oshmann's hotel room today?"

For an instant, I thought the question rattled him enough to break him. But he rallied.

"Took my lunch hour early to see an old friend. So what?"

"Some friend. The guy you hit Saturday night," I said.

He turned suddenly earnest. I think I preferred the smarmy smirk. "See? That's it. I wanted to make sure we were okay. You know, no hard feelings. And there weren't. The Assman and I go way back and—"

"*Etchells.*"

Clara and I turned toward the shout from a heavy-set man plowing his way toward us from the back of the lot.

Marcus didn't. He glowered at us. "I've got nothing more to say.

Get the hell out of here."

"Etchells," the man shouted again.

Clara and I looked at each other and moved toward her van.

Inside, we could still hear the man.

"I told you two weeks ago. No more giveaways for your women. Best vehicle in my inventory and you practically give it away for a piece of junk. I'm not in business to get you laid. One more time and…"

Clara drove us away with the man still shouting. Marcus' smirk had returned.

CHAPTER TWENTY-FIVE

FAE DESCRIBED ESSENTIALLY the same sequence as Wesley.

We caught up with her on the back porch of the B&B, typing at warp speed.

She grunted without looking up. Another couple of minutes of flat-out typing, and finally she stopped and looked up. But she didn't move her hands from the keyboard.

"More questions?"

"We're confirming the order folks arrived at the picnic area yesterday," Clara said.

Fae reported Debi and Mary Jo were there when she arrived, followed by Wesley. Then she left to go back for the dish she'd forgotten. She paid no attention to vehicles in the parking lot either time she'd arrived. Why should she?

"What time did you get back here to get the dish?" I asked.

"No idea."

"What time did you get to the picnic area?"

"No idea."

"What time did you leave the B&B the first time?"

"No idea."

Before either of us could press her, Fae spoke quickly. "When I got there, Debi was ordering Mary Jo around, just like high school. Also just like high school, she was complaining Mary Jo was late, leaving Debi to do all the work—and then she reeled off to-dos for Mary Jo.

"Thought I'd enjoy hearing someone like Mary Jo get bossed

around. Thought I wanted payback for being bullied at good old North Bend County High, but it didn't satisfy the way I thought it would.

"Anyway, Mary Jo got a break when I showed up and Debi zeroed in on my empty hands, not even noticing Wesley coming right after me. The lovely staff here at the B&B had given me a casserole to bring, but I forgot it. I told Debi that I'd go back and get it if more than twenty people showed up, but that wouldn't do for her. Ancella came during the great debate. Debi insisted I get it right that minute."

"When did you get back to Senior Hill?"

"I saw you two climbing the hill as I pulled in."

That matched my memory, too. No need to let her know that. Better to keep her slightly on the defensive. So I kept asking questions.

"Friday night, when you had dinner in your room in the B&B—?"

"About that, I might have misspoken."

My heart hammered at my ribs. "Oh?"

"I didn't eat in my room. I try not to when there's an alternative, so the room doesn't smell like food the whole night. Ottalie Bishop suggested I eat out here on the back veranda and I did."

Clara released a stream of air. Then rallied before I did by asking, "What did you have?"

"Filet with BLT risotto that was delicious."

Images of cutlery and a distinctive knife danced in my head. "Steak."

"Uh-huh. That was good, but that BLT risotto... Mmm."

"**...DOESN'T MEAN FAE** or Glenn used a Haines Tavern steak knife to kill Josepha," Clara concluded her defense of her fellow alums.

"Let's go back to the high school."

"Okay, but why? The sheriff's department will have the picnic area closed off. If they also have someone watching..."

"Word will get back to Deputy Hensen we're poking around. I know. But we won't go by the picnic area."

In fact, Clara steered well clear of it, entering the back parking lot from the north side of the building—the opposite side from the picnic area. She drove as close to the football field as possible, then we got out and walked to the bleachers, blending in with a couple dozen students and other spectators watching the team doing drills.

But when I pulled out my phone, I did not focus on the sweating teenagers. I shifted to point it at this side of the hill that held up the picnic area.

Deputies had strung police tape around the base of the hill.

Ordinary precaution to discourage the foolhardy from trying that approach to the crime scene? Or something more?

First, I found the buffet table, standing out in silhouette against the sky. Slowly, I lowered the focus down the hill, keeping it as wide as possible.

Then I zoomed in a bit and tried again.

The top part of the hill was hard to see with the contour thrown into deep shadow. But as I came low enough to exclude the light gray sky from the frame, details started to appear.

Trying to keep the camera still, I pulled my head back to survey the same area with my bare eyes.

"What are you looking at?" Clara asked.

"Just a second."

I looked through the camera again, confirming I'd seen what I thought I'd seen.

This time when I was done, I turned to her and saw she'd taken her own phone out and was studying the hillside. "I don't see any-thing," she complained.

"Pull back to a wide view. Now see the little scrub tree on the left that looks like a question mark?"

"Like a—? Okay. It does."

"Staying on a line with that, scan over to the right. If you see any-thing interesting, zoom in."

She went slowly—so slowly I began to doubt my confidence.

Then she shifted her hold on the phone and zoomed in with one finger.

"Oh… Is that…?" Slowly, she panned down toward the bottom of the hill. She lowered her phone and turned to me. "What do you think that is?"

"You first. I don't want to influence you."

"It looks like… Well, if it were winter, I'd say ski tracks or even sled tracks in snow. But it's in the grass and that kind of light brush."

"Then we see the same thing. Like someone skied—or skidded—down that part of the hill. We dismissed the idea of someone climbing *up* the hill to kill Josepha, but could they have come down this side to avoid detection after committing the murder?"

"Maybe," she said slowly.

"If so, that opens the field wide. It could be just about anyone. Except Debi."

She sighed. "I get it. Because the reason to skid down the face of the hill would be for the murderer to make his or her escape and Debi didn't. She was there when others started arriving."

I did not chide her for the note of disappointment in her words. In fact, I set about cheering her up some.

"Just because the marks are there on the hillside doesn't mean it was the murderer escaping. Could have been a kid or—"

"Word would be all over the county if a kid did it."

"Still, maybe it wasn't the murderer, but someone else wanting to get out of there fast and for reasons they didn't want to broadcast."

"Maybe." She wasn't much cheered. She pointed toward what we could see of the parking lot nearest the high school building. "Looks like students are starting to leave."

My phone rang and ID said Kit. Kit calling during her prime writing time? "I better get this."

"Sure."

"Kit?"

"Don't sound all worried. I'm reporting back with my sources' takes on your Glenn Selka."

"Not my—Never mind. What did they say?"

"Everything he told you checks out. Without being asked, they went beyond that. Sound man. Respected and liked. Not a common combo."

"Your report is that Glenn Selka's a saint?"

"These people wouldn't have included respect if he was a saint."

"You could have messaged that to me."

"Quicker this way. In case it had a big impact on what you're doing. Anything vital and new?"

Ah, curiosity. Kit's strength and her potential kryptonite.

"I wouldn't say vital—"

"Okay, then it can wait until tonight when you update me. Gotta get my words in."

"Kit, I—"

She was gone before I could complete my protest that I hadn't promised to update her, specifically not tonight.

I turned to find Clara frowning at me. "You had your great-aunt check up on Glenn? Why? We told Kirstin we'd help them. How can we help if you suspect him?"

"That's why I asked her to check. To remove doubt."

"I didn't have any doubt. Or I wouldn't have told Kirstin we'd help them clear his name."

"I didn't say we'd clear his name. I said we'd do our best to figure this out. Sure would help if we could talk to Glenn. To find out more about what the sheriff's department has on him."

"Thinks they have on him." She corrected me firmly, yet without anger. She'd make a good teacher.

"Either way—" I wriggled around our potential difference of opinion. "—it would help to know what they're asking him."

"I'll remind Kirstin that we want to know as soon as he's released."

"If he's released."

"It's our job to make sure he is."

A figure walked along an aisle between parked cars in the lot, raising a hand in farewell to the occupants of one departing vehicle.

"Is that Lovell Zelig?" I asked. "As long as we're here, what are the chances of talking to him?"

"Are you changing the subject?"

"Yes."

She gave me a stern look that didn't last long. Then she tipped her head toward more students emerging from the building. "With school letting out, it's a good time to try."

But Lovell Zelig was nowhere in sight when we emerged from behind the curve of the hill and into the parking lot.

Clara said, "We'll check in at the office and see if they know where he is."

By the time we walked around to the main entrance, the student exodus had reached full flow.

Overheard snippets of conversation reminded me of Kit's view on high schools. I reminded myself that I'd been at least that shallow at that stage.

After fighting our way against that tide, encountering a gray-haired school office matriarch who remembered Clara with obvious fondness restored my spirits. Her fondness didn't stop her from having us fill out visitor forms, taking copies of our IDs, and attaching fluorescent tags to us announcing our foreign status.

She also told us Zelig's assignment of the moment was patrolling the East Lot and directed us to the shortest route.

We found him talking to a gaggle of girls involved in solving the complex math problem of who should ride with whom, when they were all going to the mall in Stringer.

Seeing us, he peeled away from the girls and met us with a smile.

"Nice to see you again so soon, Clara."

"Hi, Mr. Zelig. I'd like you to meet my friend, Sheila Mackey."

We shook hands and expressed our pleasure at meeting each other.

"Not a North Bend alum, but you were at the reunion Saturday night," he said.

"You're very right and you're very observant."

"I asked Sheila to come with me because my husband's stuck in that hurricane disaster area because of business and couldn't come, not Saturday night and not yesterday," Clara explained.

His expression instantly changed. "I heard about yesterday, of course. And that you two… Well. It's horrible. Absolutely horrible. And hard to believe."

I raised a mildly skeptical eyebrow. "You don't think alums of North Bend County High are capable of murder?"

CHAPTER TWENTY-SIX

HE DEFLECTED MY question, saying, "Don't they say anyone's capable?"

Without waiting for an answer, he continued, "There's a lot of pressure in high school. Most kids—now and for all the years I've taught—are great, each in his or her own way. The hard part is a lot of them don't believe they are. They see through a very narrow lens. They compare themselves to actors to singers to athletes to so-called influencers. Anything I can do to help these kids shake that off and believe in their own, individual greatness is the most rewarding part of my job."

"Tell him what your aunt says about high school," Clara urged me.

I did, at the same time recognizing how successfully he'd steered away from my question about murder.

"Boy, is that true." He chuckled. "Was your aunt ever a teacher?"

"No. A close observer of humanity."

"But Sheila was a teacher," Clara slid in. "High school English, until an inheritance meant she could quit her job and move here."

I concentrated on not grinding my teeth. My general policy was the fewer people who knew anything about me, the better. More specifically, the fewer high school teachers who knew about my supposed past, the lots better.

When I'd decided on this cover story I'd debated between college and high school teaching being my former profession. High school won because people were more likely to ask the name of a college than a high school—thinking they might have known someone who was a student there or on faculty there. Always looking for those connections between people.

I hadn't counted on Teague O'Donnell being a high school teacher.

I hadn't counted on Teague O'Donnell at all.

I sure hadn't counted on Teague O'Donnell being retired law enforcement and all too adept at spotting lies, half-truths, and evasions.

And yet, as much as he threatened my cover, I couldn't regret failing to stay far, far away from him as I'd planned when we met. Especially not when he had his arms around me and we were snuggled—

"Lucky you." Lovell Zelig's comment jerked me back to the ongoing conversation, its potential pitfalls, and its possible hidden meanings.

He didn't mean it.

In fact, I'd wager he thought I was crazy to have left teaching. But was that because he truly loved teaching teenagers or for a less benign reason? A gay man was no more likely to abuse students than other categories of abusers, but that didn't mean it didn't happen.

As if to confirm my first thoughts, but leaving my questions unanswered, he added, "Any interest in getting back into teaching here? We might be able to arrange something."

"My dog would never forgive me for getting a job out of the house."

Clara solemnly confirmed my flippant remark. "That's true."

"But getting back to Saturday night…" An inelegant, but effective wrenching of the topic away from me and returning it to murder. "I couldn't help but notice what a popular figure you are with all of Clara's class."

"Not all," he said dryly.

"Yes. Well, let's say all the sober ones."

He raised one shoulder, tipping his head toward it at the same time, acknowledging my point, yet also dismissing it. And certainly not pursuing the topic.

Which left me to do the pursuing.

"Did you know Marcus Etchells when he was in high school?"

"Didn't have him in any classes, but I knew who he was. Suppose everyone did, certainly by his senior year."

"Big man on campus?"

"In his own eyes for sure."

"Did he have trouble with anybody?"

"Him? Not troubled by anybody." He looked from me to Clara. "Turn it around, though, with who he was trouble for and…" He raised both hands.

"Whom," she said.

"What?"

"With *whom* he was trouble for. Remember, Sheila was an English teacher. Who versus whom is important to her."

Right back where we were. *Thanks a bunch, Clara.*

"Was there someone in particular he was trouble for?" I know. Preposition at the end of a sentence. At least I'd avoided the who/whom issue.

Both of Zelig's hands came up. "If it was on my radar then it didn't impress me enough to remember it now."

"Have you seen him since graduation?"

"Sure. Football games. Basketball games. Around town now and then."

He said it easily and his answer was completely plausible. Although, from the corner of my eye, I saw Clara cross her forearms and look down.

"He comes back to the high school to watch games?"

"A lot do. Some have kids and come back for them, of course. Some are true sports fans. Some feel it's being part of the community. Some can't let go."

He had a trick of generalizing about the students and alums. Yet the strong implication here was that Marcus, specifically, fell into the last category.

Strong implication wasn't sufficient.

"Which was Marcus?"

He flashed a one-sided grimace. "The last. Reliving those glory days." He shook his head. "Though they weren't all that filled with glory from what I recall. Played football, but not the best on the team and no championship seasons when he played or anything."

"No. Our sports teams weren't very successful," Clara agreed.

"Why the interest in Marcus Etchells?" he asked.

I wondered if he knew about Marcus' alibi. Probably.

"There seemed to be tension between you two Saturday night."

He smiled very slowly, a knowing smile. At the same time he rocked back on one foot and tilted his head as if for a better angle while he studied me.

I bet that sequence made high school students conscious of their sins. But I'd had a lot of practice hiding my sins—and secrets.

I blandly gazed back at him.

Clara looked from one to the other of us. Opened her mouth. Then closed it.

But that seemed to edge Zelig into a decision.

He exhaled and straightened up. "Look, I've heard you—" He included Clara with a glance, but came back to me. "—were on the spot and now you're asking questions. And you've, uh, been involved in other investigations."

Wouldn't Deputy Eckles hate to hear that? Even Deputy Hensen wouldn't like it.

"Saw you interviewed on TV," he added to Clara. Then, again, he focused on me. "I'm all for catching whoever murdered Josepha Viedux. So ask your questions and we'll see where that leads."

I took him up on that immediately. "What was the cause of the tension between you and Marcus?"

"His homophobia." He said it fast enough to have been practiced.

"What form did that take?"

"He tried all through his years in high school to get a rise out of me with general would-be smart-ass comments that made him look and sound stupid. Stupid and way out of date." His mouth twisted. "Even twenty years ago, it wasn't that big a deal. But, yeah, Marcus gave me grief. You'd have thought it was the Fifties the way he carried on. As if it was some big secret that I'm gay.

"Unbelievable that he tried it Saturday night. Talk about never outgrowing high school."

His dismissal wasn't entirely believable, because I thought it had gotten under his skin Saturday night. The tension definitely hadn't flowed one way.

I glanced toward Clara. She still was looking down.

Instead of plowing straight ahead, I jagged.

"How about Debi, now Debi Norris?"

"More raw material to work with than Marcus. More raw material than you might think. But crippled her potential by limiting herself with a narrow—and shallow—definition of success. Cheering for mediocre teams was the pinnacle of her imagination. She didn't see past that. And she hasn't lived past that."

Clara's head came up. Her surprised blink reflected my reaction, too. He wasn't pulling his punches.

He flashed a grin at both of us. "One of the perks of impending retirement. Can speak my mind." His expression shifted. "Especially when it might help solve a murder."

"Did you know Josepha Viedux?"

"You mean is that the reason I'm all for you two looking into this? No. True, I had her in a class. Think it was her sophomore year. But, no, it's not personal. Except that what it does to all of us when someone's murdered is personal."

From the corner of my eye, I caught Clara's nod of agreement and fought my own. We wanted information out of him, not a kumbaya moment.

"Who were Josepha's friends in high school?"

He frowned, then his brows lifted in surprise. "Don't know that she had any."

His gaze shifted to Clara. She shrugged, tossing the ball back to him.

"If she did," he continued, "I don't remember who they were. I don't think of her as connected to a group or … anybody."

His eyes narrowed, thinking back. Somehow it made him even more attractive.

"She stayed inside herself, if you know what I mean. Didn't reach out and didn't respond when other people did, including me. I tried to pin down why she had no parental involvement. There was no pinning her down. Totally held me off. Did well enough in class to not warrant special attention. Didn't do so well that she got the other kind of attention, either, though I always thought she could have. I thought then that going down the middle was on purpose. A strategy. She liked sitting back and watching. Didn't want that interrupted by anyone focusing on her."

He jerked his head in a sort of shake that indicated bemusement and sadness. "Rather a strange girl, who became a strange woman."

"Did you know her as an adult?"

"No. I should have qualified it with *as far as I knew*. I did hear things from some people who had her company clean for them."

"What kind of things?"

With a shrug that didn't come off as casual as he might have intended, he said, "Everyone said she and her company did a good job cleaning. Yet a lot of them dropped her and didn't recommend her. Maybe nothing to it, but they wouldn't explain why they dropped her. There was one teacher here—they moved to Arizona about five years ago—who followed exactly that pattern. We were pretty good friends, but when I asked straight out why she dropped Josepha's service, she got uncomfortable, avoided answering, and ended up only saying I shouldn't ever hire them. I never did, so…"

So, why had Josepha Viedux been watching him Saturday night like the cat who had an unlimited supply of cream?

"I've finished my parking lot duty now. Going inside. I wish you success with—"

"What about Fae Ballard? Did you know her?"

"Yeah. Why do you ask?"

"Checking all the people who were at the picnic site early. Including Wesley Oshmann…"

"Knew the name and he was part of Marcus' entourage, but that was all."

"Mary Jo Anderson."

"Part of Debi's entourage. No other claim to fame that I know of. Sort of the female equivalent of Wesley."

"And Fae?"

"I knew her a little better than some of the others when she was in school. Another one I had in class. Good student. Smart and did the work. They don't always go together, but they did for her. Not happy. At least not happy here in North Bend County. But she seems to have found her place in life now. Really have to go. Good luck to you both."

He smiled at us, warmly, but impartially.

CHAPTER TWENTY-SEVEN

WE SAT IN the car, waiting for the teenage traffic to clear more.

It gave us a chance to recap. It also kept Clara's van—and the Woodrows' insurance rates—out of harm's way.

"I wonder if his being gay is quite as easy as Lovell Zelig made it sound. Some parents still might not be as open-minded as he would hope. And what about twenty years ago?"

Clara released a breath. "I'm afraid you're right for some in our class. Among that group of kids it was sort of whispered about, rather than said straight out, as if it *were* a secret. But not most of the kids. Not most of the parents from what I know, either."

"When you say it was whispered about, what do you mean?"

She looked out the windshield. After a full minute, she brought her gaze toward me, but not on me—she was still in the past. "It wasn't like with Josepha Viedux, who really knew some secrets. That group of girls—like Debi and Mary Jo—giggled about it or made sly sexual references to being the ones who'd be able to win him over to playing for the other team. But I think in some ways they were more comfortable with him than any of the other teachers."

"In what way?"

"Oh, I suppose it was partly because he seemed young even though he wasn't as young as a few of the other teachers who were just out of college." She slipped back into memories. "I wonder… Maybe the teachers closer to our age were more of a threat, in a way. The women as rivals, the men as potentially wanting sex from them—not that any of the teachers felt that way, but those girls did."

"Because they viewed the world that way, with the currency in sexual power and sexual favors?"

She nodded. "Never could have expressed it that way back then, but that's it. But with Mr. Zelig they could relax, because that was all off the table." She hitched one shoulder. "The guys—at least Marcus and those guys made rude jokes. But under their breath, sort of. Never to his face. You know, cowardly stuff."

"How did you feel about Lovell?"

"I liked him. He was funny. He is funny. I *do* like him."

Ah, Clara. What a good person she was. I truly valued her for that.

That didn't stop the Aunt Kit voice at the back of my brain, chiding me to get busy looking for motives. "Were there any whispers about him being too close to any of the male students?"

"No. Nothing."

"Don't dismiss the possibility, Clara. Think about it. No—" I told her parted lips. "—don't even try to answer now. Tell me after you've thought a while. The kind of thinking where you put it in the back of your mind and let it percolate until something comes to the surface."

"The best kind of thinking." Her grin faded. "Sheila?"

"Uh-huh."

"There was something Lovell Zelig didn't mention. Something about Marcus. I mean, I don't know for sure. I didn't see it. I heard something. And it wasn't very clear. Plus, you know how unreliable third- and fourth-hand—"

"Enough with the caveats. Tell me."

She inhaled deeply. "Marcus beat up Mr. Zelig's significant other."

I crooked my fingers. "More. Details."

"The story is that Marcus was drunk—"

Big surprise.

"—and he stumbled into John Jones outside Shep's Market and John said sorry, like you do, but Marcus started yelling and calling him names—you know the kind—and then he swung. John avoided him, but then he was wedged in somehow and couldn't get away.

"Marcus landed several punches before Gundy Vance got out there and broke it up."

Vance ran Shep's, a family grocery store and Haines Tavern institution. Bouncer was not one of his usual duties.

"Let's go see what Gundy has to say about what happened."

"I like that," Clara said, her good humor restored. "We can pick up something for dinner, too."

I put a dent in her good humor as she pulled onto Carrion Lane. "How did Zelig react to what Marcus did?"

"I heard something happened the next time Marcus showed up at a football game. He was hustled out, but the word was he had a black eye after. I didn't see him, so it's all rumor." She swallowed. "Although one of the sources was Donna."

If Donna from the dog park said Marcus had a black eye after an encounter with Lovell, I'd bank on it.

All in all, an interesting development.

Also a far cry from what Zelig described as seeing Marcus *around town*.

✧　✧　✧　✧

CLARA'S PHONE RANG. She glanced at caller ID and handed it to me. "Kirstin Selka. You answer so I'm not distracted."

"Clara Woodrow's phone."

"Is—? Is that Sheila?"

"Yes it is, Kirstin. I'm with Clara, but she's driving." On the other hand, she was driving in North Bend County, Kentucky, not mid-town Manhattan. "I'll put you on speakerphone if you'd like."

"Yes. Please."

"All set."

"Hi Kirstin," Clara said.

"Hello. I talked briefly to Glenn again. The lawyer I met at the courthouse earlier is on the job now. He got me in to see Glenn for a few minutes. Couldn't count on it being a private conversation, of course, but I was so relieved to see him."

"How is he?"

She made a sound that was three-quarters exasperated, one-quarter amused. "Him? Says he's fine. They're feeding him and gave him a break overnight. They said he could have gone back to the B&B, but the idiot said no. Said he didn't want to risk disturbing me and he wants to cooperate as fully as possible so they clear him quickly so we can go home. So he slept in somebody's office, for heaven's sake."

Going against the tide of Kirstin's tone, Clara said, "That could be smart to stay there and answer everything so they can't suspect him anymore."

"That's not what the lawyer says and I tend to agree with him. But I didn't call about that. Glenn said a couple things that might help you.

"First, he gathered from their questions that the woman—Josepha—was not killed in the hours right after the reunion. He said they're careful not to pin it down, but they're also not interested in what he did immediately after we left the hotel and returned to the B&B. They do seem interested in his ability to get out of the B&B without being seen. And he blithely told them it would be easy."

That also applied to Fae Ballard, though the sheriff's department had shown no interest in her beyond gathering her initial statement as far as we knew.

Come to think of it, Debi, Wesley, and Mary Jo also could have left where they were staying without being seen. Though it might require dodging security cameras.

"The other thing they seem to be very interested in is what Glenn ate Friday night at Haines Tavern and how he ate it," she said. "The knife he used. I know you—those of you who saw the body—said she was stabbed…"

The question she didn't verbalize was clear nonetheless.

Clara glanced at me. I shook my head.

For now, we weren't sharing the fact that I'd recognized where the knife came from.

Unless—

I swallowed an internal curse.

Why hadn't it occurred to me before this moment that other restaurants might have similar or the exact same knife?

I'd have indulged in more swearing, but had to pay attention, because Kirstin wasn't done.

"Glenn overheard bits and pieces. From that and what they asked him, he said they seemed very interested in his knife. Do you think...? But that makes no sense."

She might not consider a connection of Glenn's knife and a knife stuck in Josepha as making sense, but I'd bet the sheriff's department did.

"Apparently, the sheriff's department asked the restaurant staff if anyone had access to the knife Glenn used afterward. They said only the busboy. He's only worked there a couple months since he moved here from upstate New York. No known associations with anybody involved in the case. That's what Glenn heard."

"What about the server?"

"Not from what Glenn said. It would make more sense for a busboy to clear. In fact, I saw him leaving our table with the dishes and such."

I didn't remember that, but it might have been so normal it didn't register. "Was that before or after that drunk guy stumbled by your table?"

"Drunk guy?" Slowly, she continued, "I didn't see a drunk guy or anyone stumble. When did that happen? Do you think that's important?"

Rather than answer—because telling her who the heck knew if it was important could understandably demoralize her—I said, "Tell us about who you saw when you reached the picnic area yesterday."

"I don't know the names of most of them. Debi was there and the two women who were helping her—" Mary Jo and Ancella. "The guy with his hands dug in his pockets." Wesley Oshmann. "But beyond that it was two clumps of faces I didn't know. I do remember Fae Ballard was ahead of us as we walked up, because it surprised me. You two came right after that, followed by the woman who talked about Marcus' arrests. And then—You know what happened then."

"Go back a second. You said you noticed Fae because it surprised you. Why?"

"Oh. Because she left the B&B well before we did. In fact, it was an hour before we did. I noticed because I was keeping track of time to get ready for—I have to go. The attorney's coming out. I have to talk to him. Good-bye."

Clara turned on her turn signal to go north.

"Where are you heading? Shep's Market?"

"Absolutely. But with a stop first at Amber House B&B to see if Fae's there to explain the time discrepancy. And if she's not, maybe Ottalie can confirm what time Fae left the B&B the first and/or second time."

"How much time discrepancy are we talking, do you think?"

"If Kirstin's accurate that Fae left Amber House an hour ahead of her and Glenn, but showed up for the second time at the picnic area just before Kirstin and Glenn—"

"But with another round-trip from the high school to the B&B and back, because she didn't have a dish the first time and she *did* have one the second time. Although she could possibly have had it in her rental car and didn't—for whatever reason—take it up the picnic area and, instead, drove around a while before adding it to the buffet."

"Something else we might check with Ottalie—when Fae took the casserole. But back to the time, I'd say leaving an hour before Kirstin and Glenn, but arriving just before them, minus a round-trip to the B&B, leaves her at least forty minutes unaccounted for."

"There could be an explanation," I said, soft-pedaling what seemed suspicious to me to avoid piling on to Clara's disappointment at Fae's possible involvement.

"There could be. But it might not be one I like."

CHAPTER TWENTY-EIGHT

FAE, WHEN A B&B employee who was not Ottalie Bishop directed us to the same porch, did not deny the timeline Kirstin sketched. She did try to pass it off with a shrug.

Clara wasn't having it.

"Forty minutes, Fae." Her voice rose high with the disbelief of someone who knew local commutes never extended to that sort of time without natural disasters or alien landings. "That was enough to get here, kill Josepha, and leave before Debi arrived."

"Or Debi killed her. Depending on the time of death," Fae said immediately.

"Or Debi killed her." I jumped in with that concession, because I could see Clara's growing irritation. "But that doesn't remove the truth that you had the opportunity. Depending on the time of death."

Fae breathed out noisily. "I went to look at the house where I grew up. All right? Trip down memory lane. Absolutely ridiculous. I didn't have a good time growing up. Not abuse or any of that. My parents love me, but they ... they don't know how to connect with other people or me and they couldn't help me figure out how to—Anyway, that's where I went."

"Talk to anyone?"

"No. What was I going to do, knock on the front door and ask them to let me in to look around the old homestead for the plaque to the Ballard family? I'm sure they'd have welcomed me with open arms."

"What address?"

Her face shuttered for a moment. "You think anyone noticed me?"

"We'll find out."

GUNDY VANCE HELD up one finger, asking us to wait, before directing an assistant to take over, while he stepped out from behind the customer service counter of Shep's Market, then opened the door to a crowded office.

The three of us stood, because there was no room to do anything else.

"What can I do for you?"

Ever since we'd dealt with an issue that affected his family, he'd welcomed us warmly. Not to the point of giving away his wares, but warmly.

"Do you remember an incident involving Marcus Etchells?"

"Sure, I remember. First time we've ever had anyone beating on someone else right outside our door."

"What happened?"

"First I knew of it, Fern—" He shot a questioning look at me. I nodded. Yes, I knew the octogenarian. "—hollered from the door for me to get out there. Had no idea how it started, but Etchells had John Jones pinned in the corner between the outside wall and the display shelves out there. We attached those shelves to the outside wall so they'd never come down, no matter what was on them. John didn't have any escape. He was trying, but Marcus was—" He shook his head. "—whaling away at him."

"Why?"

"No idea. Fern might have heard something. But we were fully occupied with stopping Etchells. I'll tell you the truth, I wasn't making much progress. Not until—This can stay with us, right?"

We both nodded.

"Until Fern whacked him across the back of the knees. First with her purse and then with the handle of a shovel. His legs buckled enough that I could wrestle him off John. She tripped him and I got on top of him on the ground. I don't want word to get around about that and have Etchells go after Fern when nobody else is around, even if she can handle herself. Glad the sheriff's department showed up quickly.

"I heard John tell the deputies he'd just left the market and Etchells was walking along the sidewalk. They almost bumped. John stepped back. Etchells charged him. He didn't even have a chance to defend himself. John was battered, but more than that he was shaken. And who can blame him? Somebody coming at him out of nowhere like that."

"When was this, Gundy?" Clara asked.

"A month ago, more or less. Anything else?"

"The same question back at you," I said. "Anything else?"

He tucked in one side of his mouth. "Lovell Zelig showed up after we'd closed. Thanked me, but he wanted details. He also wanted to know if I knew where Marcus Etchells was living, because he'd moved out of his previous address and wasn't at his mother's."

The three of us exchanged looks.

He nodded. "Lovell didn't find him as far as I know, but he was out for Etchells' blood. Which does not make him a rarity among our county's population. Marcus Etchells is a master at getting under people's skin. Not that I blame Lovell. That was out and out a blindside attack. For no reason.

"But, why are you interested in him? Isn't he the one person who couldn't have committed the murder you're trying to solve?"

Clara huffed shortly. "Thanks for reminding us."

WE PICKED UP dinner before leaving Shep's Market, then stopped at my house for Gracie, before landing at Clara's.

With sweaters, we were comfortable on her deck and the dogs had a fine time chasing around the back yard in dizzying loop-de-loops. It wasn't the dog park, but they would tough it out, making any sacrifice to have fun.

As usual, LuLu led the way with Gracie at her shoulder. It wasn't that Gracie couldn't keep up with her. This gave Gracie a better angle to herd her buddy in whatever direction my fluffy beast decided on, using her presence, her nose, or nonviolent chewing on LuLu's shoulder.

Ah, and one more method. Teeth-clacking.

Gracie chomped her teeth together, with nothing between them but air, sending off a castanet-sounding rhythm that informed LuLu she needed to change direction, which LuLu did with affable and loose-limbed readiness.

Besides watching the dogs, we ate and discussed what we'd learned today. What we'd learned didn't feel like much of a haul for a full day of question-asking.

The pre-prepped dinners that Judy Vance, wife of the owner, put together for Shep's Market were delicious, as always. I lamented not being able to cook like that.

Clara patted my arm and said, "Judy couldn't solve a murder."

"At this rate, neither can we."

"It's barely twenty-four hours. We'll go to yoga tonight, relax, get a good night's sleep, and tomorrow we'll start fresh," Clara the optimist said.

HAVING DROPPED GRACIE off at my house, Clara and I were in our favorite corner at the Beguiling Way Yoga Studio, stretched out on our mats, when our pre-class peace was interrupted.

"Sheila. Clara. What do you know about this murder?"

Berrie Vittlow.

A dog park regular with an impressive pack of Boston terriers and lately styling herself as a trainer. Which took championship grade *hutzpah*, considering her dogs' behavior.

She also was the very soul of tact, having voiced her question loud enough to turn most heads, including those not yet in the studio.

I closed my eyes.

For a second, I fantasized about a tornado whirling up and my mat landing on top of her, with only her feet showing. No ruby slippers, because we were barefoot in the studio. Still, plenty satisfying.

But I also knew Clara would not close her eyes … probably didn't even fantasize about tornados.

"You must have seen the report on the news. We haven't even done that," Clara said, implying Berrie knew more than we did, without saying anything that wasn't true.

"Saw that and heard Debi Norris was there, but she won't talk about it. Slammed the door right in my face, even though we've been neighbors for years. And—"

If Berrie's Boston terriers were as barky at home as they were at the dog park, being a neighbor might not be a plus in Debi's view.

But what really struck me was that Debi's door-slamming put us on a par with Berrie Vittlow. That hurt.

"—she doesn't have anything to be all high and mighty about with the carrying-on she's been part of. Couldn't help but hear all about it during the shouting—screaming on her part—when I was walking my babies past their house not long ago.

"Didn't waste any sympathy on her over that, that's for sure. Not after she went off on me all because this guy doing work for me plugged an extension cord into their outside plug. And the guy and his wife are great friends with the Norrises for Pete's sake. You wouldn't believe the number of times I listened to them all being loud and drunk on the deck next door. They practically twisted my arm to hire him and then when he uses some of their electricity, she goes nuts at *me*. Thank heavens it was on the phone. Still upset my babies, because Boston terriers are exceptionally attuned to their human's emotions, but not as bad as it would have been if they'd heard her viciousness.

"Totally unstable, that woman. So not at all surprising she's involved in this horrible, horrible tragedy."

Debi Norris wasn't my fave, but jumping from her yelling at Berrie for whatever reason to proving she was *involved* in a murder struck me as harsh.

"Did you know Josepha Viedux?" Clara asked.

"No. I'm not one of the idle rich who can afford to have someone clean my house." The themes of how hard she worked and didn't have as much money as many who were far less worthy were two of her favorites. Though I had heard her finances were better since she started training dogs for poor, misguided souls who didn't know any better. She jerked her attention back to her main topic. "What do you know about this? You two always seem to be in the middle of these things."

"Thank you. We do what we can to help."

Clara's sincere modesty carried the day—along with the instructor coming into the studio and closing the double doors from the reception area behind her, signifying the start of class.

CHAPTER TWENTY-NINE

WE SLID OUT after class before Berrie could stop us.

But we weren't in such a hurry that we didn't stop at the café around the corner to check out their desserts.

"Let's get them to go," Clara said in a low voice as she smiled and waved at a group around the large table at the back. I recognized Linda and Carole from the thirty-fifth reunion group from Saturday night. Lovell Zelig was not there.

"Sure." If we stayed, we'd need to be even more careful than usual about what we said with that group in the small café.

As the clerk handed us the bags with our goodies—a classic double chocolate brownie for me and key lime pie for Clara—Linda and Carole came up to us.

"Since you weren't coming over to say hello, we came to you," Linda said.

Clara indicated our outfits. "We just finished yoga. We'd bring down the tone of your distinguished group."

"A few out-of-towners stayed over, so we're wringing as much fun out of this time as possible," Linda said.

It struck me that they could answer one question for us. "Did you all know about the twenty-year group's picnic scheduled for Sunday? The people at your reunion, I mean."

"Oh, yes. We all knew about it. Most of the twenty-year classes have one. The youngest alums party hard all Saturday night and the older ones aren't about to climb that hill."

So, Lovell Zelig almost certainly knew of the picnic plan, even before Josepha urged him to attend.

On the other hand, would knowing the picnic would be held on Senior Hill make him—or anyone else—more or less likely to commit a murder there?

I suppose that depended. Want the body found quickly or prefer it stay hidden longer?

My head began to throb. Possibly from lack of sugar.

"Almost decided I *would* climb Senior Hill because that girl running your reunion—" Carole nodded to Clara. "—was so obnoxious."

"Debi Norris? What did she do?"

"That's her. Made a big deal about proclaiming to one and all at the joint meeting of reunion committees to iron out any little conflicts that the hill picnic area was hers all hers and nobody better mess with it."

The women gave simultaneous tongue clicks.

My thoughts from Saturday night about blinders lifting with these longer-term alums returned. They certainly saw through Debi.

As for their fellow classmates, it seemed another layer was removed when people connected person to person, without regard to the overblown superficiality of their teens or even the practical realities of their next few decades. They saw each other as people … perhaps with a generous bit of a soft focus.

While I mused on blinders, the conversation traveled.

"…marveling how fortunate our class has been, with very few deaths, while Mrs. Ingram was just telling us your class had that poor girl who died shortly after graduation, then three more in car accidents, two in the military, two from cancer, and now this Josepha murdered." Carole shook her head.

Linda joined in, "We know you're busy trying to figure out what on earth happened at the picnic yesterday. And we certainly hope you succeed quickly. It's horrifying to all of us, but none more so than Lovell Zelig. He knows all of your class from when you were kids."

"I always think of him as a teacher. It's hard to remember he was also a student at North Bend," Clara said.

"I can imagine. Since Lovell was our classmate, we knew him in a very different way."

"Did you know he was gay?" I asked.

"It was understood, even if it wasn't as open as it is now." Linda smiled. "We're not Victorians, you know. Although I've always thought the stereotype must be overstated or how did those Victorians have kids who had kids who had kids that eventually led to us?"

"Not to mention Victorian pornography."

Linda, Carole, and I stared at Clara.

"What?" she asked. "I was researching it for a client."

"On that note, I think we should let you two get on your way," Carole said.

Linda winked. "And we'll escape the wicked ways of these youngsters."

Not so wicked. We barely nibbled on our goodies on the way to my house.

✧ ✧ ✧ ✧

"OH, HOW ROMANTIC. Look who's parked in your driveway."

Teague O'Donnell.

Even if Clara hadn't pointed him out and if I hadn't noticed his vehicle, Gracie's frenetic barking from the living room window informed me. Not only of his presence, but of his inexplicable (to her) behavior in not immediately coming in the house to pet her and to bring Murphy with him.

Her disapproval of the fact that he'd done neither was heard in every sharp bark.

My reach for the car door handle froze with Clara's next words.

"You should tell him."

I went with the classic "What" to stall, while my ribs tried to withstand the hammering of my heart.

Tell Teague? Acknowledge I wasn't who most people thought I was now? That I also hadn't been who most people thought I was when I was pretending to be the person people now didn't know I'd purported to be? That maybe I wasn't entirely sure of who I was underneath the layers?

"I think that's what's holding you two back," Clara said.

She might be right. But how did you say, *Okay, voila, now I'll be who I really am, even though I haven't had any practice for a decade and a half.*

"I think if you tell him, you'll find it much easier to write."

Oh. Tell him about *writing.*

Of course. Because that was the secret Clara knew.

"I mean, I don't know for sure, because I'm not a writer like you—"

I bit my lip to keep from grumbling about not being a writer at all. Wallowing in rampant insecurity wasn't attractive, especially when she was being so nice.

"—but from what my clients have said about the impact of what's going on in their lives, especially with their emotions, on their writing, I'm sure holding back from Teague about your writing is holding your writing back and holding back what's between Teague and you."

"Why?" I asked, to prove I was still conscious and not limited to *what.*

"Because it's hard to have a relationship when you're withholding something important to you."

Tell me about it.

"Oh, Sheila, I'm sorry. I didn't mean to make you cry."

"I'm not crying." Teary, but not crying. "It's just... You might be right, but I haven't even told Aunt Kit yet."

"Why?"

"Expectations. Too much help. Need to know I can do it first." I waved a hand. "And all the other reasons I haven't told anybody. Except you."

She sat back. "Well, you didn't tell me, either. I found out and started talking about it to you. I considered waiting for you to bring it up, but you don't talk about things—important things—much."

"I'm not very good at it."

"Only way you'll get better is practice."

She made it sound so easy. Scary easy. With the emphasis on scary.

"Right now, I think we better go talk to Teague before he bursts."

He watched us with would-be patience that had far too much curiosity to really qualify.

She chuckled. "Let's go."

CHAPTER THIRTY

WE ALL MET near the back door, with Gracie still providing the soundtrack.

"Hey, you two." Teague put a hand on my shoulder, then slid it up to the back of my neck for a gentle and welcomed squeeze. I hadn't realized how tight my muscles there were.

"Hi, Teague. You really have Gracie going."

"Uh-huh. That looked like a serious talk you were having."

"Girl talk," Clara said airily. Then she spoke to me. "He obviously needs a key to your house to spare your dog."

I avoided responding by opening the back door to the four-legged noise machine who barreled toward us.

She went straight to Teague and gave him four more sharp barks—not as bad as Debi's shriek, but still impressive—cementing her point that his behavior in remaining outside the house was unacceptable, before she danced around Clara and me.

That would teach him.

But he did not appear to be aware he'd been taught. He appeared to have other things on his mind.

"You two found the body of that woman at the picnic area at the high school?" He barely made it a question.

"No," I said strongly.

"Debi Norris found the body under the picnic table. But she just stood there and screamed. Sheila took control and kept people from contaminating the crime scene. Well, any more than it already had been by people putting dishes on the table and getting it ready for the picnic and moving around as they talked to each other and—"

"Please, Clara. Even as a former policeman you're giving me nightmares."

"Can't help you with that, but would you like some of what we brought from the café?"

"I wouldn't take your last bite—either of you."

We both looked down at our bags. Our nibbles had made significant inroads into our desserts. Exchanging a look, we each popped a final bite in our mouths.

Clara finished first. "Anyway, Sheila kept the people away after Debi found the body. And then—"

"—you gave your statements and came right home, leaving the sheriff's department to do its job. Leaving the professionals to do what they're trained to do."

Clara contemplated his wishful statement a moment. "Sometimes the amateurs beat the professionals. Look at golf and tennis and… and chess."

"Chess?" I muttered.

"And sometimes the amateurs get in the way of the professionals. Sometimes the amateurs get hurt. Or dead," Teague shot back.

"And sometimes they don't, like with us," she said triumphantly.

"*Yet.*" He went on quickly to block any response. "Listen, if you two insist on this, first you have to know if there was a crime—"

Clara tipped her head. "She was stabbed and hidden under the picnic table. That seems like a crime."

"—and what kind of crime."

"Also pretty obvious," I said.

Undeterred by our astute—or smart ass, depending on your point of view—observations, Teague said, "You don't leap in. You determine what kind of crime by the evidence. You two usually skip that step."

"We dig for evidence," Clara said.

"After you've leapt in. And here I always thought the way to investigate was to let the evidence lead you in the right direction and eventually to the right conclusion."

"Our way is faster," Clara said. "Though this time, we don't have much evidence."

"Thank you for making my point. No evidence, so you're in no position to pursue this."

"Much. I said *much*. And not yet."

I scoffed. "Is that what you did, O'Donnell, when a case came in that jangled your instincts, but no easy evidence landed in your lap, no voluntary confession walked in the door, no guess-what-clincher-evidence-we-just-found came from forensics? You gave up?"

"It was my job and—"

I tossed my hands up. Clara persisted. "You didn't give up, right? Neither will we. We don't have forensics or access to any of what the police know, so we're doing what we do have access to—talking to people."

He closed his eyes for a long moment, as if in pain. But he wasn't really in pain, so I felt no compunction about noticing how this expression called attention to long, thick lashes that—

Perhaps not wise while he was working his wiles against our investigating.

I turned away, so I didn't know how long he kept his eyes closed.

"I'm not making any headway with you two, so I'll stop trying—for now. But I do have another question for you, Clara. Why the high school wasn't built on another street. Say Possum Path Road."

I turned back. Teague's expression remained solemn while his voice vibrated with a suppressed chuckle.

Clara didn't appear to hear that. "Wrong part of the county. That's in the south where there's less population. Wouldn't make sense to have the high school down there."

"So, that's why they put a high school—or any school—on Carrion Lane? In a way it fits. Aunt Kit would tell you about researchers who studied high schools and view them as taxpayer-supported *Lord of the Flies*. For millennia, teenagers were part of family and tribal units where their teen-ness was diluted by adults, younger kids, elders. Not all packed together in a building with token representatives of adulthood."

Teague leaned back against the counter, his amusement rising closer to the surface. "Going by that, they should have borrowed another name—Sewage Disposal Lagoon Road—from Gallatin County."

"Did they build a high school on it?" I asked.

He said, "Not as far as I can tell, but who knows what the future holds. In the meantime, I found the perfect street for the dog park."

"It's already on a street. Torrid Avenue. Why would—?"

"It should move to Big Dog Way."

Clara's protest stopped in mid-breath. "Wouldn't that be cute? It would be farther from town, but—"

"Wait. Before you go packing up all the fences and leashes and poop bags, what about the small dogs?" I asked. "They wouldn't be represented. They might not even feel welcomed at a park on Big Dog Way."

"Oh." Clara's empathy packed a wallop in that syllable. "That's true. But it would be so cute to have the dog park on Big Dog Way."

"Another time, another place, it might have been possible."

"Yeah, you can laugh at me, Teague."

"Laugh? I'm not laughing at you, Clara."

"He is, too," I said. "Though I can't totally blame him. You have to admit this county has strange road names."

"Like what?"

"Like Torrid Avenue, where the dog park is."

"It marks off the town's boundaries with Temperate on the other end."

"Most towns use names like North, South, East, or West for boundaries. Not Torrid. And what about Beguiling Way where the yoga studio is?"

"That's a lovely name. It means it's charming."

"Not quite. Notice the word *guile* within beguiling? It's deceptively charming. Or using charm to mislead."

"Oh."

As long as I had her on the ropes, I added, "Or Covert Circle. And what about Shady Bridge?"

"That just means there's lots of shade on what used to be a bridge and now is a street. It's where you'd want to be on a hot summer day."

"How about the other meaning of shady? Like dishonest."

"That's a reach, Sheila. Shady, like dishonest." She chuckled. "All right. I'm leaving. Good night, Teague." To me she added, "I'll see you tomorrow."

After Clara left, I offered Teague a drink. He said yes to sparkling water.

I asked how the accessibility project went over the weekend and what kind of day he'd had teaching today. He answered, but was abstracted as he watched me getting him the drink.

After I handed it to him, he shifted the glass to his other hand, then took hold of my hand and ran the tip of his thumb over my short nails.

"When I met you, you said your nails were usually long and raggedy, but I haven't seen them that way in months."

"I said that to you?"

"No. You said it to Clara. The first day, at the dog park." That sounded more likely.

"You remember?"

"I remember a lot of things you've said. And not said."

When he said things like that, I had the feeling he'd tuned his investigative abilities into me. Not a comfortable feeling.

"You didn't try very hard to talk us out of investigating."

"I don't try to talk you out of it. We've been through that—I know I can't. I point out the issues it can raise—"

"For law enforcement."

"—and the dangers."

"We're careful."

He eyed me for a long, discomfiting, and disbelieving moment.

"Can I ask you a question?" I asked only partly to break the tension.

"Sure." He took a long drink.

"No, I mean a ... an important question. A nosy question." I almost added *A question about your history.* But no sense erecting a giant, neon pointer to the fact that we didn't talk about our personal histories.

He lowered the glass.

I could have backtracked then, but I was so far in now…

"You said your eyesight wouldn't have stopped you from moving to a different police department, that you'd still qualify for most, but not for the one you'd worked for."

I didn't even know which department it was among the many in the Chicago area. I suppose Clara must, since she'd talked to Teague's former partner, even met him in person for lunch months ago when she and Ned were in Chicago.

I'd meandered far enough off the main point, that his, "Yeah," jolted me back.

"That sounds like you had good grounds to fight the medical retirement. Why didn't you?"

He looked at me for what felt like a day and a half, while my muscles screamed to be released from my will's hold so they could take me far away from the danger in his gaze. *You opened this door. You're not going to get to slam it.*

"I could have fought," he said slowly. "It was my first instinct. I was ready to rub their noses in it—the higher-ups."

"Why didn't you?" I asked again.

"Because winning would've left me someplace where the top guy didn't want me. And that nose rubbing? It wouldn't have been just the higher-ups. It would have been the whole department, affecting the officers and staff I worked with. You know what they say about stuff rolling downhill.

"Plus, my partner—Harris—said something wise." His mouth quirked. "He didn't mean to. In fact, he meant something totally different, but it got me thinking. He came over one night for a football game and we were knocking back a few and talking about how the lawyers would take apart the department's action in forcing me into medical retirement. And then he said, 'Sure, you'll spent the next few years fighting this, but when it's over, you'll be right back where you were.'

"The lightbulb over my head should have lit up the entire block.

When he put it like that—being on hold for several years with a legal battle and then the best-case scenario getting me right back to where I'd been… It didn't appeal. At all. I wanted to move forward. Didn't know to where, but definitely forward. That started the process."

"The process?"

"Thinking. Eventually took me to wanting to teach, which meant courses, looking for jobs, then coming here."

"Why didn't you stay in the Chicago area?"

He turned toward the counter, placing his glass down carefully. "New place for a new career. Besides, I got on the subbing roster here first. You know, money. That evil necessity for living." He added, over his shoulder, "Or maybe you don't, considering your financial situation."

I froze for half a beat—a quarter beat—maybe less. The realities of what Aunt Kit had earned with her writing as the person I was supposed to be, then invested with comfortable-for-life success for both of us flashed into my mind.

He didn't miss it.

I chuckled anyway. Not half bad, either. "My inheritance? I'm grateful and can't lie that I love it and the life it's given me here in Haines Tavern."

He pivoted back to me.

I braced.

He kissed my forehead. "I'm grateful, too. It brought you here, letting our paths cross."

Then he kissed my mouth and talking was done.

But I felt a strange ache in my throat. Possibly the result of muscles clamping tight against the urge to tell him I knew exactly what he meant about wanting to move forward, even without knowing exactly where it would lead.

Possibly the result of knowing that at some point, he'd ask me questions I wouldn't be able to answer with anything like his honesty.

TUESDAY

CHAPTER THIRTY-ONE

CLARA NEEDED TO finish a project for an author client this morning. Teague was teaching again. As a writer, I wasn't viewed as doing anything important, so I was nominated to, first, go door-to-door through Fae Ballard's childhood neighborhood with no payoff and, second, collect the three dogs and take them to the dog park so they'd be exercised before Clara and I started the day's sleuthing.

Okay, I was self-nominated and I truly wasn't doing anything except the very taxing job of not writing. Plus, I figured the neighborhood canvass and the dog park visit were better for me than another dip into reactions of never-before-heard-the-Righteous-Brothers listeners. Though a young woman from Nigeria was adorable when—

No. Not going down that rabbit hole.

As I detangled leashes for the second time in my attempts to get the hirsute trio out of the back seat of my sedan, I remembered Kit waxing bitterly eloquent on the phenomenon of non-writers not considering writing real work. She'd relayed instance after instance of writers being imposed on by nine-to-fivers—especially women writers—to pick up packages, meet home repairmen, ferry children, and more since they "weren't doing anything else." And how unfair that was to writers, who lost precious time beyond the actual interruption because of the effort needed to recreate a lost train of thought—if it was possible at all.

"That's why I don't answer the phone, emails, messages, or the doorbell."

At the time, I'd thought her reaction extreme. Now, I thought I'd been too harsh.

I couldn't claim to have had my writing interrupted. On the other hand, my train of thought about the murder of Josepha Viedux certainly had been cut, frayed, and tattered by the time I loosed the three hounds into the big-dog area.

My mood lifted at seeing Donna was here and Berrie of the Boston terriers was not.

Donna's aged golden retriever ignored the rambunctious trio doing the canine version of wheelies across the open area and ambled serenely to meet me. I fondled Hattie's ears as she liked, and told her what a good girl she was. Satisfied with my obeisance, she led me back toward the humans near one picnic table.

Donna met me out of earshot of the group.

"Surprised to see you here. Thought you and Clara would be hard at work."

"She is. Deadline for a client. I have dog duty."

She *huh'd* her comprehension. "Making progress?"

"Depends on your definition. No answers so far."

"Answers would be my definition. Heard you were at the library yesterday looking at articles about Heidi Holmes' death."

I arched my brows. "Amy?"

"Amy Kackley? No. More roundabout route. People know I have an interest. I knew the couple who owned the building where Heidi lived. Her death devastated them. Felt entirely responsible. They paid all the expenses for her funeral, the headstone, and for Josepha Viedux to sort through her things and clear out the apartment. One of her first big jobs when she started her business. They also put up an impenetrable fence so it could never happen again.

"They wanted to sell right away, but they felt obligated to one particular tenant who had been there forty years. From what her relations said, she used to stay up most of the night, looking out her window. If she looked past the parking lot, there were trees, and lots of sky above them. Rarely went out and didn't throw out much. So it was quite a job for Josepha when the time came to clean out that apartment. Not like poor Heidi. That wasn't much of a job for one person alone, while this long-time tenant was a chore even though she had expanded her company by then."

She reached down and patted Hattie's head. "After that, they sold. It was a shame because they were good landlords. Not enough of those around. Good people torn up about that accident."

"Sad all the way around," I said.

"It was."

For a couple of minutes, we watched Gracie dashing from LuLu's shoulder to Murphy's as she herded them to some mystery destination. Then all three would abruptly stop. Panting and tongues lolling, they sniffed the grass or the air. Before they took off again.

"That explains my interest in you and Clara looking up the articles," Donna said, as if there'd been no interruption, "but not yours and Clara's."

"Following up because it was a seminal event for their class, coming so soon after graduation."

I aimed to steer her away from Glenn with those words. But as I spoke, it struck me they also were true. I'd overheard several conversations Saturday night that included the death of Heidi Holmes.

"Did you know Heidi?" To her shaking head, I added, "Or Josepha Viedux?"

"Neither. Not dog owners, different generation, and their parents weren't long-time residents."

"You still might have heard things—"

My phone pinged.

"Very little," Donna said.

I held up an apologetic finger while I checked the phone. "Clara," I explained. I stepped away and answered with "I got nothing in Fae's old neighborhood. Zilch."

"Where are you?"

"Where am I? Exactly where you sent me. The dog park."

"Oh. Right. Get back here. We have to get to the B&B. The sheriff's department's released Glenn."

✧ ✧ ✧ ✧

"I THOUGHT IF I kept answering their questions as openly and honestly as I could, we could clear up their mistaken belief that I stabbed Josepha." Glenn's mouth went grim. "It didn't work very well."

We'd joined him and Kirstin in the same dining room where we'd talked to Kirstin before. Wearing the khakis and casual shirt he'd had on Sunday, now adorned by networks of wrinkles that served as topographical maps of his experience, he ate leftover breakfast casserole with enough gusto that he didn't immediately question our presence or our questions.

"But they released you."

"I think they had to if they weren't charging me. But they asked me to stay in town and I agreed to remain a few more days. From the way they acted, they think they'll arrest me before that, after they've worked up more evidence, enough to charge me."

"I knew it, I knew it." His wife's voice skidded up beyond her usual calm.

"I said that's what they think, honey. Not what's going to happen. They can't find more evidence because I didn't do it."

"You shouldn't have cooperated. You should have waited until I found the right lawyer—"

"It wouldn't have changed that they see me as a suspect, Kirstin. I had to try cooperation. I have nothing to hide. But proving that is surprisingly difficult. At least it's surprising to me." Shifting his attention from his wife, he said, "I appreciate you coming to show your support, Clara, and, uh—" I didn't bother to fill in my name. "—but I need to talk to that lawyer and—"

Kirstin interrupted. "They're investigating for you, Glenn."

Confusion drove his eyebrows high. "Investigating?"

"Clara and Sheila have solved murders before. I thought if they could find out who did this, that would be the fastest way to clear you."

"The lawyer you hired—"

"Yes, yes, we're talking to him, too. But he's focused on showing you're not guilty. They can prove you're innocent."

With Glenn looking thoughtful, I took the opportunity to ask, "Why would the sheriff's department think you had a reason to kill Josepha Viedux?"

He shook his head once. "That might be why they released me. They couldn't find a reason to explain why I'd come back after twenty years and stab someone I barely knew even when I did live here."

"What about your connection to the knife?"

His head jerked to his wife, then back to me with a frown. "I'm not talking to you about that. It was nice of you to come, but if you'd please leave now so my wife and I can talk in private."

"Glenn—"

Ignoring Kirstin, he stood, went to the door and opened it.

✧ ✧ ✧ ✧

ON OUR WAY out, we saw Ottalie Bishop. Even better, no one else was around.

We deserved a break after getting nowhere with Glenn.

"We understand your staff kindly supplied Fae with a dish to bring to Senior Hill for the picnic," I said to Ottalie. "That's going the extra mile for a guest."

Clara picked it up beautifully. "But then she forgot it and came back."

"She did. When we saw it on the table by the front door, I thought for sure it was too late, but one of my staff said, no, she'd heard the picnic wasn't starting until later. Fae had left early enough the first time that she had plenty of time to come back and get it."

By the end of her speech, I was ninety-five percent certain Ottalie Bishop knew exactly what we were fishing for and was willing to supply it. But not directly.

"But you couldn't know she'd come back during the—what?— forty to fifty minutes before she returned to pick it up? With you worrying all the time that it would go to waste."

"It was a long forty-five minutes, wondering if we should call her or send someone after her."

Clara and I shook our heads in sympathy. "What a shame we never got to taste it at the picnic," Clara said.

"We make it every Sunday. You'll have to come one week and try it."

We left with the satisfaction of confirming Fae's timeline without compromising Ottalie's hostess duties and with an invitation to sample the vaunted Amber House B&B cooking. Win-win-win.

YOGA TEACHERS SAY to leave your day off your mat. To bring your mind and your body solely inside the confines of its edges.

Yeah. Not so much.

Don't get me wrong. I get a lot out of yoga, well beyond stretched muscles and loosened joints. But limiting my mind to what's within the edges of a yoga mat?

No. Not so much.

So, I was busily thinking about the morning as we settled into sleeping swan in the second half of our lunchtime class.

No one in Fae's old block remembered seeing her or her rental car late Sunday morning, including the family who now lived in her old house.

"So much for neighbors being on the alert," I'd grumbled in detailing that non-result to Clara right after Glenn's closed-door policy.

Charitable Clara said, "Maybe they took off Sunday."

"And then there's Glenn's reaction, which has to raise suspicions."

"Not necessarily. Oh, look at the time…"

I suspected that was a ploy, but it was true.

We rushed to get to yoga on time.

After class, a fellow student stopped us. Fern, the octogenarian who'd teamed with Gundy Vance to bring down Marcus and who routinely out-yogaed the rest of the class.

"My, my, my, the two lady detectives back on the job after that girl was found dead."

Another example of our business being everyone's business in

North Bend County.

I countered with, "We heard you were there at a recent confrontation between Marcus Etchells and John Jones at Shep's Market."

"No confrontation. Two people almost bumped. John backed up like normal people do. Etchells started beating on him, like he'd exploded. He wasn't even looking at John."

"Did he say anything?"

"Might've mumbled something, but I doubt it made any sense. Smelled like he'd been swimming in a vat of booze."

My nose twitched at the reminder.

"But why're you interested in him?" she added. "He's got an airtight alibi."

An unnecessary reminder of that inconvenient fact.

Moving on, I asked, "Did you know Josepha?"

"By sight. Someone once recommended I have her company come to clean for me. I cut that acquaintance."

It wasn't entirely clear to me if she cut the acquaintance over the suggestion of Josepha or the intimation that she needed help of any kind.

"So, you were asking around this morning about Fae Ballard being seen at her childhood house Sunday."

No sense denying it. Phones probably started burning up before I reached the first door. "I was. With no success."

"Good reason for that."

And then she stopped.

I had to pay the toll. "What reason?"

"She wasn't there."

"How do you know that?"

Her eyes glinted. "Because I know where she was."

CHAPTER THIRTY-TWO

"**Where?**"

Her expression shifted, as if something distant now claimed her attention. "*Where* matters less than *who* in this case. You know, I have the strongest craving for a little something from the café."

Another toll to pay.

At the café, Fern couldn't decide between hazelnut cream cake and lemon chess pie, so she ordered both. On us, of course. The upside of this toll was Clara and I also sampled those offerings on the café's often-changed dessert menu and swapped tastes. Fern ate both her slices herself.

"Tell us who," Clara urged after we ordered.

"Not in here," Fern said in a super-spy whisper.

So we had to wait.

With all the desserts consumed and paid for, Fern had us accompany her to her car. There, after looking all around with care, she said, "She was in a car—must've been her rental car because I didn't recognize it—in back of the renovation of a place two blocks behind the tavern and one over. Good spot for a rendezvous, actually. Trucks and such are usually back there when they're working, but not on a Sunday. Between the scaffolding and the trees, none of the neighbors could see the car, much less the people in it. Along with being convenient for the person she was meeting."

Clara's eyes narrowed. "You couldn't see that location from your house."

"Of course not. I saw them during my power walk when I check on neighborhood construction. Go that way a couple times a week to see what they're up to. Turning it into a single family home. Looks real nice, but got my doubts they'll turn much of a profit."

"Good for the neighborhood, though. And—"

I interrupted Clara's detour into the welfare of Haines Tavern, which Fern would happily pursue, and dragged the conversation back to the main point. "Who was she with?"

"Didn't I say?" Fern asked with full-bore mischief. "Lovell Zelig."

To Fern's obvious satisfaction, that flummoxed Clara and me.

"And…" She dragged out the syllable for full dramatic effect. "…he had his arms around her and her head was on his shoulder."

More flummoxed silence.

Fern continued, "Couldn't get a good enough angle to know if he was consoling her or they were in an amorous embrace."

"Amorous embrace? But he's—" Clara broke off in abrupt confusion.

"Married. I know. And to a man. Know that, too." Fern muttered something about the younger generation being the only ones who thought they knew anything. "I often see him jogging around there, because he and his husband live three, four blocks away in one of the original workman's cottages—now there's a nice renovation job, only they've done it themselves, bit by bit. Looks—"

"Fae and Mr. Z? No way," Clara said.

"Well, I did say he could have been consoling her."

"But they were never close. Not to mention…"

"His husband, John," Fern supplied. "Married when the Supreme Court said all the states had to let them, but they've been together more than—" She raised one eyebrow, signaling that what she was about to say was significant. "—two decades."

"IN OTHER WORDS, he was in a committed relationship when you all were in high school. Fae hadn't been back since graduation. Yet they were embracing," I said after Fern drove away.

"It could be entirely innocent," Clara said. "A chance to catch up, because there wasn't much time Saturday night, not with everyone else wanting to talk to him and having his own reunion next door."

"Then why park behind a construction site? And why wouldn't Fae have told us, instead of lying about it? It sure explains why I couldn't find anyone who'd seen her in her old neighborhood Sunday."

Her defensiveness crumbled. "You're right."

"She had to know we'd asked about what she was doing at that time because it was possibly the time of the murder. Yet she chose not to tell us there was someone who could vouch for her whereabouts."

"And his own. So, what could be worth hiding?"

"Let's ask her."

Clara sighed, but messaged her former classmate with the traditionally ominous words: *We need to talk.*

"Now that we've had dessert, let's have lunch at The Tavern while we wait for an answer."

Figuring she opted for that as a kind of solace for feeling disappointed by—and possibly worried for—Fae, I gladly went along.

✧　✧　✧　✧

WHEN OUR SERVER on the bar side of the Haines Tavern went to the bartender for our soft drinks, he said something back to her, with a nod in our direction. She turned toward us, her mouth forming an O.

But to my relief, she said nothing when she delivered the drinks, took our orders, and departed.

With a couple occupying a nearby table, we confined our conversation to Clara's accomplishments this morning and the dogs' antics.

The couple finished shortly after the server brought our salads, leaving us the only customers in the bar area for now.

"I get we're focusing on who was here for the reunion because someone who's around here all the time could have killed her whenever they wanted. But people temporarily here from out of town for the reunion are on a tight schedule and had to do it now." She took a forkful of her Caesar salad. "What? Why are you looking at me like that?"

Between tangy bites of cranberries and Granny Smith apples, along with bacon-wrapped salmon, I said, "That's it. We should be looking more at motives for people who are here all the time. Motives and opportunity."

"Why? Didn't you hear what I just said? And that's repeating what *you* said before—they could have killed her at any other point in the past twenty years."

"But they couldn't have killed her at any other time when the focus would be *off* them and *on* all those people here for a short time."

"That would be really devious."

"Murderers tend to be devious. At least the ones not quickly caught. You saw that way before I did. It's like Dorothy in *The Wizard of Oz*."

She gave me a slightly wary look. "Is it?"

"Where she had the red shoes on but didn't know the power until the Good Witch of the North pointed it out."

"Does that make me the Good Witch of the North?"

"Absolutely."

Her face cleared. "Okay. Don't know what I said that told you how to use the shoes, but I'm good with being Glenda. Always liked her."

"Of course, you did." I, on the other hand, had been smitten with the doorkeeper to the city of Oz.

The server returned to refill our glasses and remove our empty salad bowls.

But she didn't immediately leave. She said to Clara, "Excuse me, but you're the woman who's solved murders and been on TV, aren't you?"

"We both—I mean, I've been on TV, but that's because my friend is—"

"Yes, she's the one," I said before she dragged me into it more.

The young woman nodded solemnly. "I thought so."

Then she left.

Clara and I looked at each other a moment, before she chuckled. "I got all flustered because I thought she was going to say something about how brilliant I—*we*—have been. Serves me right for getting big-headed about it. When you're really the brains, which people would know if—"

"No, no, no. On all counts. I'm much happier with you as our public face. You are not big-headed in any way. And we're both the brains."

"That's very nice of you to say, but you—"

"The proof is I feel completely stymied on this one. What do we do next? Start talking to everybody all over?"

From the corner of my eye, I caught movement and turned. Our server stood in a doorway to the right of the bar that led to a few private rooms. Next to her was the man I assumed was the manager of Haines Tavern, having seen him directing traffic and employees on several previous visits.

The server nodded toward us. The man said something that looked like *thank you* and came to our table.

"Would you two mind coming in back with me?"

Clara immediately said, "Of course not."

Committed by her agreeableness, I suppressed my desire to protest that we'd done nothing wrong and followed her example by getting off my stool.

CHAPTER THIRTY-THREE

THE MAN PICKED up our soft drink glasses and directed us toward the private rooms, so it seemed unlikely he was going to kick us out, since the door was in the opposite direction.

Why I defaulted to thinking he might be throwing us out might take some exploring. Later. For now, I concentrated on looking casual for the benefit of the server, bartender, and three arriving customers.

Inside the smallest private room, he put our glasses on the table and gestured for us to sit. His next gesture invited us to drink, then he set his hands on the table.

As I took a sip, he said, "I know what you two have been doing."

I gulped reflexively. It took a hard swallow to stop from choking.

In the meantime, Clara said in her normal voice, "Do you, Rich?"

"Yeah. Hear you're looking into that reunion murder."

Clara flicked me a look.

No time for more before Rich continued, "Like you've done be-fore. The things you've been on TV for. I asked my staff to keep an eye out for you and let me know when you came in again."

Clara nodded encouragingly.

"Is there anything you need, anything to help you figure it out?"

Rich's question stopped even Clara. "Uh… That's nice of you. But are you saying you know something about it? If you do and—"

"I'll tell you what I know. I know a knife from here was used to stab that woman."

"*What?*" That came out of my mouth before I could stop it.

How had he learned that? We sure hadn't leaked it.

"How do you know that, Rich?" Clara's follow-up was smooth, but Rich looked a little doubtful after my outburst.

"I hear things." His vagueness sharpened my focus.

Of course, he heard things. Lots of people—especially important people—spent a lot of time at the Historic Haines Tavern and much of it involved imbibing alcohol. But there was more.

His name. Rich. As in Richard *Haines* Chafford.

For being well-connected in North Bend County, he might even top Donna from the dog park.

"And what I don't like hearing is the *Historic Haines Tavern* connected to a murder, especially one of our knives being used as the murder weapon."

"Could the knife have come from somewhere else?" I asked. "Another restaurant or—?"

"No. It's our design. Not allowed to be sold east of the Rockies, west of the Appalachian Mountains."

That is a lot of territory.

"Do you sell them? Merchandise to keep the tavern's name—"

"No, thank God. Wouldn't that be nice—get a knife from the Historic Haines Tavern just like the one used to murder that woman on a picnic."

"Did the sheriff's department tell you they know that for sure?"

"Say it? No. But it didn't take anything to put it together." He dropped his voice. "They found fingerprints on it. And they matched them to the guy they were holding."

"They told you—?"

"Not officially, but good enough."

I asked, "Wouldn't there always be fingerprints on it? All the people who handle a knife—the servers, the busboys, the customers. How could they get a fingerprint from all that?"

Rich's substantial jaw became more prominent. "After *a* server, *a* bus person, *a* customer—*singular* for each of them—every piece is sterilized, including our signature steak knives. And our sterilizing would not leave smudgy fingerprints. There'd be *no* fingerprints from a previous use. Just went through this with the sheriff's department."

I'd want to check on that.

Rich wasn't done. "I don't want customers wondering who else held the knife they're using on their prime rib. I don't want customers thinking about murder at all when they're eating here."

He blew out his lips in an explosive exhale.

"I'm not unreasonable. I know people are talking about this. And when word gets out that the murder weapon came from here…"

"It might increase business."

He sent me a sharp look, then shook his head. "You might be right and I don't say this often, but I don't want that kind of business. It's not the kind that sticks around. Lots of traffic that pisses off regular customers, then it's gone. I want this cleared up and fast. I'm not saying the sheriff's department isn't good. They are. But they'll take it slow and steady. That's great for a lot of things. Not for this, not for the Historic Haines Tavern. You ladies have had success at beating the sheriff's department to the punch and that's what I need now. The fastest solution possible."

"The fastest correct solution."

How did Clara do that? If I'd said those words, it would have sounded like I was calling him morally bankrupt to go for speed over the right solution. An implication sure to put anyone's back up.

But she had him nodding and saying—with apparent sincerity— "Absolutely. The correct solution. So, will you do it?"

Clara glanced at me, as if inviting me to answer. She was far better at this. Not to mention I wasn't sure what he meant, either.

"Do what?" she asked.

"Take on the case for me. For Haines Tavern." Pretty sure he meant this establishment, not the town, but he gave it enough import to cover the town, too. "What are your fees?"

"Oh, we don't do this for money." Clara not only meant that, but it was a totally different matter for her than it was for me.

She and Ned weren't starving, but added income would not go amiss. Her VA job offered some. On the other hand, most profession-al authors laugh at the rolling-in-it stereotype Hollywood's cooked up of their lifestyle. There's frequently an edge of bitterness to the laugh.

In other words, Clara wasn't going to get rich working for authors.

"This isn't a business for us," she clarified. "Besides, we're already looking into it for someone else."

From looking slightly bewildered, Rich shifted to pleased. He might not understand Clara's altruism, but he didn't mind reaping benefits while someone else paid the freight.

"Well, if there's anything I can do to help you two ladies with this, you let me know. Need a private place to meet with, uh, witnesses or whatever, you let me know. Anything at all, you let me know."

BACK IN THE bar, we didn't linger long over finishing our drinks.

It was not my imagination that staff from the dining room and kitchen kept coming into the bar to stare at us. Clearly the word had spread.

I did keep an eye out for the server from Friday night because he might be worth talking to, but didn't see him. With our glasses empty, we left to walk back to where we'd parked a couple blocks away.

Which gave me the first opportunity to say to Clara, "You didn't have to tell him we don't charge. We could, you know."

She turned wide eyes to me. "Why?"

"It's hard work. Some people don't value other people's hard work unless they pay for it. Also, it's nice for paying bills."

Concern immediately shaded her face. "Are you short on money?"

"Me? No, no, I'm fine. Don't worry about me." I might have been too vehement. "I mean, everybody can use money, right?"

"But that's not the reason we do this. Even if it is hard work." Head erect, shoulders back, Clara added, "We aren't doing this because it's easy, we're doing it because it needs to be done."

"And we like to know what happened," I added.

She grinned. "And we like to know what happened. Isn't that amazing that Rich knew about what we've been doing?"

Not the word I would have chosen. More like another nail in the coffin of keeping a low profile.

"And—" Her excitement edged up another notch. "Did you hear

what he called it? The reunion murder. I told you."

"*That's* what struck you about that conversation? Not that he talked like we were Batman and Robin."

"Did they solve murders? I thought they stopped them. Oh. We—"

"No masks. No Batmobile. No Bat Cave. No Alfred. No—"

"A butler would be awfully nice."

"Okay, if we can wrangle a butler, I won't fight that." I pulled in air to emit a sigh, but turned it to better use. "Let's consider suspects."

"You're going to say Glenn, aren't you? But, look at it this way, Deputy Hensen's considering him plenty. Our time's better spent considering other angles."

Not a bad argument. Plus, she really, really didn't want to consider Glenn a suspect. That didn't mean I wouldn't consider him one outside our discussions. "Who else, then?"

"I suppose, after what Fern said, we need to at least find out Fae and Lovell's explanation for why they met and why Fae didn't tell us they met."

"Lied to us. And, yes, they're suspects." I ignored her grimace. "If Josepha knew about whatever it was they were up to Sunday morning, that's a potential motive. Although, being seen by Fern cuts into their potential time to commit the murder."

"Lovell could have been comforting her after one or both of them did the murder." A game offering, but lacking in conviction. Clara didn't want them to be murderers. She'd said the words from a sense of fairness because I agreed to steer clear of Glenn for the moment.

"True. What about Wesley?"

Her eyes widened. "He has no motive. Especially since he's no longer Marcus' follower."

"We're running out of people, Clara. Mary Jo?" Then I answered my own question. "But people already knew about her husband and Debi, so is Mary Jo hiding another secret? Also, it would make more sense for Mary Jo to kill Debi than Josepha."

"What about Debi? Josepha could have found out something even worse than we know. Debi had the best opportunity. She could have met Josepha *hours* before anybody else got there, committed the murder, set the scene, then pulled the curtain up when she chose, so to speak. After all, she was the one who found the body and you said your aunt said the person who finds the body has to be a strong suspect."

"True, but Debi couldn't have faked that shriek."

Clara flung her arm out to stop me, then almost hopped to bring us face to face on the sidewalk. "Oh, *yes*, she *could*. She absolutely could."

"I know you're not best friends, but that shriek—"

"No, no. I mean, you're right, I don't like her. But I *know* she can shriek like that on cue. She tried out for *Oklahoma*. I was there, waiting to try out myself. Debi was trying for the lead, but then they asked her about Ado Annie and told her she got excited—wound up—about things. And when she read the part, she produced a shriek *just like that*."

I stepped back. "Wow. And then you got the part?"

"Uh-huh."

"Did she get any part?"

"Nope."

"That explains the nametag business."

"She didn't even remember me."

"Oh, yes, she did. Or she wouldn't have done a song and dance— pun intended—about *not* remembering you and she wouldn't have egged on Marcus. Aside from that, you know what Debi being able to fake that shriek means?"

"We have to consider her a suspect."

"Uh-huh. And that means…"

"We talk to Berrie again. At least the dogs will be happy, because at this time of day we can almost certainly catch her at the dog—"

"Clara?"

"—park."

We both swung at the male voice calling from the direction of the town square. We had no time to do more than exchange a quick glance wondering if we'd kept our voices low enough to prevent being overheard before Wesley Oshmann hurried up to us.

"Hi, Wesley," Clara said carefully.

He rushed past the niceties. "Do you know why the sheriff's department is holding Glenn Selka? I just heard. That's awful. But why—?"

"They released him. Although they're saying he has to stay in town."

"Like he's their prime suspect? Why would Glenn do it?"

"That's exactly what I keep saying. He has no reason to murder Josepha and I have no idea why the sheriff's department would think he did. Although they did find one of those knives from Haines Tavern—"

"Like every house in this county doesn't have one."

"—with his fingerprints on it."

"*What?* My God."

"I know. It must be a mistake."

I gritted my teeth to stop from saying the mistake—*major* mistake—was sharing the fingerprint information.

"Yeah. You must be right. A mistake. Look, I've gotta go. Thanks."

He included me in his nod and walked quickly away.

"See, Sheila? He's shocked, too. He knows Glenn couldn't have done it."

"I agree he was shocked, but not that he believes in Glenn's innocence. He couldn't get away fast enough after hearing Glenn's fingerprints were on the knife."

"No," she protested.

I said nothing.

She turned to watch his departing figure. "Oh, dear. And I'm the reason he thinks that now." Another layer of *stricken* slid over her face. "*And* I blabbed about the fingerprints. Oh, Sheila, I'm sorry. I could run after him and say he can't tell anybody or would that call more attention…"

"Better leave it as is, I think."

In her van, after picking up both dogs and heading to the park, I realized she remained in the dumps over spilling the fingerprint info.

Casting about for something to distract her, I asked, "I've been meaning to ask, why was Wesley's nickname Assman?"

"It seemed to be some big joke among that group and I don't know why it would have been if the obvious explanation was the reason." Eager to make amends, she said, "You know who might know? Ancella. I'll call and see if she's back at the hotel."

She had her phone out. "Hi, Ancella? It's Clara—Clara Prentice Woodrow… Uh, yes. It is true. In fact, we're trying to clear some niggling questions. You know, underbrush, sort of."

As opposed to us being stumped by bigger questions.

"We were wondering why Wesley was called Assman? … Uh-huh. But she checked out. … Oh. … It would be. When are you leaving? … Will you send that to me? … Thank you. … Yes, you, too."

She clicked off in time to accelerate away from a four-way stop before the vehicle behind us became impatient.

"She doesn't know about the nickname, but thinks Mary Jo will. And Mary Jo hasn't left town. She's with her brother in Stringer. Ancella—she's leaving this evening—gave me her number and Mary Jo's."

She wisely pulled over before we reached the dog park. Trying to make a phone call from that parking lot with two park-crazed dogs in the back is not conducive to communication.

Again, Clara's side of the conversation filled me in.

"Who was at Senior Hill when you got there Sunday? … Debi was alone?… Uh-huh. Was there a box of supplies or—? … Always did, huh? And the tablecloth… Already on the table. I see. … One more quick question, do you know why Wesley was called Assman?" Clara turned pink. "Okay. Thanks. Yeah, I have to go, too. Bye."

She clicked off.

I told her, "I got everything but the answer about the nickname."

Clara turned pinker. "He was Assman because he licked Marcus'."

CHAPTER THIRTY-FOUR

GRACIE AND LULU were as ecstatic about being at the dog park as they would have been after a month away, rather than a few hours.

As usual, Berrie's patriarchal Boston terrier named Marcus carried on like I was Cruella De Vil, bent on kidnapping Boston terriers instead of Dalmatian puppies.

For once, though, I didn't mind him barking madly at me when I entered the "foyer" that connected the two large-dog and two small-dog enclosures' gates. Because it caught Berrie's attention from the other side of the small-dog enclosures where she was lecturing a pleasant-looking owner of a well-behaved Scottish terrier.

"It never hit me before, but this Marcus—" Shouting her comments over the din, Clara gestured to the barking ringleader, who'd drawn several of his fellow Boston terriers into the frenzy. "—is a lot like the human one. Especially volume."

"At least this one doesn't drink to excess," I shouted back.

"You shouldn't shout." Berrie out-shouted us and the barking from across the gate into the small-dog area. "It excites your dog. No wonder Gracie is tangling her leash."

She had tangled her leash during an ecstatic circle at getting this close to her doggy Valhalla. But since she was sitting and waiting for me to unhook the leash, open the gate to the large-dog enclosure, and give her the release command, I was good with tangling.

Gracie had to wait a bit more, because Clara tilted the screen of her phone toward me to read, with her body blocking Berrie's view of it.

Fae had written: *I'll talk to you in 90 minutes. Not at the B&B.*

Okay. Will let you know where in a bit, Clara typed. I nodded and she sent the message.

"Just a minute, Berrie. Let us get our dogs in, so we can talk." Clara was buttering her up by attributing our inability to talk to our dogs, rather than Berrie's. I approved the tactic, but couldn't bring myself to join in.

However, with our dogs set free to gallop into the big-dog enclosure, I diplomatically moved along the fence, which—for no reason anyone had figured out to date—stopped canine Marcus' barking at me. I didn't even mention the abrupt cessation of noise. I was on my best behavior.

"The leash is the direct line of communication between your dog and you," Berrie lectured happily. "You must not allow it to have twists or kinks."

Actually, I found the most direct line of communication between Gracie and me was looking at each other. She read me well— sometimes scarily well—and she expressed herself fluently.

But we weren't here to set Berrie Vittlow straight. Who had that kind of time?

"That's so interesting, Berrie." Clara was effective because part of her believed it. "Do you practice leash control with your dogs when you walk them in your neighborhood, like in front of your neighbor's house?"

"Of course. It's vital to practice at every opportunity. Though I prefer the term lead hygiene. Just the other day—"

"*Lead hygiene.* That's perfect. You're always so busy here at the park." She didn't even add an edge to those words. "You must think of terms while you're walking your pups at home. Like when there were those carrying-ons at Debi Norris' house you mentioned before."

She looked at Berrie with limpid interest in Berrie's dog-walking creative time. I needed to learn that technique.

"Carrying-ons when she closed her door in my face, you mean, which is no way to treat a neighbor when I was saying how sorry I was she was caught up in all this and must be a prime suspect because she found the body."

Yeah, boy, why would anyone not want to talk to *that* neighbor?

"Now, that was the second time, wasn't it? Because there was another time you mentioned there were carrying-ons at her house," Clara said.

"Second, third, twentieth. She and her husband were at each other all the time and so loud it was impossible not to overhear them."

I didn't roll my eyes, I didn't say what I was thinking, I didn't even let my expression change. So, while Clara was knocking it out of the ballpark drawing Berrie along, I contributed in my own way.

"But that time a week ago got especially nasty. He said she'd been sleeping around." Her voice dropped. "With Marcus Etchells. Her husband definitely said that name and about how she was welcome to keep living in a second childhood for all he cared, but didn't she have anyone better from her past to, uh, have a *relationship* with—"

Have a relationship with did not sound like an accurate quote.

"—and she'd slept with her supposed best friend's husband, which was low even for her. Not that her husband cared, but if she thought the friend wasn't going to find out she was even stupider than he thought she was. He moved out. I saw him piling things into his car. Tried to chat with him, you know, for a minute to express my sympathy, but he was in such a rush to leave he couldn't take the time.

"Though he did take the time to clear out the joint bank accounts from what I heard Debi screaming about."

FAE ARRIVED AT the designated rendezvous spot by the fountain at the center of the town square on time. Not alone.

"Lovell insisted on coming." She frowned at him.

His presence likely explained why she'd delayed the time—waiting for the end of the school day.

"It's just as well." I interrupted myself to gesture to two stone benches set at right angles to each other that were generally occupied earlier in the day by a group of male retirees. They'd either gone home for early suppers or it was happy hour somewhere. "This concerns him as well."

I wasted no time once we all sat.

"We know, Fae, that you did not spend the forty minutes Sunday morning between the time you left the B&B the first time and when you returned there for your potluck dish by visiting your childhood home and neighborhood. You were seen elsewhere. Together."

Lovell made a sound low in his throat.

Fae raised a commanding hand. "That doesn't mean anything. Because it was entirely innocent. We were *talking*."

"And hugging." That came out of my mouth before I considered that making hugging sound like cause for suspicion in a murder inquiry was a stretch.

"And hugging," she flung back at me with a mocking smile.

"Why wouldn't you tell us?" Clara asked.

"Because it's none of your business. It *isn't* any of their business." She directed the last at Lovell, who had touched her arm.

"It wasn't so innocent that you didn't make up a story about what you were doing," I said.

"It's none of your—"

"Business. Got that part. But when someone's been murdered all sorts of things become all sorts of people's business."

That stopped her, at least for the moment.

He put a hand over hers. "She's right. A murder investigation… I won't let you be suspected to cover my ass, Fae."

"Lovell—"

He kept talking. "There's no reason to make this a big secret. Clara and—"

"Sheila," I supplied into his momentary blank.

"Right. They won't spread this around for sport. Not like… Anyway. I'm asking you both to consider that the feelings of a good man who's done nothing to deserve it could be deeply, deeply injured if this gets out."

We looked back at him without saying anything. It would all depend on what he said.

Lovell Zelig cleared his throat. "It was a rough time for John and me, back twenty years ago, but that's absolutely no excuse for taking advantage of a student." He grimaced. "All those rumors about me and boys. But Fae's the only student I ever—That's not an excuse, either. There shouldn't have been any … any—"

"I seduced you."

"Stop saying that. You didn't."

"Not with any great feminine wiles, but with my neediness."

"You did not. You were stronger than you knew. That's what drew me to you."

"Not until you made me believe in myself."

Clara sputtered, "But… But… What about…? I mean, aren't you…?"

"Gay?" Lovell filled in, not unkindly. "If we're going to discuss my sexuality, might as well spell it out. I'm probably technically bi. But I love John. He's the love of my life. He's my husband. That doesn't mean I'm never attracted to other men or women." He rested a hand on Fae's shoulder. "Or girls."

"I was grown up enough to know what I was doing—and to be the aggressor. And you were *not* my teacher anymore." She practically spat at us, "It was after graduation."

He shook his head—not at her, at himself.

"You've stayed in touch?" I asked.

"We message, but it's surface because…" His words slid away.

Because they didn't want John to know of their long-ago liaison and to be hurt by it.

"It's why I suggested we meet Sunday morning. I wanted to talk to her, really talk to her, and find out if she truly was okay. A teacher never should have—"

"I'm more than okay, as I've told you all along, Lovell." A slight smile lifted her lips. "I wouldn't have the relationship I have now if we hadn't had that time together."

He still looked concerned. He did care about her.

I wondered if he cared about something else, too. Like his job.

"I'm retiring next year." It took a beat to recognize he hadn't read my thought, but connected his words to our conversation. "If I weren't, I wouldn't blame you two for feeling you needed to expose this, even though it was twenty years ago."

"We won't say anything to anybody unless it's necessary to expose a murderer," Clara said.

His brows rose. "I suppose that's fair. Certainly don't deserve any better promise."

I asked, "Did Josepha say something to either of you?"

They exchanged a look. "Not directly. But we discussed if her urging me to come to the picnic meant she knew and was going public to try to harm either or both of us because of what I did twenty years—"

"Stop that. Stop beating yourself up." Fae scowled. "You changed my life for the better. Opened it up. Gave me confidence I *never* would have had otherwise."

"It was wrong."

"Yes, it was," Clara said firmly. "No matter what good Fae believes it did for her. On the other hand, she's an adult now and if she doesn't want to pursue it…"

"I don't, for God's sake. How many times do I have to say it? To you, to him, to anybody. It was a brief time—after I graduated, mind you—and it would only hurt John and Lovell to have it come out now. There is no justice in that, especially since I wanted it. Desperately."

CHAPTER THIRTY-FIVE

WE WATCHED THEM walk away. Not touching, yet connected in what struck me as a rather sweet way.

Not something I would say, because Clara would strike them off our potential suspect list, which was already thin. And I wasn't ready to strike them off.

"So they alibi each other," she said with satisfaction.

"Unless the murder happened earlier, say daybreak, which it might have when you consider someone easily could have spotted them committing murder on Senior Hill later in the morning."

"Who would've spotted them? No football practice Sunday morning."

"A jogger using the track, a dog walker," I suggested.

Her eyes narrowed. "A jogger using the track would only be able to see for a brief part of each lap. The rest, their back or side is to the hill. Even when they face the hill, they aren't very close, so it would be hard to tell what was going on or who was up there without stopping their jog and using zoom. Remember how little we saw from the bleachers without zoom? Not much closer on the track. And a jogger's moving.

"A dog walker wouldn't be moving as much, but would be farther away, because they're supposed to stay outside the fence around the football field area."

"Okay, okay. So, someone familiar with all that might not have worried about committing the murder after full light Sunday. Still, riskier than earlier or at night."

"Granted. But how would someone persuade Josepha to meet

them there at an odd hour?"

"I think it would depend on what Josepha wanted from them," I said slowly.

"Money?" Clara's expression cast doubt on her own suggestion.

"That would fit with what she said about a bill needing to be paid. But do you think there's something more likely than money?"

"Power. Control. A hold over people."

"She'd certainly have control over Lovell, because she could tell John. Not so much over Fae."

"But Fae cares about Lovell and wouldn't want him to suffer. Sort of a hold once removed. Or maybe it could hurt her professionally."

"Would Josepha be satisfied with controlling only Lovell Zelig?"

"No." Immediate and sure. "She'd want to control as many as possible."

"You know, I was thinking about how she could have found out secrets. I wonder if it was from cleaning for people."

"That's *brilliant*. You. Not Josepha," Clara emphasized. "But how can we know *whose* secrets?"

"It sure would be easier if she'd gone after cash and we had a money trail to follow. We might not be able to eliminate people, but—"

A message came in—on my phone this time.

"Check the message. Maybe it will be a clue," Clara said, only half kidding.

Not a clue. Teague.

Leaving school. Want to meet up?

"He might know something." She truly had this optimism thing down pat.

I snorted. "Not that he'll share with us."

"Worth a try."

Sure. Clara and I at fountain. Town square.

Even as I typed, my mind recalled Josepha's voice from Saturday night.

Their reasons centered around that they were the class leaders and you were a nobody.

My mental playback pressed a faint emphasis on the first word.

Their reasons. Were there others with different reasons for trying to unseat Glenn? Did Josepha herself have reasons? Did I misremember and that emphasis never existed?

"Clara, remember what I told you about the voice in the hallway talking about bad memories?"

"Yes, though first you just said memories. It wasn't until Josepha was murdered that you told me the voice said *bad* memories. Like you needed to protect me or something."

"Didn't want to ruin your reunion vibe." I continued quickly before she expressed more miffedness, "I was thinking about the other part of what she said—about a nightmare coming and a bill you have to pay. Especially that last phrase. Why a bill you have to pay?"

She planted her elbows on her knees and snapped her open hands forward. "*Yes*. So maybe she *was* blackmailing somebody for money? But who?"

We lapsed into a silence. My thoughts circled around the tracks we'd already covered, not making any progress.

Clara cleared her throat. "I remembered something." She didn't sound happy. "When you asked Mr. Zelig about people at the high school yesterday, he didn't answer right away about Fae."

"Why do you ask?" I quoted.

"Exactly. You had to ask him again, after he'd answered about Debi, Marcus, Wesley, and Mary Jo."

"That's good, Clara. And there was something else. He'd been talking about Josepha as an adult, but when I asked him about Fae, he went back to high school. It seemed understandable at the time—that's how he knew her. But maybe it was something else. Like an effort to lead us away from Fae as an adult."

"That could make sense, even though I hate it. I always liked Fae. Not like we were good friends, but I admired her, you know? She stood apart, as her own person. That's not easy to do in high school."

"From what people have said, you did the same thing."

"It wasn't the same. I didn't make waves. I was careful. Fae wasn't. She—" She waved a hand. "—let the chips fall where they may."

Could one of those chips include murder?

"Let's go back over what we know about the things Josepha could have been holding over people."

"Debi's husband was running around on her. Debi apparently slept with Mary Jo's husband—now ex. Mr. Z cheated on his partner by sleeping with Fae shortly after graduation." She huffed. "As for Marcus, there's a lot about him cheating on his wife—wives—and not keeping jobs. Why are you frowning like that?"

"I'm frowning because … Does something strike you about all these things?"

"Hmm. Most didn't happen real recently, except Debi sleeping with Mary Jo's husband and even that was last year. So why kill Josepha now? But that brings us back to focusing on the reunion goers from far away who hadn't been back before."

"Right, right. That's good about not recent, hold onto that thought. But what I was thinking is that none of these were particularly hard to find out. I mean, other people besides Josepha knew about them and most of those people talked. So, while the information wasn't exactly something *everybody* knew, if the murderer wanted to hold onto their secret, they shouldn't have stopped with Josepha."

"Do you mean…? We're looking for a secret only Josepha knew?"

"Maybe."

"How do we find that out?"

"I don't know." I flopped back against the unyielding stone bench and immediately regretted it. "It was relatively easy for us to find out about Debi's husband's philandering and her revenge-or-otherwise motivated philandering."

"Berrie. Which means it's known by enough people that Josepha knowing wouldn't give her power over Debi."

"Unless Josepha knowing—I mean her specifically—would bother Debi for some reason?"

Clara shook her head at my Hail Mary attempt. "I can't imagine why. It's not like Debi ever cared what Josepha thought." She gusted out a breath. "So where does that leave us? Debi's no good because too many people knew what she'd been up to for Josepha to wield power. Marcus wouldn't care if people knew he'd slept with Debi. One more notch on the proverbial bed post. Not to mention he was in jail at the time of the murder. Fae and Mr. Zelig alibi each other, no matter—"

"What if they lied? One provided the alibi, the other did the murder. Fae or Lovell."

"I was going to say no matter what we thought about whether the motive was strong enough in the first place, which I *don't* think it is."

"Because you like both of them."

"And know both of them."

"Or did."

She opened her mouth. Closed it. "That's fair."

She sank into a silence.

"What if," I started slowly, "there's another pair trying to protect the same secret. Like Fae and Lovell, but not them."

"What secret?"

"I don't know, but don't you think it's a little suspicious that Marcus Etchells has a cast iron alibi? Nobody else does."

"I'm willing to suspect Marcus of just about anything, but what could he have done that he wanted kept quiet—he brags about his misdeeds—and that someone else would commit murder in order to protect Marcus' secret? To take that terrible risk. I mean, how much would you have to love someone to risk being caught and charged for murder, not to mention actually doing the deed? It's one of the reasons I've never thought Fae or Lovell was likely. They clearly care a lot about each other. But that much?"

"You've never thought they were likely because you like them."

She didn't hesitate. "That, too. Would Mr. Z feel as guilty about his relationship with Fae—even as an ex-student—if he weren't a good guy?"

"Or pretending to feel guilty."

She clicked her tongue. "You are so untrusting."

"I really do need to introduce you to my Aunt Kit."

"Yes, you do. In fact—"

"But this isn't the time to discuss that. To get back to Marcus and play out the idea, is there someone who'd be willing to protect him?"

Clara shook her head slowly. "I can't think of anyone. I know he's divorced three times, but beyond that and what we know about his carrying on with Debi—*Oh*. Could Debi...?"

We looked at each other for several beats, then said in unison. "No."

She expanded it. "Not for anybody but herself."

"Hmm. Remember Linda and Carole saying Debi warned the other reunions away from Senior Hill?"

"Yes. She could have been planning it then. And if self-interest pushed her, she *might* kill for Marcus... But we'd have to figure out why."

"We haven't eliminated anybody." I exhaled from my toes. "But you know who else could have something hidden? Glenn Selka."

CHAPTER THIRTY-SIX

TO HER MULISH doubt, I said, "I think… No, I can't even go that strong about whether or not the *bad memories* exchange was Josepha talking to Glenn in the hallway. But I am sure she thought he had a secret. We have to talk to him, Clara."

Slowly, she shook her head.

"We do. And this time we have to press him. No more Ms. Nice Investigators. We have to get him to tell us why he came back, what he's hiding. What else the sheriff's department knows. All of it."

"Okay. But I was shaking my head because Teague's coming toward us and we have to stop talking about this."

"WHAT HAVE YOU two been doing today?" Teague asked with good-cop friendliness, which still vibrated with cop-ness.

"Clara's been working for her clients. As for me—"

Clara talked over me. "The knife that stabbed Josepha came from the Haines Tavern. Can you believe it?"

"How did you hear that?"

"Oh, we've known—"

I returned the favor by talking over Clara. "A reliable source, but not, perhaps, as reliable a source as *you* have."

"What do you mean, Sheila?"

That was Clara asking. Because Teague knew what I meant.

Watching him, I answered her. "He wasn't surprised to hear Josepha was stabbed with a Haines Tavern steak knife because he already knew that. He *was* surprised that we knew. Which means he had the information from a law enforcement source. A source he's quite sure would never share it with us. And that's why he's surprised we know. He's also not happy we know, whether for himself or on behalf of his official source."

Clara looked at him. "Is that true? That's like … like you're working *against* us, not with us. Well, not exactly with us, because you won't. Which is another thing. But I'm not holding that against you. But—"

"Thank you. What we should be talking about is how you two know something law enforcement is holding back to further their investigation."

That dry response lit tinder in Clara.

She propped her fists on her hips. "I've been sticking up for you. When Sheila said we should keep our distance—"

Teague shifted his gaze to me and hiked one eyebrow.

"—I said you were a nice man. I thought she was being paranoid, but now you act like this?"

I closed my eyes. Not long enough. When I opened them, his brow had rejoined the other at their normal height, but they rested above an assessing stare.

"Keep your distance? Paranoid?" he asked me.

"Clara's point was that I *wasn't* paranoid." A glint in his eyes acknowledged I'd scored a point. "Despite that, I will tell you that our knowing about the knife is not through a law enforcement leak."

"And you won't tell anyone about it."

Clara and I looked at each other. "We won't tell anyone about it from now on."

That covered her spilling the beans to Wesley. Of course, we couldn't stop other people from telling us, as Rich had.

"How about going for some dinner to seal the deal—my treat. Want to go to The Tavern?" Teague asked.

"Sorry. We can't. We have somewhere else to be."

I held Clara's gaze. She swallowed. "Uh-huh. Right now."

We waited until Teague was out of sight after an easygoing acceptance of our decision before striking out across the town square in the direction of the Amber House B&B.

"GLENN, YOU SAID you have nothing to hide."

"Yeah."

"I don't believe you. Everyone Josepha approached Saturday night had something to hide. And she approached you. What are you hiding?"

He said nothing.

"Okay, then I'll hypothesize that it has to do with Heidi Holmes' death and whether or not that was an accident."

Kirstin gasped wordlessly. Clara protested with "*Sheila.*"

I didn't pause. "But what I don't get is why that's worth hiding. You'd been gone—what? two, three months when she fell on that rainy night and died. You weren't here. Were you?"

"No. God, no."

"Then why come back? Why look up articles from the time? Why—?"

"Guilt," Kirstin said. "Misplaced, unwarranted, unresolved guilt. You want to know why we came to this accursed reunion? Because all these years later, he was still caught by a dead girl. *Because* she was dead. He needed to be free of wondering. Tell them."

He said nothing.

"Tell them, Glenn. Tell them how you broke it off with her, thinking she was seeing someone else, but blamed yourself that maybe that was an excuse you made up because you wanted to be free of her to go on to your new college life. Tell them how you've tortured yourself she might have committed suicide because you left her pregnant and deserted her. Tell them that I hounded you into coming to this reunion to finally—finally—have resolution over Heidi Holmes. You are not being disloyal to me. You are not—"

"Stop."

No one moved as his sharp word echoed into silence.

Looking only at the table, he spoke slowly.

"When we broke up…" He rubbed at the back of his neck with

one hand. "When I broke it off, she'd been pushing for more. Getting engaged, married even. I said I was going to college. She said she'd move with me, we'd get an apartment, I could still go to school. I panicked. Felt like I'd be trapped. I broke it off right then. Wouldn't answer her, none of the ways she tried reached out. Slipped out of classes early, took roundabout routes to avoid her. She stopped trying to contact me before the end of the school year and I was so relieved, I never wondered…"

He left a long enough pause that I said, "Not mature, but not un-heard of for teenagers."

"Yeah. But when you say not mature… It wasn't until years after she died, in fact, after we'd married and Kirstin mentioned a friend who became pregnant by a long-time boyfriend who ghosted her after she told him, that it finally hit me that Heidi could have been… Could have been pregnant with my baby and didn't know how to tell me, what to do.

"If she was and with the way I cut her off, then left, could she have been so desperate a few months later that she'd committed suicide?"

"But she didn't kill herself, Glenn," Clara protested. "The official reports—"

"They've been known to get things wrong."

I added, "There also wasn't anything about her being pregnant."

"No, no there wasn't."

"That's not enough for you?" Clara asked.

He rubbed his neck again. "I don't know. I read those articles. Everything you said was right there in black and white. But … I don't know."

I jerked my head side to side. "No. That isn't what Josepha needled you about. It doesn't fit. There's something else. That might be why you came, that might be what matters to you and to Kirstin, but it's not what Josepha was after you about."

He shrugged.

The gesture lit my fuse.

"We are trying to figure out this murder. If you really didn't com-mit it, you are hindering our finding out who did by keeping secrets.

And not telling us makes it more believable that it was something worth killing Josepha over."

"It isn't."

We all waited. We all watched him.

He shot a look at Kirstin. She looked back at him steadily.

"Fine. Here's the deep, dark secret Josepha thought she had on me. I didn't graduate from high school," he said.

"Of course, you did," Clara said. "You were valedictorian."

"Yes. But I didn't graduate."

"I saw you walk across the stage and get your diploma."

"Yes, that, too. Though what you saw me receive from Principal Ingram was a diploma placeholder. Officially, I did not complete the state requirements to graduate."

"How is that possible?"

"I took a few college courses my junior and senior years. I filled in high school classes where I could. By the end of senior year, I'd missed one requirement. I was going to make it up over the summer, but then my family moved."

"What did you miss?"

"Half a credit of PE."

"Gym? You didn't graduate over a *gym* class?"

"That's about the size of it."

"But then how did you get into college?"

"I'd been accepted early. Based on my academics, not PE," he added dryly. "Apparently they never went back and checked my transcript. My parents were so terrified I'd lose my scholarship they made me swear not to tell anyone. It's still a taboo subject in the family. Though I did tell my PhD advisor. She said she didn't care that I hadn't sweated enough in high school, she'd make me sweat plenty. And she did."

He took Kirstin's hand.

"As it turns out, I came to appreciate fitness and health when we met, then married, and started having kids. It became vital to me to extend my time on earth with all of them as much as I can."

I saw Clara melting at the sentiment.

I stuck with practicalities. "You mentioned your transcript. Does it show you didn't graduate?"

"I have no idea. I've never checked."

"Would this affect your other degrees? Could they take them away?"

"I doubt it. I know of students who started community college without a diploma or a GED and went on to a bachelor's degree or more. Nobody raised a stink about that. But try to convince my parents of that. They still live in dread it will come out."

So much so that they barely mentioned him in their updates—to people here in North Bend County. Doing everything they could to keep a spotlight off him that might reveal this.

Kirstin said, "The only instances I've ever heard of a diploma being revoked involved cheating, plagiarism, or something else that tarnished the integrity of the school. Glenn has only reflected well on his alma maters, including North Bend County High School."

He tightened his hold on her hand and she squeezed back.

"You knew all along?" I asked her.

"From our third date."

"Some pickup line, huh?" He almost grinned. It faded quickly.

"Kirstin, your family, your advisor, who else knows?"

He shook his head. "I honestly rarely think about it. If I did, especially to the extent of being paranoid about it, would I have risked coming to the reunion?"

"Possibly not." I didn't want him to dismiss this. "But Josepha found out and that points to someone else here knowing."

Would it be a motive? Not the way he told it now—but how accurate was that—and what about to spare his parents the realization of their twenty-year nightmare?

"She didn't say she knew," he objected.

"She wouldn't have. Not overtly. That wasn't how she operated. But the comments she made to you… She knew. Still, it comes back to how she found out."

"School records?" Kirstin asked. "Would she have had access to those?"

"Not that we know of. And I'd think she'd have to know about it first to go searching. Scrolling through decades and decades of school records on the off chance of finding something like that? I don't think so."

"Mr. Ingram knew," Glenn said.

"The principal," Clara filled in for me. "But he moved to Florida right after he retired and he died at least five years ago. If Josepha found out from him—not that I could see him sharing something like that—"

Glenn's head shake confirmed her opinion.

"—she would have had to hold onto it on the chance Glenn came back someday and she'd have the opportunity to use it against him."

That fit my take on Josepha Viedux, but I'd save that observation for when Clara and I were alone.

"If she thought I'd crumple at the knees, she'd've been disappointed," he said with satisfaction.

"That might have made her more dangerous," I said. "But we still have the question of how she could have found out."

Clara jerked upright. "Mr. Ingram's widow lives here. After he died, she moved back to be near their children. Maybe Josepha knew her."

"Or cleaned for her?" I asked.

She pointed at me. "Or cleaned for her. Exactly. Although that's if Mr. Ingram had papers that included Glenn missing half a credit in PE, moved those papers to Florida, his widow kept his papers, and moved them back up here…"

"Not likely," Glenn said.

"All we can do is ask, starting with if Josepha's company cleans for her," I said.

CHAPTER THIRTY-SEVEN

"Of course I remember you, Clara Prentice. Mr. Ingram always liked you. Said you were solid gold."

Proof the late principal had good judgment.

The short woman peered up at me as Clara and I stood outside Mrs. Ingram's front door. "I'm sorry I don't recall…"

"I didn't attend North Bend County High School, Mrs. Ingram. My name is Sheila Mackey."

"She's my friend, Mrs. Ingram. And we are hoping we can come in and chat with you."

"Come in, come in."

She insisted we have tea or coffee or something. She wore us down to water.

After we settled in chairs around a coffee table, Clara said, "We wanted to ask you if Mr. Ingram kept records after he retired?"

"Oh, my, yes. He kept pretty near everything. Not official records, of course, but his informal notes and thoughts."

"We know it's a long shot, but did you take the records with you and—this is even a longer shot—bring them back here?"

The woman chuckled.

Clara and I exchanged confused looks.

"We didn't take the papers to Florida then bring them back. They never left here."

In response to our continuing confusion, she said, "We didn't sell this house when we went to Florida. Our oldest boy and his family were preparing to build a house at the time, so they lived here for a while, then a niece for a couple years, and a teacher whose house burned down—poor soul lost everything—then a cousin. And when I came back, it was here, waiting for me." She looked around at the comfortably lived-in room, her gaze resting on a photograph of a portly man with a warm smile. "Home."

She gathered herself and focused on Clara again. "Was there something of yours you're looking for?"

"Not exactly. But… Mrs. Ingram, you heard about the woman who was killed at the reunion picnic Sunday?"

"I did. Horrible. Horrible."

She meant that. At the same time, a bit of reserve cloaked her openness.

"Did she clean for you?"

"She did at one time, but we did not suit."

An old-fashioned phrase that could cover considerable territory.

"Was there a particular reason?" Clara pressed.

"As I said, we did not suit."

And that was where she was prepared to end this conversation.

Clara sent me a look.

I nodded.

Clara quickly told her about Glenn, making it sound more like he'd failed to clear out his locker than failed to complete the requirements for graduation.

"My. How did you hear that?"

"Glenn told us."

"Did he?"

Clara glanced at me, recognizing that question as a placeholder while Mrs. Ingram thought through the situation. And decided whether she'd tell us anything she knew.

I leaned forward. "Josepha said something to Glenn on Saturday night that indicated she knew he didn't officially complete high school."

"Giving him a motive?" she asked sharply.

"Perhaps." I held her gaze. "But knowing how she knew about his situation would help us figure out how she found out other things, which could help us figure out who killed her and that would clear anyone who didn't commit the murder."

"Glenn also told us that even if this became widely known—which it wouldn't from us—it wouldn't hurt his career," Clara added.

"I shouldn't think so with all that boy has achieved," she said tartly.

Time ticked by as we watched her consider the matter.

Suddenly, despite my deep interest in this conversation, my brain piped up with a snatch of a Righteous Brothers song that included a line about how much time can change and the singer wondering if his honey was still his.

Maybe it was a good sign it wasn't *You've Lost That Lovin' Feeling* this time. On the other hand, seeing how people reacted to *Unchained Melody* for the first time…

No. I *had* to get these guys out of my head—

"She was going through his papers."

"What?" I gabbled.

Clara stayed on track. "That's why you fired her."

"As I said, we did not suit," Mrs. Ingram said dryly. "I came home early from lunch three weeks ago yesterday because my friend had a terrible toothache. I walked into the office and there Josepha was, rifling through his records. She tried to pretend the drawer came open on its own when she fell against the file cabinet. Hah! I have no idea how much she had already accessed, but she was reading through his personal notes about your senior year."

MRS. INGRAM TOLD us she fired Josepha Viedux on the spot and made sure she didn't leave with any of the papers the former principal filed along with updates about each graduating class. What she took away in her memory there was no way of telling.

"Would your husband have written about Glenn's situation?"

"Yes. He thought quite highly of the boy's potential and kept track of him in school and after."

✧ ✧ ✧ ✧

"**THIS DOESN'T REALLY** help Glenn," Clara complained when we were back in my car.

Anticipating a return to my house, we'd left both dogs there to entertain each other. But first we were picking up pizza for dinner.

"That's not our goal. Figuring out who committed murder is." But I said it half-heartedly.

For some reason my brain kept replaying one phrase of Mrs. Ingram's.

She tried to pretend the drawer came open on its own when she fell against the file cabinet.

The entire drive to my house, it played over and over in my head. And it didn't quit when we sat at my small kitchen table.

Clara went over what Mrs. Ingram said, pointing out that Josepha could have read almost anything from Mr. Ingram's notes about that school year.

She tried to pretend the drawer came open on its own when she fell against the file cabinet.

What about Josepha's lame excuse had caught me?

She tried to pretend the drawer came open on its own when she fell against the file cabinet.

Lame and bad acting, from what the principal's wife said.

Bad acting…

"The guy who stumbled. That was bad acting." I heard the words come out of my mouth.

"What guy? What acting? What are you talking about?"

"Friday night. At The Tavern. The guy who stumbled into Glenn and Kirstin's table after they joined us. You didn't see him?"

Clara shook her head.

"Damn. I thought at the time I was the only one who noticed, but I hoped…"

"You sound like this is really important, but I don't get it, Sheila."

"I saw this guy stumble into Glenn and Kirstin's table after they joined us, but before it was cleared. I thought at the time the guy was drunk. Our server came and helped him. The server sort of scooped him up, with the guy holding onto a napkin—and maybe more—and rushed him out the back."

"Okay, but what does that have to do with—*Oh*, you think this man who stumbled into the table took Glenn's knife?"

"It's possible. He had the opportunity."

"Who?"

"That's the thing. My memory could have been tainted—or two memories blended together. It's not like when I saw him again I thought, *Oh, that's the guy who stumbled into Glenn and Kirstin's table.* Although I did think he was familiar."

"But who was it, Sheila?"

I didn't answer. I was running the scene back through my head.

And then my mind jumped from that scene to one outside the hotel Saturday night.

"I should have recognized him then," I said. "The same kind of stumble. Except what held him up the second time was Wesley's shoulder, instead of the server."

Marcus wasn't that *drunk.*

My own thought about his outrageous behavior outside the hotel echoed in my head.

But if he wasn't *that* drunk, then…

He did both on purpose?

Stumbling into the Haines Tavern table.

Yeah, okay. He could have staged that to pick up the knife. Specifically, the knife Glenn Selka used? Or would any knife have done?

The scene outside the hotel, what did that get him?

That was easy.

A night in police custody as a rock-solid alibi, which meant he knew when the murder would happen.

And what had it taken? Goading Fae Ballard. Stumbling around, saying obnoxious things. That, really, was all he'd done until the sheriff's department vehicle pulled up. Only then did he shove Wesley, adding actions to his words.

"*Marcus.* You're talking about Marcus. But he's the one person who *couldn't* have killed Josepha. And why would he?"

An idea had started to form about that. But I wasn't ready to put it into words yet.

"Before we go any further, let's see if there's a way to confirm. It sure would be nice to have someone else who saw his opportunity to take the knife. Maybe the server. Though he was behind, so Marcus' body blocked his view—*Teague.* Of *course.* Teague. He had almost the same angle I did."

"Great. Let's call him and—"

"Wait. We have to figure out a way to ask without outright asking him. You know, without tainting his reaction… We need to find photos or video from the reunion to show him."

Clara had her phone out, already searching. "There's lots online."

AFTER WE WENT through possibilities, I downloaded two videos with all the relevant people, editing them into one clip on my desktop upstairs before loading it on my phone.

I called Teague on our way.

"Can Clara and I come over?"

"Now? Why?"

"We'll tell you when we get there."

"I'm teaching in the morning."

"We'll be there as fast as we can."

Murphy was much more pleased to welcome us to the small, utilitarian, yet comfortable apartment Teague rented in a building with eight units not far from the yoga studio.

He opened the door with a dry smile. "That was fast. Almost like you were already here when you called."

I didn't waste any time. "We're going to show you a short video clip."

"Is this something I'm going to like?" He had a wicked gleam in his eyes.

Clara giggled.

I said a stern, "No."

"Is this going to explain why you're here?"

"Yes." I clicked play.

At the end, he looked from me to Clara and back. "The reunion?"

"Yes. Did you recognize anyone? Before you answer, do you want to see it again with sound this time?"

"We kept it off in case it muddled your memories," Clara added.

One side of his mouth lifted. "Nope. I'm good."

"So, did you recognize anyone?"

"Yeah. You want a list?" He barely waited for our twin nods. "You two, of course. Three—no, four—people from around town. Don't know their names."

"Can you describe them?"

"Give me the phone." He went back to the beginning, playing it at time and a half.

"Her." Debi Norris. "Works in the liquor store."

I snorted.

"This guy. Works at the hardware store."

I vaguely recalled the guy from the reunion. "He left early," Clara said. "Didn't come to the picnic. Never heard anything bad about him. Anybody else, Teague?"

"Seen her around. Post office, I think." Josepha Viedux.

"And him."

He'd stopped the video with Marcus in the center of the screen.

"Which color shirt?" I asked carefully.

"Blue. Untucked to cover a gut. Cuffs rolled back. Showy watch. Cheap knockoff."

I felt Clara's excited look, but didn't return it. I was playing this carefully right out to the end.

"Someone else you've seen around town?"

"Might have. But for sure saw him Friday night at The Tavern."

CHAPTER THIRTY-EIGHT

Clara started to burble. I clenched her arm.

"When did you see him?"

Teague had been paying close attention to our reactions from the start, but now he let it show.

"In the dining room. After Glenn and Kirstin joined our table. He came in from the hall door in the back room. He leaned partly across the table Glenn and Kirstin had been at. Our server was right behind him. Got him upright and out of there."

"Because he was drunk and fell against the table," Clara said in triumph.

"It might have been a fall—" His tone added that it might not have been, too. "—but he wasn't falling down drunk."

"Not drunk?" came out of my mouth.

"Not falling down drunk. Fifty-fifty he could have passed an FST—field sobriety test. When he came forward across the table, he put his hand around Glenn's water glass. Didn't knock it over. Didn't juggle it. And as the server drew him back upright, he had the presence of mind to take a napkin with him to dry his hand."

I hadn't seen that part with the water glass from my angle. But I had seen the napkin.

Possibility thudded hard in my chest. A napkin could have been right near the steak knife and used to cover it.

"Anything else?"

He studied me a moment. "Yes. The server was tailing him. Not an accident he was there that fast."

"Oh, that's so interesting," Clara burst out, unable to contain herself. "Don't you think that's interesting. Sheila?"

I kept my eyes on Teague. "Anything else?"

"Your guy held onto the napkin. Slid it into his jacket pocket. The one away from the server."

"Did it…? Did he fold it into his pocket?"

"No."

"So it could have held—?"

"Clara."

"No reason to stop her, Sheila. I can put a clue or two together. You're thinking he pocketed Glenn Selka's knife off the table. Used that as the murder weapon without wiping out the prints."

And then he stopped, darn him. I prompted more with, "*Could* he have done that from what you saw?"

"Yes. But I also can't say he *did*. Who is the guy? Other than one of your former classmates, Clara."

"Marcus Etchells. Exchanged less than pleasant words with Josepha."

"Also other people. I mean he exchanged less than pleasant words with other people, but so did she."

"So no smoking gun … or smoking knife in this case." He stood.

"Where are you going?"

"You know I'm going to the sheriff's department to tell them what I saw."

"No smoking knife, as you said. You don't know anything more than you did before we came over and—"

"I know there's a possible connection to the case. I wasn't looking for connections, because it's not my job. But it is my responsibility to report what I saw after you two pointed out the connection."

Clara opened her mouth, then closed it.

Eventually, back at my kitchen table and administering chocolate to ourselves, she said, morosely, "It is one of the reasons we like him so much, his doing the right thing even when we'd rather he didn't."

"I don't know about like. But I respect it. And we can't complain too much, since he's going to the sheriff's department to tell them that the person who mostly likely took the murder weapon from The Tavern is the person whose alibi is them."

"OHHHHH." CLARA'S EXHALATION made the word multi-syllabic. "You're right. That's awful."

I couldn't resist. "Especially for them."

"But even if Marcus did those things to get the knife and give himself an alibi, how did he commit the murder?"

"He didn't. We saw Josepha Viedux leave the hotel after he was in the deputy's custody. He wasn't released until half an hour or so before the body was found. She'd been dead longer than that. Not to mention, there were already people at Senior Hill, setting up before he was released. He couldn't have done it. But he must know what happened to the knife next. How it got in the hands of the murderer and who that murderer is. All we have to do is figure out how to get him to spill the beans."

"That's all."

Ignoring that uncharacteristic pessimism, I added, "We need to talk to our server."

"Oh, I forgot. Rich called while you were editing the videos to show to Teague, and said he'd talked to every server except the guy who had our table Friday night. He finally came in for a shift tonight and Rich plans to talk to him after."

The young guy with the hair over his forehead.

I jerked upright, unable to stay seated. Aware of both dogs jumping up and looking at me with a mixture of concern, confusion, and hope that I'd do something interesting.

Cursing myself did not meet their definition of interesting.

"What an idiot. Total, absolute, complete idiot. I thought he looked familiar, but I didn't connect it with what happened. He was right there and I saw clear as anything when the server—"

The scene came sharp before my eyes.

The server's expert retrieval of the drunken stumbler, the two faces almost beside each other. Almost…

"A double, triple idiot. Total, absolute, complete idiot. I almost had it Saturday night, too, then it slid away."

"What are you talking—?"

"Do you know what that server's name is?"

"No. Why?"

"Can you call Rich and ask?"

"Okay." She said it carefully, as if mollifying a lunatic.

"Now. Call him now."

"Okay, okay. I'm getting my phone." She found a number with maddening deliberation. Rich apparently answered immediately. After far too many pleasantries for my taste, like saying hello, she finally asked the question. "Rich, that server, the one you haven't talked to yet, what's his name?"

Her eyes and mouth went round.

"Yeah? … Okay. That would be great. Thank you, Rich. I'll talk to you then." She ended the call. "His name is Toby. Toby Etchells. And he's Marcus' son. How did you know, Sheila?"

"Know? I didn't. I haven't *known* anything."

"Don't go on a doubting tangent. How did you know that kid was Marcus' son?"

"That's why I'm such an idiot. I should have recognized Marcus at the reunion as the table stumbler. I should have spotted the resemblance when I saw them together at The Tavern. When he scooped up Marcus, their faces, were right there, close together.

"That stumble—what I *thought* was a stumble Friday night—was deliberate. Marcus grabbed the knife, with that napkin over his hand to cover it. But it wasn't until the fact that Rich *hasn't* talked to him sparked the thought the kid was avoiding him that I envisioned it again, seeing their faces together, and recognized the resemblance. And holding up Marcus was a practiced move—"

"Because he'd done it a lot considering how much Marcus drinks. Wow. Just, wow. So, a son—that's someone who might have killed for Marcus out of love. And that's how Marcus could have an airtight alibi, but still be behind it, though *why* would he kill Josepha?"

"A secret. Just like we've thought all along. The bill Josepha was going to make people pay, including him."

"But *what?*"

Something flickered at the edge of my mind.

Clara said, "You saw them—Marcus and his son—together. Gut feeling, do you think the son's in on it?"

"He was angry, embarrassed. Trying to get out of a potentially awkward situation as quietly and quickly as he could. We have to confront him. Tomorrow—No, wait. We're running out of time. They'll scatter. We have to confront them *all*. All at once. Call Rich back. See if he can arrange for a farewell breakfast tomorrow for—us, Marcus, Debi, Mary Jo, Fae and Lovell, Wesley, Glenn and Kirstin— that's ten, with Marcus' son serving."

"But—"

"Just see if he can do it."

He could.

Now all we had to do was get him to confess so the murderer would, too.

CHAPTER THIRTY-NINE

I HAVE NEVER been so relieved to have my great-aunt call me.

Clara had left with us both saying we needed to get a good night's sleep to be ready for tomorrow.

No way was I sleeping. And my pacing was getting on Gracie's nerves. She went as far as leaving her bed in the bedroom and taking up a spot at the top of the stairs. Flopping down there with a deep sigh at the inexplicable weirdness of humans.

Then Kit called.

In a rush of words and nerves, I covered everything that had happened since the last time we'd talked.

Partway into it, Gracie returned, circled tight into her bed, gave me a warning look, and closed her eyes.

"…though why I instinctively thought the owner might be throwing us out of The Tavern, when such a thought never occurred to Clara… Maybe that's it. Because she's secure here. She knows she belongs, while I'm an outsider."

"More like you still wrestle with guilt over being the author of *Abandon All*. Which—"

"I'm *not* the author of *Abandon All*."

"—you should have been over ages ago if you'd had any reason for guilt in the first place, which you didn't. You and I were business partners. We had success, for which we both worked very hard."

"You wrote the book—"

"And you presented and represented it."

"If it comes out—"

"It will be a very minor sensation for a very small group of people for a very short amount of time. And, yes, I know *very* is a weak intensifier, but it gains power by the rhythmic repetition."

That was my author aunt, editing her own conversation.

"Better for it to not come out." Before she could respond, I kept going. "But to bring this back to the murder—"

She snorted at the change of subject.

"—Rich said no fingerprints would survive their dishwasher. The knife was brought out with the steak, so it should have prints of the server and the diner. The killer's prints would show over those of the server and diner?"

"Depends."

"Depends on—? Gloves."

"First, if the killer isn't the server or diner, of course. Also, gloves. They could smudge earlier prints. So could blood."

"How likely that the earlier prints would still be identifiable? That's the impression Rich gave us that the sheriff's department gave him."

She scoffed lightly. "Like a game of telephone, but they could be identifiable."

"It explains their great interest in Glenn."

"Glad you're putting your brain to *some* use."

"*Some* use?" Oh, how I wanted to take those words back. But there's no use fighting gravity when you've already stepped off the cliff.

"Solving murders is all well and good but writing should be where you're putting most of your energy."

My light laugh came out surprisingly believable. "Kit, you're the writer, not me."

She snorted. "You're sure not a good liar. You are writing."

"Why would you think that?" I hedged.

"Because you should be and you're resisting it. The Righteous Brothers rabbit hole. Classic writer avoidance," she said, as if that were proof. "What are you writing?"

"Aunt Kit, I don't know why you'd think—"

"Because it's about time."

"Wh—what?"

"You think I didn't know you wanted to write? Why do you think I asked you to be my partner in *Abandon All*? From the time you were little, making words with your blocks while your brothers built forts. And living in the brownstone, with you listening hungrily to my band of reprobate friends talking writing. Why do you think I've kept blithering on about writing? You know I don't do that with people who aren't interested."

I had no response. Kit didn't need one.

"So, what are you writing?"

"I haven't figured that out." Was this what I needed, acknowledging to Kit that I was writing? Or... "I start one thing, then another. Sometimes in the same genre, sometimes a different one. I know, I know, you're going to tell me to pick one genre and push ahead."

She tsk'd. "Not yet. You haven't written enough. Keep going. Even if it's not what you end up wanting to do, you'll learn a lot. Starting is one big hurdle. Finishing is another. Keep going over those hurdles. No lollygagging."

"Lollygagging?"

"It's an excellent word and it's what you need to avoid, because you get caught in a cycle that's hard to break. I won't go on at you about what you write, but write, you must."

"You brought this up to distract me, didn't you? To make me stop thinking about tomorrow. If I had something stronger about who—"

"What does your gut tell you?"

"Marcus Etchells." I heard my breath gust into the mouthpiece. "But he was in the drunk tank until—"

"Sobering cell."

I conceded her point. Don't argue words with Kit. "Whatever they call where they had him sleeping it off, he was in police custody from the time we all left the hotel—with Josepha Viedux definitely alive—until just before her body was found, with no opportunity to commit the crime. He's the one person who couldn't have killed her."

"Tell me about him. Is he attractive?"

"More like repellent. But he seems convinced of his own appeal."

"Was he attractive in high school?"

Thinking of his son, I said, "I suppose."

"Anything else you know about him?"

"The guy he seemed happiest to see didn't reciprocate. And I can't blame him, since Marcus made a big deal of how this supposed friend was a great wingman because he never offered any competition when Marcus went after—and I quote—*babes.*"

"That's well-observed, Sheila. Wait. Hold on." I heard her tapping on her phone. "Gotta go. A guest—"

In other words, the cute widower she wouldn't tell me anything about. Apparently arriving for a booty call—though his call or hers, there was no telling.

"—will be here any minute. I have one more thing to say. You need to tell your policeman all about it."

"What we're going to try tomorrow? No way."

"About writing."

"But—"

"That and your *Abandon All* life. Bye."

The woman hung up. Drop a bomb, then hang up.

Tell Teague? Was she nuts? What if we broke up? What if we kept going out, but he knew of some obscure law Kit and her legal team missed and it tormented him whether to overlook law-breaking or turn me in?

No.

No, no, no, no.

Well, maybe. Eventually. But certainly not right away.

WEDNESDAY

CHAPTER FORTY

I DIDN'T SLEEP much, but Kit's declaration took my mind off what I hoped we'd accomplish at this breakfast.

When I did sleep, I dreamt over and over of the Righteous Brothers singing *You've Lost That Lovin' Feeling* to the Wicked Witch of the East's legs sticking out from under Dorothy's house.

✧ ✧ ✧ ✧

"WHAT'S THAT YOU'RE humming, Sheila?"

It took a couple beats to yank my thoughts back to the moment and Clara's question as we arrived at the Historic Haines Tavern, plus another one to recognize the tune.

"*You've Lost That Lovin' Feeling.* The Righteous Brothers."

She gave me a *Really?* look.

"It's a classic. Their voices are perfect for it and the lyrics catch the signs of a relationship going down the tubes. The girl's not closing her eyes when they kiss, and there's no welcome when he touches her, and her fingertips…"

A short interaction flashed into my brain like a snippet of video. Action and reaction, then reaction to the reaction.

"Sheila?"

"And the Wicked Witch of the East dream was telling me to go back to the beginning. To the very beginning."

"You're starting to scare me, Sheila."

"It might get even scarier. Remember what I told you I thought I heard in the hallway?"

"Of course. About it being *all set*."

"And more. We need to get Mrs. Ingram to this breakfast. And I need to tell you some things Donna told me yesterday morning that almost got lost in the shuffle."

RICH CHAFFORD PUT us in a larger private room with a large square table.

Clara and I sat on the side closest to the door.

On the side to our left, were Lovell, Wesley, and Kirstin.

Opposite us, Glenn sat just around the corner from his wife, then Mary Jo, and Marcus.

The fourth side held Fae, Debi, and Mrs. Ingram, closest to us.

Rich stood by the door.

"Thought we were getting fed," Marcus grumbled.

"First, let's get our water glasses filled," I said, as arranged.

Rich took the cue and opened the door, beckoning to someone.

Our server from Friday night, Toby Etchells came in pushing a cart with several pitchers of ice water.

He startled at all eyes being on him. He spotted Marcus then immediately away. Rich murmured something about placing the pitchers.

With his eyes down and his neck red, Toby went to work. We all watched as he set two pitchers on the farthest side of the table, then the side to our right, next the side to our left, and, finally, on the side where Clara and I were.

"Hello. You were our server Friday night, weren't you?" My gesture included Clara.

"I guess." He looked toward his boss, who stood between him and the door, then down.

"As well as for the couple back there at the corner." I pointed to Kirstin and Glenn. "Is there anyone else you recognize who was here Friday night?"

"What the hell is going on?" Marcus started to stand.

"Sit down, Marcus. We'll get to that."

The kid ducked his head.

"Is your name Toby Etchells?" I asked him.

That sucked air in, but I didn't take my eyes off him to find out whose. Clara would tell me later.

"Yeah."

"Is Marcus your father?"

"Yeah. Officially."

That added word made my heart jump. This might be smoother than I'd feared. Especially for this boy.

"Did you see him here Friday night?"

"Showed up. Told him before I didn't want him here. Told him before he could cost me my job." Another quick look toward Rich.

"He didn't listen to you?"

"Never does."

"You took him out of the back dining room?"

"Yeah." His face turned painfully red.

"Did you think he was drunk?"

"Usually is."

"Thank you, Toby." To Rich, I said, "I think you should take Toby out now."

The boy's glance toward his father didn't make it all the way there. Marcus never looked his way at all.

He leaned back in his chair, hooking one elbow over the back. "So what? What's the big deal?"

"The big deal is that it fills in some of the journey taken by a knife. A Haines Tavern steak knife that started here—"

Rich reentered the room and walked to the other end, standing against the left-hand wall.

"—and ended up in Josepha Viedux, killing her."

Marcus' smirk had returned. "In case you didn't notice, I couldn't have done that. Even you have to get that."

"He was in jail," Debi said harshly. "You're just trying to pin it on him to save your friend Glenn. You're all trying to dance on Marcus' grave like the goons you are."

Fae asked the question in my head, "Do you mean ghouls?"

"I know what I mean."

"Maybe, but we don't."

"Always so smart, aren't you? Showing off your brains to the rest of us. You and Mr. Valedictorian. Thinking you were so much better than everybody else."

"He *was* better than everybody else. That's what valedictorian means," Fae said matter-of-factly.

"Yeah? Well, I know you screwed Lovell Zelig." She flung a look around without connecting with anyone as far as I could tell. "Did the rest of you high and mighties know that?"

Clara's head pivoted toward me. I got the message—another secret that wasn't so secret.

"And—" Debi drew it out with pleasure. "—Glenn Selka might have been the best student, but not of *our* graduating class, because he didn't graduate."

Fae and Wesley jerked toward Glenn. He shrugged with would-be casualness.

"Did Josepha tell you that? Before she started using your secrets against you?"

Debi ignored my question. Maybe she didn't hear it. She had more venom to spill.

"Wesley wasn't innocent, either. Always presenting himself as Marcus' most loyal friend, but when he had a chance to screw me, he did it fast enough."

Wesley flushed fire engine red. "You'd broken up by then," he mumbled.

"You mean she'd found out he was cheating on her with a nobody," Mary Jo said.

"Temporary," Debi snapped. "He came back to me. He always does."

"After you were married and he was married, you mean? He used you, the way he uses everybody who's not Marcus. As for Wesley—"

Debi jumped in. "He screwed me. His best friend's girl."

Fae came to Wesley's rescue. "How did he get that chance, Debi, if you didn't give it to him? Not to mention Wesley might have been

Marcus' best friend, but Marcus was never a friend to him. I bet Marcus didn't even care."

"Maybe Mr. Z didn't screw you," Debi shot back. "Maybe you screwed him. Maybe you held him down and—"

"Quit working it so hard, Debi. You're not going to shock them. They already know Lovell Zelig and I qualified for carnal knowledge diplomas after I graduated. It's old news—*ancient* news. Not like the fact that you slept with Mary Jo's husband last year—"

"*Ex*-husband," Mary Jo emphasized.

"He wanted it. And she went away."

Fae got in, "She was away to care for her sick mother and he wasn't ex at the time."

"*Finally.*" Mary Jo thumped the table. "Finally, you admit it."

"All right, all right, quit whining about it. He wasn't much of a lay, anyway. Had to fake the whole thing."

"My heart bleeds for you," Fae muttered.

Lovell cleared his throat with teacher authority and everyone quieted.

"What does this have to do with the reason you presumably gathered us here this morning, Josepha's murder?"

"Ah," I said, as if I welcomed the question, when I would have preferred to let the airing of dirty laundry go on longer in hopes of more useful tidbits. "It goes back farther than that. Much farther. Back to another death, shortly after this class graduated. Heidi Holmes."

Everyone stared at me, except Clara, who was hard at work on her assignment of watching for reactions.

"Did you all know Josepha cleaned out Heidi Holmes' apartment and the apartment of another renter after their deaths? The other renter was someone who would sit in her window at night and watch the activities of other residents. Every night. And she took notes."

I felt Clara's lightning glance at me, but didn't return it. I'd told her I was going to expand beyond what I knew into the realm of conjecture. I hadn't told her what conjecture, nor that it also extended past conjecture. Because if Josepha *had* known what happened that night in the parking lot of Heidi Holmes' apartment, she would have applied pressure to Marcus long ago.

But Marcus didn't know when the other tenant died. And I hoped—prayed—that if he ever thought to ask, it would be much too late.

This way, too, we had a better shot of keeping our promise to Mrs. Ingram to keep her husband's personal notes out of this.

Still, I didn't dare look at Clara, in case it drew attention to her innate honesty illuminating my fibs.

"The tenant saw what happened that night and wrote it down. That's how Josepha found out and why she started turning the screws on Marcus."

"That's bull—" Marcus stopped when Rich strode to behind him and grasped the back of his collar.

I turned away from him and toward one of his classmates. "And why Marcus blackmailed you into killing Josepha Viedux."

CHAPTER FORTY-ONE

WESLEY OSHMANN'S FACE twisted.

"Or did you do it to help him?" I asked.

"Help him? *Him*? No. He had nothing to lose, because he's made nothing, built nothing, achieved nothing. I'm the one who had everything to lose. All because twenty years ago I helped an asshole who's never grown up. And he used it against me."

"Shut up. Don't—"

Rich twisted his handful of collar and Marcus couldn't get out further commands.

It felt like no one else moved, or even breathed.

Quietly, I said, "Tell us your side of what happened the night Heidi Holmes died, Wesley."

"He called in a panic. I should have hung up. I should have told him to go to hell. God. I should have stayed the hell home that night. One more day. Just one more day, and I'd have left for college.

"But no. Marcus calls and I go running. Like always. I thought it was his car. It was always breaking down. And he was always calling me to rescue his butt, even though I didn't have a car. I'd ask my parents and after a while they got fed up with him calling, always wanting things from me, never giving anything, saying he was using me." He laughed harshly. "No shit. But I was too stupid to see it."

"He called you that night and you went … where?"

"That apartment building where Heidi lived."

"Where she died?" I asked quietly.

He dropped his head. "Yeah."

"You helped him kill her."

His head snapped up. "Me? No. *No.* I liked her. I'd never—"

Have killed someone he liked.

But he hadn't liked Josepha.

"God. One night. One lousy decision."

"What happened?" I asked.

"All he said was he needed a ride. Like he did all the time. I couldn't possibly have known. I was looking for his worthless junker and he came jumping out of the bushes like a wild man, gibbering and waving at me. And then…"

He sucked in. "And then he said he'd killed her."

"I didn't—I didn't. That's a lie. She was going at me, that's true. She was crazy. I told her to just give me her keys and I'd go. If she'd done that… But she threw them. Down there."

Nobody even looked at Marcus.

"That's why I had to call Wesley. Because she wouldn't give me her keys."

"Kill her *and* take her car. Nice," Mary Jo said.

"She was grabbing at me," he whined, "and I gave her a push to get her off me. Like self-defense. She didn't even try to catch on anything, went straight down. Wasn't anything I could do."

"You mean when you went down after her," I suggested.

He calculated, searching for the better story.

"I did go down after her. I tried. But she'd slid all the way. I heard a kind of a scream and a thud, but I still climbed down to see if I could save her. Only she'd gone over the edge. I could see from there she'd broken her neck. I freaked."

I didn't believe any of that except the last sentence. Possibly the scream.

"That isn't what he said then. He said he hadn't gone after her," Wesley said. "If I'd used my head, I would have stopped the car right then, pushed him out, and called the cops."

"But you didn't."

"No. I didn't. I listened to him. I couldn't stop him talking. And I couldn't stop listening. His car broke down—of course. She picked him up and brought him back to her apartment. Booty call and that jackass made her pick him up. And then, he said she had to take him home and couldn't understand why she was pissed. It's a thunderstorm, rain coming down like crazy. He gets her out in the parking lot and they're yelling at each other and she said something and he pushed her. He said that's all he did. Push her. One push and she tripped over the curb by where her car was parked. That's what he said. And she must have slipped on wet leaves, and went down fast. He said he tried to catch her but she was already gone.

"I yelled at him. Why didn't he go down and look for her? He said it was too steep. By this time, we'd left the apartments. He was shouting and shouting at me to get away from there. I couldn't. I drove to where I thought she might be. It took a couple tries, but I found the street. She was lying on a running path alongside it. Marcus kept screaming that we had to get out of there. I remember thinking I couldn't leave the car running, couldn't leave the keys in the car or he'd take off. I remember squeezing those keys in my fist. Squeezing and squeezing as I got out and went to her. But…"

But her neck was broken.

"Her head was at such a weird angle and she wasn't…" he gulped in air. "Her eyes… She was dead."

"It could have been an accident," Clara said.

"No," Wesley said. "He wasn't just wet, he had leaves and mud on him. His shoes were full of them. He went down that embankment and pushed her over the edge. I knew it that night. And I still kept his secret. I kept his damned secret until Josepha Viedux got her teeth into it, and he came after me again to clean up after him."

"I didn't stab Josepha," Marcus shouted. "He did. I was at the jail. All the deputies, everybody knows I couldn't have done it."

"I think you'll find, Marcus, that stealing the knife and providing the murder weapon involves you in conspiracy to commit murder."

"I didn't. The knife—I didn't do that. The kid—Toby—"

A sound came from every other soul in the room. Not a sigh. Not words. If revulsion had a sound, that was it.

I said, "You were seen taking that knife, Marcus. Two witnesses."

"And I'll damn well testify you gave it to me, not your *son*," Wesley said. "It was conspiracy all right. He told me when and where to meet her—instead of him. And if I didn't, he'd go to the sheriff's department and tell them I'd been his accomplice in killing Heidi, because he had nothing to lose. While I…" His voice shook, and tears slid down his cheeks, into grooves around his mouth, then off his jaw. "…I would lose everything I'd built. My family, my life, everything."

"So, you went to Senior Hill in place of Marcus Etchells and stabbed Josepha Viedux?"

"Yes," he sobbed. "Yes."

I don't think any of us could look away from him.

At last, Kirstin spoke, sounding as if she were in a trance. "You were going to let Glenn take the blame?"

Wesley wiped at his face with one hand.

"I didn't set him up. That was Marcus. I didn't know he'd picked up Glenn's knife. I had no idea, until you told me." He jerked his head toward Clara. "I didn't know what to do… I couldn't *think*. But Marcus… Marcus thought it was funny."

"You were going to let Glenn take the blame?" Kirstin repeated in the same dead voice.

A sheen of fire across her eyes was the only warning before she stood up and swung.

AFTER THE SHERIFF'S department left with Marcus and Wesley, the rest cleared out, one by one, except for Fae and Lovell Zelig, who walked out together. He was giving her a ride to the airport.

Mrs. Ingram hugged Clara and said, "Mr. Ingram would be proud of you—of you both—for finding out the truth and pleased he helped in some small way."

That left Clara, me, and the Selkas.

Glenn gripped Clara's arm and put his other hand on my shoulder. "Thank you both. For proving I didn't do this, but also for giving me the answers. As sad as they are, they are answers."

Kirstin, worn but relieved said, "But thank you most of all for proving he didn't do this." She slid her non-slugging hand around his arm. "Come on, Glenn. Let's change our flight and go home."

We shared hugs.

And then only Clara and I were left.

"I wonder if any of them will come back for the twenty-fifth reunion," she said.

I groaned.

EPILOGUE

WE HAD DINNER Friday night at Clara and Ned's, including Teague.

Deputy Hensen had asked us a lot of questions all through the rest of Wednesday.

Ned came home that night and I only saw Clara in passing at the dog park the next two days.

Teague completed the week subbing and we'd had short *how are you* phone calls in the evenings.

I gave Kit the full blow-by-blow rundown.

And I wrote.

Don't get too excited. I also deleted. Still, by the time Teague and Murphy picked up Gracie and me for Friday dinner at the Woodrows'—true friends also invite dogs to their dinner parties—I had more words than a week ago.

I also thought a lot about telling Teague my secrets—the smaller one that I was writing and the big one about how I'd spent the fifteen years before we met.

I was going to do it.

Soon.

Take the plunge both Kit and Clara recommended. See what that did for this relationship.

Because I wanted a true relationship.

I wanted him.

We filled Teague and Ned in on the murder of Josepha Viedux. Heidi Holmes' death was less clear-cut. We believed we knew what happened, even had Wesley's account, but the chance of the evidence of that twenty-year-old death moving a prosecutor to act was slim.

"Tell them the words you overheard in the hallway Saturday night," Clara urged me. "If she hadn't heard them, we might still be trying to figure it out."

"*...truth... hiding. I go, you go. ... Want to lose...?* Then after the other person said something, *Told you. It's all set.*"

"Okay, I give," Ned said.

"Not *hiding. Heidi.* That was Marcus' accent and bourbons at work when he said *the truth about Heidi.* He was telling Wesley he had to kill Josepha or the truth about Heidi would come out and ruin Wesley's life."

"But, how did you know it was Wesley? You said the scales had fallen from his eyes about Marcus," Ned objected.

"They had. But Marcus had that hold on him. And he reminded Wesley of it right before the deputy took him away Saturday night. He kept saying Wesley wouldn't complain, that Wesley did what Marcus said because he knew what was good for him. Marcus was reminding him he better go through with the murder, right there in front of all of us and the deputy.

"Besides, at the time of Heidi's death, Wesley was the only one who would have helped Marcus if he was involved with Heidi's fall."

"That's another thing. How did you get to Marcus and Heidi being together?"

"Bits and pieces. Bits and pieces. Clara saying Heidi said she was happy on graduation day, Debi talking about finding out after prom that Marcus was seeing—to quote her—a *skank.* Josepha mildly taunting Glenn about it being good he didn't come back because of *how things changed...* which made me think about a song where a guy's asking if the girl's still his. In this case, the answer was no."

I did not mention that the Righteous Brothers got me thinking about how thoroughly Wesley had lost his idolizing "loving feeling" for Marcus.

"But Josepha was saying things to a lot of people at the reunion, wasn't she?"

"Pretty much," Clara agreed. "But Sheila also noticed Josepha's nearly-new van in the high school parking lot with a temporary sign for her business on it. Temporary, because Josepha had just gotten it, while Debi said she used to have an old compact. And then Marcus' boss yelled at him about giving away a vehicle in a trade for a junker so he could get laid. Not that he and Josepha… But she did squeeze him to get the van. Josepha mostly used information in other ways, but she wasn't above getting a deal, either. Isn't she brilliant? Sheila, I mean."

"Brilliant," Teague echoed with a trace of dryness. "That's pretty thin for going into that breakfast with two people who didn't stop at murder—"

"Another advantage of amateurs over professionals, like Clara said," I reminded him. "We didn't need prosecutable evidence. Also, we had Mr. Ingram's notes from when Heidi died. We called Mrs. Ingram that morning and asked her to look at them to see if they offered confirmation."

Clara picked up, "She didn't have to look. Turns out she read all his notes as he made them. We promised her we wouldn't use them unless absolutely necessary, because she'd rather people don't know he kept those personal notes—just imagine the things in them. Of course, Glenn not graduating. And Mr. Ingram suspected about Mr. Zelig and Fae, though it was after she was a student… Anyway, you can't tell anyone."

She looked from Ned, who nodded, to Teague, who didn't.

"What did the notes say about Heidi's death?" he asked.

"Nothing directly," she said. "But Mr. Ingram knew Heidi and Marcus were … hooking up. He caught them in a parked car at school. That was even before Glenn broke up with her. Mr. Ingram was relieved when Glenn left town—and her. When she died, everything said it was an accident, so Mr. Ingram had no reason to suspect. He wrote that, if Marcus woke up, at least one good thing might come out of the tragedy. But we didn't need that Wednesday morning, because Wesley told the truth under Sheila's brilliant questioning."

Teague shook his head, not completely in awe at my brilliance.

But then he smiled a little.

Neither man asked as many questions as I'd have expected. I figured Clara had already told Ned what happened. But I wondered about Teague.

Ned told us about the storm damage, somehow making it amusing to have spent more than a week roughing it while trying to help people and businesses in worse shape.

Teague added anecdotes from his full week of teaching.

The dogs, who'd had another romp in the back yard before dinner, curled into an adorable tangle under the table during our meal.

We gave them extra treats as we cleared to prepare for dessert.

As we sipped wine and finished slices of apple pie, Gracie came to me and rested her chin on my forearm.

"Oh, isn't that sweet," Clara said.

"Just wait," I said.

"She's thanking you for dinner," Ned said.

"Just wait."

"Or asking for more dessert," Teague said.

"Just wait."

Gracie lifted her head slightly to look soulfully into my eyes. I met the melting brown gaze.

"Awww." Clara led the sound, but almost certainly the men joined.

Without breaking Gracie's look, I murmured, "Just wait."

Certain she had my attention, Gracie's milk chocolate eyes widened slightly as she let out a resounding belch.

The guffaws didn't bother her in the least. Wagging her tail, she trotted off.

"She definitely was thanking you for the treats," Clara said.

"Or expressing her opinion of the menu," Teague suggested.

"She must be a Chinese collie. I've heard it's considered a compliment to the chef there," Ned said.

"MIND IF I—we—come in?" Teague asked back at my house.

"I was hoping you would. I have something to tell you." My heart jammed itself into my throat, but delaying wasn't going to make this any easier.

"Me, too."

Inside, with our coats off and sitting on the couch with Gracie and Murphy curled together on the rug, I said, "You go first."

Instead, he said, "You don't talk about teaching."

"I've left teaching."

"Most people talk about what they retired from."

"Ah, but I didn't retire, unlike you." The first time he'd told me he was retired, he'd had a slight pause, as if debating if that was the right word. "I quit and embraced decadent freedom."

"Uh, talking about retiring, that's what I want to... They want me to work for them."

"Teaching full-time?"

"No. The sheriff's department."

"The sheriff's department? But you're teaching."

"Subbing. Sheriff's department would be part-time, too. I can still sub other days. Why do you look like that? You were the one asking about why I didn't go to another department. Got me thinking. So I took them up on having a conversation, and this offer's what came out of it. I was going to talk to you about it after school Tuesday, but Clara was there..."

And we talked about finding the killer of Josepha Viedux instead.

"...and then with the department so busy with this case and me teaching, the only time Hensen and I had to hammer out a few things was last night. Talked to the sheriff after school today."

"Is this what you want, Teague?" I ventured carefully.

"If I were teaching full-time, maybe not. But... yeah, I want to give it a try. I'll still have time for other projects." He pulled me close. "Including some very difficult and demanding ones."

He kissed me.

I ended it sooner than either of us wanted. "What kind of work?"

"Consulting on investigations, big cases. So, no more wheedling information out of me."

"As if we ever succeeded at that." But my mind raced with implications that had nothing to do with the murders we'd encountered. "More like we'll have to be more careful about letting you wheedle information out of us."

"I can live with that. Now, what were you going to tell me?"

"Oh, nothing that can't wait."

Because how could I tell him and ask him to keep a secret that— even if not technically—could be viewed as fraud or at least scandal? It would put him in a terrible position, possibly hurt his professional reputation. I couldn't.

"Sheila—"

"What we need to do now is toast your new position. Another great thing I learned from Aunt Kit—always have a bottle of champagne chilled, just in case."

The End

For announcements about upcoming Secret Sleuth books, as well as other titles and news, join Patricia McLinn's Readers List and receive her twice-monthly free newsletter.

patriciamclinn.com/readers-list

You can buy this book and all my others, including print editions and audiobooks, from my online store. I've added direct-to-you buying options to better control how my books reach you, while having lots more elbow room to give you special bundles, early offers, and exclusive bonuses.

Patricia's Bookstore

shop.patriciamclinn.com

Thank you for reading Sheila, Clara and Teague's latest adventure! As winter approaches, an eerie Haines Tavern legend is tested against the reality of murder.

Join Sheila and Clara, and their now not ex-cop friend Teague, along with their canine crew, for the next mystery in small-town North Bend County, Kentucky, in

Death on ZigZag Trail

Sheila, Clara, Teague and friends ask if you'll help spread the word about them and the Secret Sleuth series. You have the power to do that in two quick ways:

Recommend the book and the series to your friends and/or the whole wide world on social media. Shouting from rooftops is particu-larly appreciated.

Review the book. Take a few minutes to write an honest review and it can make a huge difference. As you likely know, it's the single best way for your fellow readers to find books they'll enjoy, too.

To me—as an author and a reader—the goal is always to find a good author-reader match. By sharing your reading experience through recommendations and reviews, you become a vital matchmaker. ☺

More Secret Sleuth mysteries

DEATH ON THE DIVERSION

Final resting place? Deck chair.

DEATH ON TORRID AVENUE

A new love (canine), an ex-cop and a dog park discovery.

DEATH ON BEGUILING WAY

No zen in sight as Sheila untangles a yoga instructor's murder.

DEATH ON COVERT CIRCLE

A reviled supermarket CEO meets his expiration date.

DEATH ON SHADY BRIDGE

A cold case heats up.

DEATH ON ZIGZAG TRAIL

A spooky legend twists grave matters.

DEATH ON PUZZLE PLACE

Season's greetings: Whodunit?

"McLinn has created a fabulous new murder mystery series with … wonderful characters, both human and canine, [and] an interesting backdrop. I highly recommend." —*5-star review*

Caught Dead in Wyoming mysteries

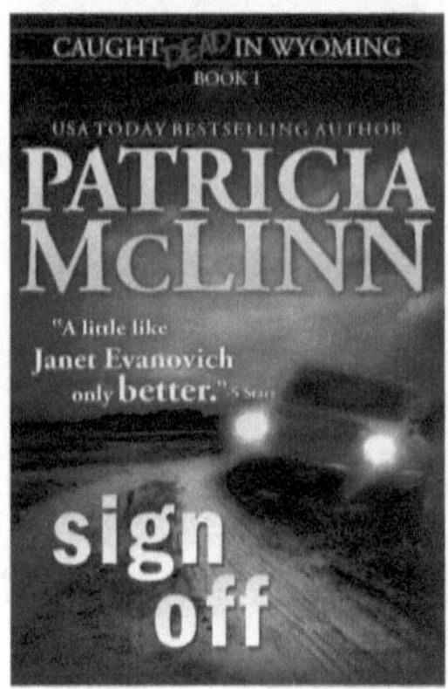

SIGN OFF

Divorce a husband, lose a career … grapple with a murder.

LEFT HANGING

Trampled by bulls—an accident? Elizabeth, Mike and friends must
dig into the world of rodeo.

SHOOT FIRST

For Elizabeth, death hits close to home. She and friends must delve into old Wyoming treasures and secrets to save lives.

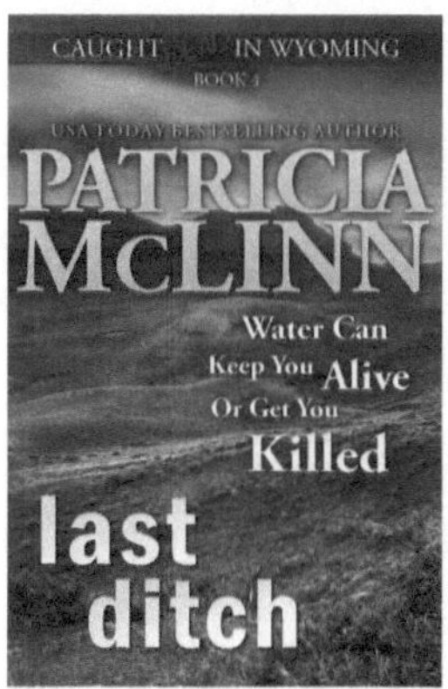

LAST DITCH

KWMT's Elizabeth and Mike search after a man in a wheelchair goes missing.

LOOK LIVE

Elizabeth and friends take on misleading murder with help—and hindrance—from intriguing out-of-towners.

BACK STORY

Murder never dies, but comes back to threaten Elizabeth, her friends and KWMT team.

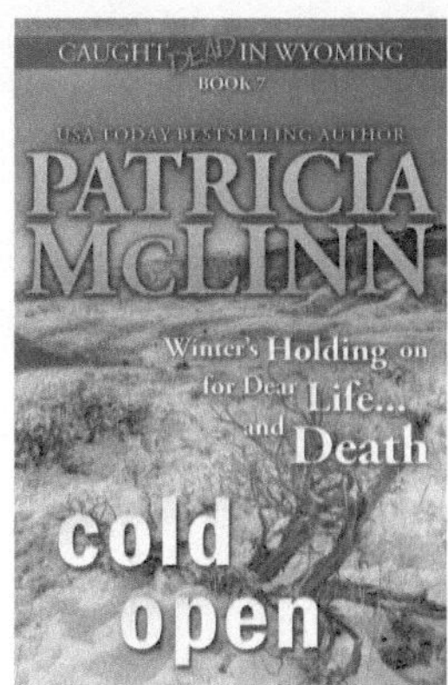

COLD OPEN

Elizabeth's looking for a place of her own becomes an open house
for murder.

HOT ROLL

One of Elizabeth's team of investigators becomes a target.

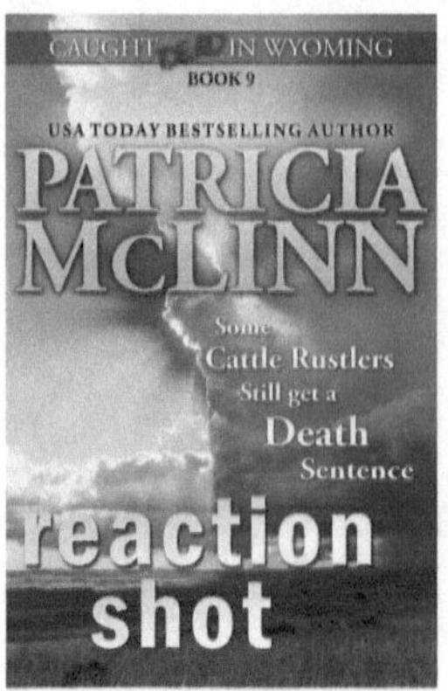

REACTION SHOT

Homicide on the range, where clouds darken over Elizabeth.

BODY BRACE

Everything can change … except murder.

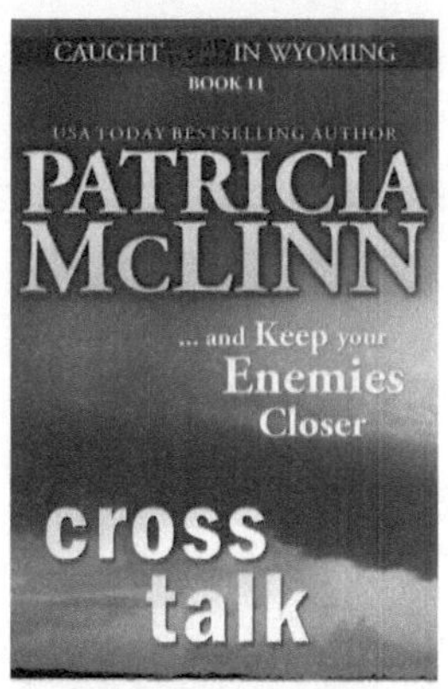

CROSS TALK

Storm clouds at the TV station.

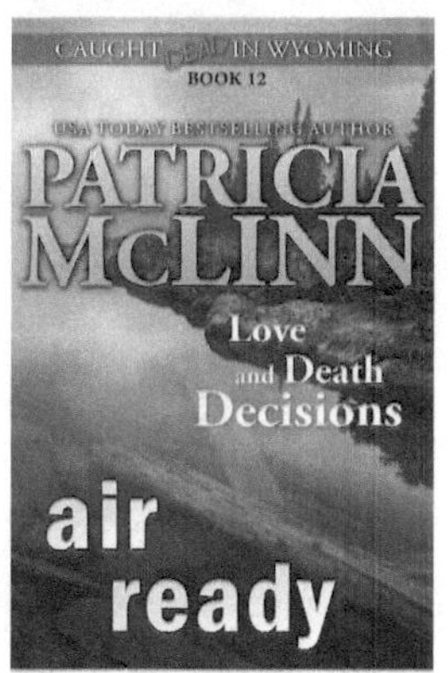

AIR READY

Love and death decisions.

HOLIDAY BULLETS

A Christmas wish with Elizabeth's name on it.

CUE UP

On the trail of murder.

PREMISE OF INNOCENCE
The last woman Detective Landis is prepared to see is the one
he must save.

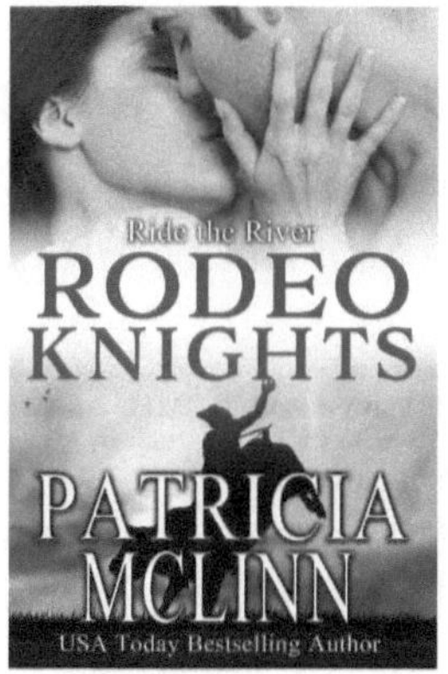

RIDE THE RIVER: RODEO KNIGHTS
Her rodeo cowboy ex is back … as her prime suspect.

Explore a complete list of all Patricia's books
patriciamclinn.com/patricias-books
Or get a printable booklist
patriciamclinn.com/patricias-books/printable-booklist

Patricia's Bookstore (buy online directly from Patricia)
shop.patriciamclinn.com

About the Author

Patricia McLinn is the USA Today bestselling author of more than 60 published novels cited by readers and reviewers for wit and vivid characterization. Her books include mysteries, romantic suspense, contemporary romance, historical romance and women's fiction. They have topped bestseller lists and won numerous awards.

She has spoken about writing from London to Melbourne, Australia, to Washington, D.C., including being a guest speaker at the Smithsonian.

McLinn spent more than 20 years as an editor at The Washington Post after stints as a sports writer (Rockford, Ill.) and assistant sports editor (Charlotte, N.C.). She received BA and MSJ degrees from Northwestern University.

Now living in Kentucky, McLinn loves to hear from readers through her website and social media.

Visit with Patricia:

Website: patriciamclinn.com

Facebook: facebook.com/PatriciaMcLinn

Pinterest: pinterest.com/patriciamclinn

Instagram: instagram.com/patriciamclinnauthor